From the Ashes

Kathleen Suzanne
&
Jeanne Sumerix

LOVE SPECTRUM

Love Spectrum is an imprint of
Genesis Press, Inc.
315 Third Avenue North
Columbus, Mississippi 39701

ISBN 1-58571-001-6

Manufactured in the United States of America

FIRST EDITION

We dedicate this book to each other...
for without the other,
it would not exist

One

"Oh my God." Paige Turner's fingertips pressed against her trembling lips and an anguished cry ripped from her throat. She stared in horror as her turn-of-the-century house burned, illuminating the onyx sky. Angry, crackling hisses of the greedy inferno echoed vengefully, mercilessly consuming the northern Michigan historic landmark. This was her childhood home, her only connection with the past and her family.

The hellish spectacle reflected an eerie red-orange glow against the inky backdrop of the cool May night. Onlookers from every direction edged their vehicles along the road to watch, mesmerized by the blazing firestorm.

Shrouded in shock, Paige helplessly watched as a lifetime of good and bad memories was savagely devoured. Her father's gentle face floated before her, urging her to be strong. His kind voice echoed from the past. Tears threatened in the back of her eyes, but she wouldn't allow them to fall. Oh how she wished she could talk to him once more, the fruitless wish making her loss that much more agonizing.

Other memories flooded in. The long ago voice of her stepmother lashed out at her from the flames. You're weak. Don't expect anyone to feel sorry for an undisciplined, oversized black moose! The cruel words filled her with added despair.

The five alarm fire brought more fire trucks. Sirens seemed to come from every direction. The wailing tried to drown out the frenzied shouts of harried firemen doing their best to save a part of Harbor Spring's history. Their efforts soon gave way to the unrelenting blaze. Still the firefighters fought on, driven by sheer adrenaline. It was obvious their efforts now were only to contain the fire.

The scorching air burned Paige's cheeks, and the acrid fumes seared her nostrils. Her fingers pressed tighter against her lips to suppress the consuming despair as an all-encompassing grief engulfed her. She was alone. Her knees weakened, and then buckled. She felt strong arms slip around her waist like an iron band. With little effort she was righted and held steadfast.

"Are you all right? Is there anyone I can call for you, a friend or family?" A deep, male voice penetrated her numbness.

Through blurred vision, she looked at the man who had kept her from falling. Probing olive-black eyes gazed at her, waiting for a response.

"Call someone?" her voice sounded distant to her. Who could she call? There was no one. She settled against his strength.

A compassionate, tender smile lifted the corner of his mouth. "Is there someone I should notify for you?"

Blinking, she floundered. "No. No one. I just came back for a visit." Her gaze turned once again to the out-of-control inferno. "Now what will I do?"

Before he could answer, another voice penetrated Paige's bewildered world.

"You're needed, Cross, I'll take over here." The voice that issued the order was loaded with ridicule.

The fireman hesitated, glancing from the intruder to the woman. Paige noted his set face, his clamped mouth and fixed eyes. For a brief moment she wondered what he thought. Then he shrugged, released her, touched his fingers to his hard hat in a gesture of compliance, and turned abruptly. She watched him gracefully lope across the lawn. A sudden blanket of cold emptiness surrounded her with his departure.

Frenzied sickness twisted in the pit of her stomach. Her gaze followed him as he disappeared into the thick smoke. "What am I going to do now?" The hoarse, whispered question escaped her lips.

"Are you a friend of the family or . . . have you been sent to open the house?"

"Friend of the family? Open the house?" Bewildered, Paige turned toward the newcomer. She found herself staring into ice blue eyes. Eyes that didn't reflect the smile on the lips below. Then it hit her like a bolt of lightning. Because she was African-American, he automatically assumed she was hired help.

She slowed her breathing and lifted her shoulders to straighten her five-foot, ten-inch frame. Knowing she had regained some of her composure, she extended her hand to the stranger. "I'm Paige Turner."

He accepted her hand. "Jack Devlin. Do you know the folks who own this place?"

"I own this place." She noted the surprise in his face and then pointed in the direction of what was left of her home. A heaviness settled in her chest. "I guess I don't have much left to own."

"Turner? Any relation to Joseph Turner?" he asked, uneasiness etching his features.

"Yes, he is my father . . . I mean was, he's deceased."

His blue eyes narrowed speculatively. "Daughter? I don't remember Joseph having any children."

"I haven't been here in years. We left when I was twelve."

Uneasiness clouded his face, but he shrugged matter-of-factly. "Perhaps I was in college at that time. Anyway, this has been one hell of a homecoming for you."

She offered him a weak smile. The sound of voices unwillingly drew her gaze back to the fire. Some of the firemen were leaving. The house had burned so fast there was no need for such a large crew. A tumble of confused thoughts assailed her. "I have no place to go."

Words were being spoken, but she didn't hear them. In the gutted center of what used to be her family home, a blackened beam collapsed.

"I saw a nice inn when I was in town." Her voice trailed off as she stared at the dying fire. She wiped her soot-smudged cheeks and looked at the dark streaks on her fingers. "I must look a mess." Warmth seeped into her sooty cheeks. With all of the problems she had, she still worried about her looks. Her years of modeling had made her constantly aware of her image.

Paige glanced at the man and tried to retrieve some semblance of common sense. She had wanted to leave her job in New York and enjoy her vacation. "I just had the house opened and then went to dinner. When I returned . . . I found this." Dazed, she pointed to the catastrophe that earlier had spewed thick, black smoke into the sky.

He gently tapped her shoulder to gain her attention. "Miss Turner, there's nothing you can do here. It's late. You can stay at my place tonight. Tomorrow is soon enough to worry about anything else."

His place? What was he talking about? She couldn't just go to a strange man's house and stay. She shook her head.

"No . . . I couldn't."

His expression reflected understanding of her hesitation and he smiled. "Like I said before, my place is a bed and breakfast. My manager and housekeeper would appreciate the diversion. This is the slow time of year."

Paige felt embarrassment rise to her face. "Oh. I'm sorry, I thought . . ."

"I know." He held up his hand to stop any further explanation. "I'll tell the fire chief where you're going in case he needs you and then I'll take you there."

"Was that the fire chief?" She glanced across the lawn at the man Jack Devlin had called Cross.

Jack followed her gaze. "No. He's just a volunteer who loves to play fireman from time to time."

The cynicism in the remark grated on her. "I think it's very courageous to volunteer, especially when you're putting your life on the line."

"Perhaps you're right."

The abrupt answer surprised her.

"He was kind to me. I want to thank him." It was obvious to her there was no love lost between these two men. And she didn't want to become involved in a small town battle. She had enough problems of her own.

Jack shook his head. "No need. It's what he volunteered to do; no thanks are necessary."

Paige didn't answer but she knew she would thank him eventually. She watched Jack speaking to the fire chief as if he were the one in charge; the chief glanced in her direction and nodded. Somehow she felt the look was more than interest in where she would be. Of course, there were not many black families that owned property here in this northern resort. Hers had been one of the first. Those had been hard times and she didn't need to think of them right now.

When Jack returned, she let herself be guided to the large, extended-cab pickup parked at the end of her long drive. She climbed in beside him, her gaze still drawn to the smoldering rubble.

Jack drove his truck down the road about a mile and pulled into the tree-lined drive of a large Victorian mansion and stopped. Silhouetted against the night sky, the house looked very romantic, like something out of a Victorian novel. The turret on one side was lit so well it gave the impression of a candle glowing in a window. It was all so majestic yet inviting.

Paige followed him out of the truck and up the steps to the wraparound porch.

"Emma," he called, taking her by the arm. "We need some help here."

Paige pulled away. "No, really, I'm fine."

An older woman with white hair done up in brush rollers came from the long hall behind the staircase, wiping her hands on her full apron.

"Emma, this is Miss Turner."

Paige held out her hand, forcing a smile she didn't feel. "Paige, please, call me Paige."

"I'm pleased to meet you, Paige. The older woman's face puckered in thought as she shook her hand. "Turner?" she mused, tucking a wispy strand of hair behind her ear. "I remember Joseph Turner who bought the old Clayton place some years back. After his wife died, he married a young woman who used to work for a family on Harbor Point. I remember him as a good man."

Paige nodded. "He was my father. He married Ada when I was twelve."

"I remember him well. I remember you too. Always a quiet thing." The older woman's faded eyes glanced at Paige's disheveled appearance. "What in the world happened to you, child?"

"Her house burned tonight," Jack intervened.

Emma rushed toward the side window and peered out into the night. "Good Lord, it must have lit up the whole sky. You'd think I'd have seen that." She turned back to them, letting the gauzy curtains drop into place. "But then, the kitchen is on the other side of the house and I had the TV blaring as usual."

"I told her she could stay here until she gets things straightened out."

"Of course. We don't have any bookings until Memorial Day." She smiled reassuringly at Paige. "You've had quite a shock. Jack, would you show Paige to the sitting room? I'll bring refreshments. Coffee, tea or something a little stronger?"

"Coffee's fine," Paige answered.

Jack ushered her into a brightly flowered, wingback chair next to a crackling fire in a fieldstone fireplace. She lifted the soot-smudged cape from her shoulders and carefully laid it on the stone hearth. "Everything was fine when I left. I just went to dinner and when I returned . . ." Paige fought the overwhelming desire to give in to her weak side. She wanted desperately to sit down and cry. She needed a strong shoulder to cry on, the shoulder she'd leaned on earlier.

Her host sat in the matching chair by the fire. He offered her a sympathetic ear and a few well-placed nods. Here she sat with a stranger, spilling her story. She glanced in his direction. And he didn't seem to be the least bit interested.

Paige stared into the orange flames. Somehow this fire was welcoming. Funny how some things can be comforting and frightful all at the same time. That's exactly how she had felt about returning to her childhood home. Her mind drifted into semi-numbness and it felt good. She was startled out of her reverie by Emma's quick reappearance.

"Here we are." She sat the tray on the coffee table, then said, "You've lost all your personal belongings then?"

Paige shook her head. "What I really lost was my past. Thankfully my luggage was sent in one direction and me in another. It should arrive in Pellston tomorrow." Exhaustion and weariness washed over her. Her heavy work schedule, the long trip and now the fire. "I can't tell you how grateful I am for your assistance, but I don't want to be any bother. I should go to a hotel."

"Nonsense. We wouldn't hear of it—would we, Jack?" Emma handed the cup of hot coffee to Paige. "We have plenty of room right now. You're more than welcome."

Jack cleared his throat. "Emma's right. I'll show you to your room as soon as you finish your coffee."

Paige glanced at the grandfather clock and then down at her soot-smudged clothing. "I think I would like to clean up. May I take my coffee with me?"

"Of course."

She rose and turned to Emma. "Thank you again.

"You're most welcome, dear. I think you'll find every-thing you need. If not, just let me know." She patted Paige's arm. "The Princess Room is ready. Breakfast is served between seven and ten during the season, but you come down whenever you want."

A smile spread across Paige's face. "Thank you, Emma. You make me feel right at home."

Emma's smile widened. "You make this your home as long as you need." She sniffed and glanced toward the hall. "Oh, Lord, my cookies." She hurried toward the kitchen.

"She gets a little forgetful sometimes, but she's one heck of a manager. Follow me, I'll show you to your room." Jack headed for the stairs. "Since no one is here yet, you can choose any room you want. There's the Hemingway Suite at the back of the house or the Captain's

Room at the head of the stairs. Actually there are fifteen themes to choose from."

Paige followed him. "I don't want to be any bother and Emma did say the Princess Room is ready."

"It's in the turret. But I think it's too small and definitely has too many windows for someone who likes to sleep late."

To her, sleeping in a small round room would be comforting, but she wasn't about to tell him that. "I think it sounds just right. And I don't sleep late." His statement had raised her hackles. What gave him the idea or the right to think she slept late? Because she was black she was lazy? Was he prejudiced? She groaned inwardly. She didn't want to deal with that too.

Still, there was a magnetism about him. He was sinfully handsome and tall with a powerfully-proportioned body. He must be well over six feet tall. He could be one of the models she worked with. His eyes were sky blue, not icy as she had thought earlier. His Roman nose and the set of his chin suggested a stubborn streak.

Jack turned on the hall light and motioned for her to follow him. He opened the tall, white paneled door. "Welcome to the Princess Room." He bowed, ushering her inside, flipping on the overhead light as he did this.

"This is enchanting," she said in a breathy voice. Windows encircled the room and stopped just short of meeting at the door to the hall. Even at night the room was airy and bright, almost bringing the outdoors inside.

On the little bit of wall that wasn't windows, delicate morning glories on a white background stretched from the highly polished hardwood floor to the ornate woodwork just below the ceiling. White Irish lace curtains were pulled back in a soft sway from the tall windows. A thick comforter matching the wallpaper covered the bed, com-

10

plemented by white lace accent pillows with blue ribbon ties.

"This is lovely. I'll be very comfortable here." She ran her hand over the softness of the comforter.

"I'm glad you like it." He moved across the room in giant strides. "This is the bathroom." He opened the door and switched on the light, casting a soft glow on the deep, claw-foot tub.

"And there is a small dressing room through here." He opened the ivy stenciled, white paneled door into the large walk-in closet.

"This is perfect. I'll be quite comfortable...at least I will when I get my things." She glanced down at the Liz Claiborne suit she had worn for the last of her shoot. She'd been in such a hurry to catch her flight, she hadn't changed her outfit. Smudges from the fire now marked the beautiful emerald green silk.

"I'll call the airport first thing in the morning and find out when your luggage is expected," he offered.

"They said tomorrow, but you know how the airlines are."

As if reading her mind, he said, "I think perhaps we might find something clean for you to wear. My cousin leaves clothes here for when she visits. I think she is around five-seven. How tall are you?"

"Five-ten," she answered. She knew she was nice looking and she had come to terms with her stature and size years ago.

"A tad taller than Lisa. Are you a basketball player?" he joked, a teasing glint in his eyes.

"Why? Do I look like a basketball player to you?"

Again, his eyes twinkled with teasing. "Could be. Want to shoot a few?" He made the gesture of doing a hook shot. "I used to be pretty good in high school."

"I think I'll pass. I never was any good at sports."

He regarded her with a speculative gaze. "Too bad. It might have been fun."

"Fun for you, maybe. You'd win hands down." She smiled.

"I'll be going now." He stepped outside the room, but turned back again. "I almost forgot. He handed her an ornate, brass skeleton key."

"Thank you." She paused in shutting the door. "Jack, could you do me one more favor?"

"I'll try."

"I just remembered that my carry-on bag is in the trunk of my car. I have some clothes in it." She held out her car keys. "Could you retrieve it for me?"

Jack hesitated. He was nobody's servant but he wanted to ingratiate himself. He was very interested in her property, so he reached out and took the keys. "Anything for a damsel in distress."

She smiled warmly, "Thanks again. I owe you a lot."

He returned the smile and strode down the hall.

Jack descended the curved staircase with a decisive gait and a whistle on his lips. Yes, he was going to make the lady a generous offer for her prime real estate, one she couldn't refuse. With the house gone, she wouldn't want to keep one hundred and eighty acres of empty land. Lady luck is with me tonight and soon that choice piece of land will be mine, he thought to himself.

Within minutes he had returned with her bag and left it outside her door. Again she had been extremely grateful. Still whistling, he entered the kitchen where Emma was busy with her cookies.

"Did you get her settled?" She scooped the last cookie from the pan, placing it on the cooling rack.

"Yes." He took a mug from its hook and poured himself coffee.

"We finally have a real princess in that room." Emma glanced at her long time employer. "Don't you think she is beautiful?" He gave no response. She held out the platter of cookies. "Would you like some?"

Without thinking, he accepted them. His mind wasn't on cookies or anything else the older woman was suggesting. It was on the land adjoining his. If he could just get her to agree to sell it, he'd put in that golf course he needed to make the rest of the resort a more profitable venture.

"Poor child. She's lost everything." Emma bit into one of her cookies. "And such a pretty little thing."

"I hadn't noticed." Little? I'd hardly use that term to describe Miss Turner, he thought.

"Such a shame."

Jack nodded. "Too bad. But perhaps she'll want to sell, now."

Emma eyed her employer. "Jack, that child has just lost her home, you can't ask her to sell, not right now."

"It isn't her home. She's here on vacation, from God only knows what. If it was that important to her, don't you think she would have been here before this?"

"Nonetheless, it was her home. And I could tell she was devastated." Emma's eyebrows peaked. "She's on vacation, you say?"

He nodded. "That's what she told me. Looks like she could use some exercise too. She probably has one of those sit-on-your butt-jobs."

"Jack!" Emma scowled in his direction.

He held up his hands in a sign of peace. "She's a little rounder than I like, that's all I'm saying."

"She's certainly not what I call fat. Tall, maybe, and well-endowed, but certainly not fat."

"But not thin, either. Besides I prefer blondes and she's definitely not blond." He took another bite.

"Jack! You sound bigoted. She's a sweet girl, I can tell." Emma's smile was triumphant.

A shadow of annoyance crossed his face. "Emma, don't start. You're worse than my own mother ever was."

Emma laughed. "I'm only saying she's a beautiful woman. Anyone with half an eye can see that."

"If you say so. But don't get any ideas about match-making," he warned. "I'm not interested." At least not in the woman but definitely in her property.

"It wouldn't hurt you to get interested in a nice girl. You have a biological clock, too, you know. At thirty-four you should be thinking seriously of settling down."

He held up his hands in mock surrender as he slid off the stool at the breakfast bar. "I'm leaving before you have me married." He pushed open the back door. "Call me if you need anything."

Paige closed her eyes as she slid under the warm, deli-ciously-scented water. Leaning back, she rested her tow-eled head against the rim. It felt so good to get the ashes and smoke from her hair and now from her body.

It had been a long time since she'd been back. But when she stepped from the car and gazed at the house, all her memories had come flooding back, some good, some bad.

So many familiar things; the lilac bush where she'd played house with her dolls still stood at the edge of the lawn. The buds were swollen and preparing to release those delicious, purple flowers.

Her mother had sat under the shade of the tall pine trees and read for hours. As her illness progressed, she could do little else. Paige remembered sitting quietly with her, not realizing the extent of her mother's infirmity. At eleven she was aware her mother was ill, but she didn't know how soon she would lose her.

That was the first tragic blow in her life. The emptiness caused by the loss of one's mother could never be put into words. Just as she had become accustomed to living alone with her father, he re-married. When he died he confessed to Paige that the second marriage had been a mistake. He was lonely and he thought she was too. They were lonely. But for Paige's mother, not the witch he married.

This had to stop. She had to control the bitter recollections and concentrate on the good. She could re-build the house just as it had been. She could be happy there again. When the water began to cool, she climbed from the tub, reached for the large bath sheet and for the carry-on bag that Jack had retrieved for her.

She tipped her head upside down and ran her fingers through the long, tangled mane of dark hair, applied conditioner and then blew it dry. Then she threw her head back letting the curls and waves fall softly around her face.

She glanced in the mirror. As she applied moisturizing cream, she studied herself. At twenty-six she didn't have many years left as a model for the Big and Beautiful Agency. They wanted beautiful women over size twelve now, but she didn't think they would want big, beautiful and wrinkled women.

She pulled the pants to the blue and silver windsuit over pink silk bikini panties. Her nose wrinkled. Wearing panties that didn't match her outer clothing bothered her. But she was sure it was better than anything Jack would have come up with.

She pulled on her top, slipped her feet into her running shoes and headed for the door. She needed to work off some of her pain. Grabbing her purse she started to tuck it into her carry-on bag when she saw her cell-phone. Automatically she dialed Mara's number.

"Hello," her friend's sweet voice answered. She could see the tall blonde's face waiting expectantly.

"Hi, it's me."

"Hi, you. How's the vacation going?"

Hearing Mara's voice, Paige spilled out the evening's events. She finished with, "I really don't know what to do."

"Girlfriend, it just so happens my next shoot was canceled. I have some time off. I'll be there as soon as I can."

Paige breathed a sigh of relief. "I don't really want you to use your time off to baby-sit me, but I know there's no use in arguing with you."

Mara laughed, "You are absolutely right. Besides, the guys you mentioned don't sound too bad."

"Like you have to come to a small town to find a guy." Paige giggled at the thought of Mara with a small town man.

"Variety is the spice of life. I am growing weary of guys who think they are as good looking as I am."

"They're models. What do you expect?"

"That's exactly why the change will be good. Now I have to make a dozen phone calls. Take care. I'll let you know my ETA as soon as I find out."

"Okay." Paige snapped the phone closed, returning it to her purse. It was good to talk to Mara. Mara had a way of making things seem better, even if they weren't.

She stuck her nose into the kitchen and told the housekeeper where she was going. Emma smiled, promising refreshments when she returned. She opened the front door and stepped out into the cool May breeze which carried the pungent odor of her burned home. And the fireman who had helped her, who was standing on the porch with hair still wet from a shower he'd obviously taken after the fire. He was now in jeans and a denim chambray shirt.

Now with his hat off she could see his gleaming, thick, raven hair tapering down to his collar. Olive black eyes were set deeply in a face bronzed by sun and wind. She shivered lightly and drew in a deep breath. Stop this, she chided herself, forcing herself to look at the item in his hands.

He smiled and held out a thick, leather-bound album that had obviously been in the fire. "I thought you would sleep better if you knew we had salvaged something."

"Oh, thank you. How did you save it?" She tenderly took the album in her hands.

"I saw it on the porch. It must have been thrown out in the frenzy."

Paige glanced into his soft, dark eyes, feeling as if she could drown in them. "I can't thank you enough." She looked down at the book, feeling a warm glow flowing through her body. "I didn't lose everything. I'd like to repay you for saving this for me, but I don't know how."

"You don't really owe me anything." He shuffled his feet, then looked directly into her eyes. "I would like to know the name of the woman with such dark golden eyes." His mouth quirked with humor.

Heat stole into her cheeks. From any other man she would have taken this as a come-on line, but from him it seemed honest. "I'm so sorry, I wasn't thinking. I'm Paige Turner." She shifted the album to her right hand and stuck out her left. Then realizing she had made another error she shifted the album back and offered her right hand. She was glad of the semi-darkness that partially hid the flush in her cheeks.

"Lincoln Cross. It's great to meet you." Amusement flickered in the eyes that met hers. He sat on the edge of the porch rail and stretched his long legs casually before him. "Do you mind if I sit? It's been a long day."

She shook her head. An electrifying shock reverberated through her. She shivered. His gaze was as soft as a caress, warm as a summer evening. Damn, she thought, this guy has everything a girl could want . . . that is, if she wanted a man right now. "Ah . . . Lincoln, would you like to come in for a cup of coffee? I know Emma has a fresh pot ." She spoke in a hushed whisper.

"Linc." My friends call me Linc." He stood as if to accept the invitation, then said, "I don't think that would be such a good idea."

"Linc..." she whispered. She remembered him leaving when Jack had come on the fire scene. Now she was sure the two men didn't care for each other. She was dying to ask why, but she knew from living here that outsiders should not involve themselves in the politics of a small town.

Smiling her brightest, I'm-on-the-runway-smile, she asked, "Would you like to have dinner with me...I want to repay you for being so nice to me." She met his gaze. The mystery in his eyes beckoned irresistibly.

"Does this mean you would like to take the whole fire department to dinner?" He turned up his smile a notch.

He was teasing her, affectionately not maliciously. "If that is the only way to get you to dinner, then yes," she poked back.

His eyes grew openly amused, and he came close, looking down at her intently. "Why don't we start out small, with just the two of us and then add the rest of the firemen one at a time." He stared at her for a moment longer, then burst out laughing.

She batted her eyelashes and said, "Whatever you say, Linc. I'm sure we can arrange that with little difficulty." Her lips tickled with the need to laugh.

His laugh broke off and his eyes smoldered. "I think we'll have to have several dinners before we entertain the rest of the guys." His gaze drifted over her and then back to her face. He tapped the side of her nose with his finger. "Wouldn't you agree?"

Their gazes locked as her fingers brushed the heated imprint on her nose, and her heart pumped faster as she read the double meaning of his gaze. She stepped back toward the door and mustered her very business-like voice. "All right then, you first, then the rest of the guys. When would you like to begin this gratitude marathon?" She tried to suppress a giggle.

Linc glanced at his watch. "I guess tonight is out of the question. How about tomorrow night?"

"Tomorrow will be just fine." Oh, yes, it would be just fine indeed.

Two

Linc stared at the door that closed behind the golden-eyed beauty. In his youth, his grandfather had told him his future rested in the hands of the woman with golden eyes, and here she was. His heart warmed thinking of his grandfather's prediction. The old man had sat by the fire and read the ashes, passing on ageless wisdom. This was destiny. He felt it when he first held her at the fire, first was drawn in by those haunting eyes.

He inhaled deeply. The pungent odor of burnt wood clung on the evening's dew. A full moon hung in the sky like a fine painting, illuminating the land in mystical, silvery light. Surveying the sky he laughed to himself, "Now all I need is a soaring eagle." His Native American heritage was an integral part of his life. Sometimes he regarded the old beliefs with a heavy dose of skepticism, which he blamed on his Caucasian half. Still, more often than not, the tribal elders were right.

He smiled to himself as he bounded down the steps of the porch. That was one beautiful woman. No, not beautiful, knock-dead gorgeous. He loved the way her soft, sable-colored hair hung in waves down her back and glistened like well-polished mahogany. Her dark golden eyes snapped and twinkled when she smiled. And she was tall, with legs that wouldn't quit. God, he loved a tall woman.

She intrigued him. He had been compelled to reach out and touch her satiny skin the color of a rich mocha cappuccino, so drawn to her that he had an overwhelming urge to know all about her. In fact, he was going to find out everything he could.

Did he believe in love at first sight? He never had before, but his mother had told him it happened to some people. Was that what had happened tonight? It was, if the zing in his veins was any indication.

He could still hear the sadness in her voice and the lost little girl look that had creased her face when she watched her home burn. The tinkle of her laughter just now rang in his ears and heart. Oh, yes, he definitely was going to learn a lot more about the girl with mysterious, golden eyes.

❋ ❋ ❋

Paige tossed and turned, trying to find solace in sleep, trying to put the horror of the fire from her mind. But the more she tried, the more awake she became. The fire wasn't the only thing that haunted her. In the dark, visions of Jack and Linc played before her eyes. One pair of mocking, blue eyes, and one pair as black as the darkest night. Two mouths. One cynical, stubborn and arrogant, the other sensuous, tender and laughing.

What was there about these two totally different men that kept her awake? They were worlds apart, not only in looks, but in personality. Linc made her blush and feel giddy like a school girl. Jack made her feel cautious and vulnerable. They both disturbed her, much more than she wanted.

Stop this! she thought. Now wasn't the time to get involved with any man. She had her career. Men didn't enter the picture, not right now.

Her house. If she thought about her house, she wouldn't allow room for romantic thoughts and surging hormones. She tried to pull plans for rebuilding from her mind but Linc's face got in the way.

Damn, this had to stop. She wasn't interested. She was here on a well-earned vacation without complications.

Her career was at its peak. One day, probably sooner than she'd like to think, she would slip in popularity, but for now her career was all-important with no room for romance.

Sometime during these disturbing thoughts, Paige drifted into a restless sleep. But even her dreams were plagued with Linc and Jack vying for her attention.

Her eyes fluttered open as the warmth of the rising sun caressed her face. A bright orange glow which swallowed the remnants of night drew her to the windows. A slight mist crept over the land from the lake but the day promised to be beautiful.

Paige stretched, then reached out and thrust open the window. The cool morning freshness drifted over her, and the morning breeze made her feel alive. Slowly at first, then with great vigor, she did her workout. It felt good to do something normal. She knew she must keep her routine normal to keep from feeling vulnerable.

After showering, she pulled on the blue and silver windsuit. It was odd not having to decide what to wear. Her whole life revolved around her apparel. Her luggage better get here pretty soon or she'd have to do some shopping, something she really didn't want to do.

She glanced at the clock. Five-thirty. Obviously by the silence, Emma wasn't up. She quietly slipped out the front door and began walking toward what used to be her home. She'd come to the bed and breakfast with Jack, and her car was still parked at her place. But she loved to walk. It was part of her daily routine.

The heavy scent of northern pines was carried on the breath of an early breeze. Birds awakened from their sleep called to each other, announcing the new day and the human intruder. Off in the distance, a lonesome owl answered in his sorrowful hoot as if refusing to give up his nocturnal watch.

The gravel beneath Paige's feet crunched softly as she made her way through the still morning. This was like Heaven with only the voices of nature to greet her approach. There were no horns honking, no sirens screaming, no milling crowds, only silent harmony and the soft voices of nature.

At the edge of the drive was her car, right where she'd left it when she'd come home from dinner and found her house in flames. Her gaze was drawn to the still smoldering mound that had once been a house. The heavy, biting smell of charred wood stung her nose, but it was the empty feeling that consumed her.

Sure, she had an apartment in New York City, but it had never been home. She'd always thought of the old Victorian house and the tall pines that protectively surrounded it as her home. Now it was gone.

"Good morning." A familiar, deep voice interrupted her solitude.

Paige whirled around, coming face to face with Linc.

"You took ten years off my life, coming up on me like that," she accused teasingly. She glanced around for a vehicle. "Where did you come from?"

The smile on his face faded. "I'm sorry if I startled you. I was out jogging when I saw you."

"I didn't realize you lived around here."

Linc's gaze turned to the road. "Back toward Harbor Springs, about a quarter of a mile." He pointed. "You're up early."

"I couldn't sleep." She turned back to the blackened heap. "I had to see it. To try to remember what it looked like before, to imprint it on my brain, my house as it used to be."

"Why?" He followed her gaze to the blackened debris.

"Because I might forget and I don't want to forget. Too many things in my life seem to fade with time." Her face reflected grief and despair as she bit her lower lip to keep it from quivering.

"What things?" he asked softly.

She turned to him, her eyes glistening with unshed tears. "Have you ever lost someone and in time their image began to fade? No matter how much you tried to remember them, the details became a blurred shadow?"

He shrugged. "I haven't thought about it."

"When you lose important people in your life, you struggle to hold on to what you have for fear even your memories will abandon you and you'll be totally alone. Sometimes I can't remember my parents' features." God, what was wrong with her? Why did he make it so easy to open up to him? She had always prided herself on being strong and independent and here she was laying her troubles at his feet.

He moved beside her. "I'm sorry your homecoming turned out like this."

She nodded. It felt good having him close. "It's not as I imagined when I made my plans. I pictured a summer of relaxation in my own house and now I don't have a house at all. I keep thinking I'll lose the image of the house, same as I sometimes do my parents. When I close my eyes and try to remember them, their features become unclear—like I'm losing them all over again."

"Your memories will always be alive in your heart." He spoke in gentle assurance.

She smiled at him. "Are your parents still with you?"

"My mother. She lives with me."

"Take good care of her. You never want to regret not doing for her."

"What do you regret?" he asked, his voice low and understanding.

"This." Her hand swung wide. "Everything came to an end before I had a chance to...to..." She shrugged. "Now even the house is gone." A heavy silence hung between them for several moments. "I remember my mother sitting with me by that lilac bush reading." She moved toward the bush that promised large, purple blossoms in a few weeks. "Even when she was so very sick she spent time with me."

"See, you have memories. If you think about something long enough it becomes clear."

His voice faded into the background. It was as if time slipped away and her mother was going to come out any moment with a book in her hands and begin reading in her soft, melodic voice. Her sweet, gentle mother with a short cap of dark curls and kind eyes. And her perfume, she always smelled so sweet, even when she was confined to bed.

"I'll always have wonderful memories, but I want them to be as sharp as yesterday's fire. I don't want to lose any of this clarity."

"None of us can live in the past. We have to go forward. Those who have left us would want that."

The past? Live in the past? She'd come here to capture the feelings of the past only to have it disappear before her eyes.

"This was all I had of my childhood. And now it's gone."

"The land is still here. It's only the house that's gone." When he spoke his voice was tender, almost a murmur.

She glanced at the pile of smoking rubble. "I'm going to rebuild. It will be exactly as it was right down to the wicker furniture on the porch." But it wouldn't be the same, of course. All the memorabilia, pictures, and antiques her father collected were lost in the fire. There was no way she could replace all that.

"Rebuild?"

She nodded. "Exactly as it was." She kicked a stone scorched by the intense heat.

The two chimneys stood tall, reaching from the charred debris toward the morning sky, an ugly reminder of what had happened. She inhaled deeply. All of her losses had taught her resilience. She reached within and pulled on that strength. Like the chimneys, she too would reach for the sky. She too would rise from the ashes. Her chin rose from her chest as she gained her resolve.

"You know," Linc's deep, velvety smooth voice wrapped around her bringing her attention to him, "I've heard my mother say, 'Your troubles aren't as dark as they seem if you just pull them into the sunlight and take a good look at them.'"

"Your mother is absolutely right." She visored her eyes against the rising sun. "See, the new day makes my troubles look better already."

Linc laughed. "Yes, I can see that."

His smooth laughter rolled over her, the warmth erasing the wrinkles of sadness. "Mothers always know best."

He tapped her nose. "You'll have to meet my mother. I'm sure she would agree with you one hundred percent."

"I'd like to meet her." She smiled lightly.

Shoulder to shoulder they began walking down the drive. Even with her house gone she now realized she'd come home. "It's been too long," she said more to herself than to him.

"How long?" His voice was soft and unobtrusive.

Paige glanced down the road at the stand of trees that separated her property from the inn, the place she'd played as a child, building magical kingdoms. "Those trees were half their height when I was here last."

Linc studied the row of trees for a moment. "That would be about ten or twelve years?"

She nodded.

"That's a long time to stay away from home. Why did your family leave?"

Paige pulled on a long piece of dead grass left from the previous summer and began twisting its brittle stem between her fingers; the pieces crumbled to the ground. "My stepmother didn't like it here. She didn't feel comfortable in a community of white people that knew she was black when she could easily pass for white. She liked going to New York where she could hide her ethnicity. And when her mother became ill, she had the perfect reason to insist father move to New York to help care for her. He intended to return, but it never happened." Her soft voice echoed a bitter past.

"That's too bad. It would be difficult to never return to your home." He fell silent. She followed his gaze and studied his profile as he stared at the landscape that boasted rolling hills dressed in forests and lush spring meadows. Why did he have to be so damned handsome? He was not only handsome, but he was kind and gentle, yet there was a strength that radiated from him that told her he was no pushover. The silence between them was not uncomfortable.

"Have you had breakfast yet?" he asked without looking at her.

"No."

"Want to go have a bite to eat?"

She threw him a teasing grin. "Breakfast and dinner all in the same day? Are you sure you can stand that much of my company?"

"I'll give it a try." His eyes twinkled with merriment.

She lowered her gaze to her windsuit, fighting the warmth that rose to her cheeks. "I'm not dressed to go out."

"You look fine to me." His eyes roved over her appreciatively. "Besides, this is vacation land. People come and go without much thought to how they look." He smiled down at her. "My treat."

Who could refuse an invitation like that? "All right, but don't blame me if people laugh at you for taking this inappropriately dressed person out in public."

"I think the public will love you." He stretched his arms out wide so she could see his clothes. "I don't look so good myself. I'll go in my sweats if you stop worrying about what you look like."

She laughed and shook her head. "I couldn't ask you to do that. You've been exercising. If you want to change, I'll understand." Her eyes settled on the wet stain of perspiration on his gray sweat shirt.

"I think you're telling me I need a shower." The beginning of a teasing smile tipped the corners of his mouth. He glanced in the direction of her car. "Do you want to take that or jog to my house."

"What?"

"Your car, unless of course, you'd rather jog."

"Oh. I think we'll drive. She pulled out the single key with the blue tag and then ran to the car. The small car jumped to life as she turned the key. She leaned her head out the window, "Come on, I'm starving."

He climbed into the small car and gave her directions which led them deep into a dense forest. She gazed over the thick trees that made a natural tunnel over the road. "It's beautiful through here."

"Mother likes her privacy. She should have been born a hundred years ago or more."

"Why?" Paige asked.

"She's one of those people who love the past. I swear, if she could find a time warp, she'd go back and never be seen again."

"I can understand that. Sometimes I'd like to live in the past, too. It seems a lot less complicated than the present." Less complicated if she could live in the past before slavery raised its ugly head, she thought.

A rich laughter echoed through the car. "Now you're beginning to sound like her."

"I'm sure your mother is very nice but the last thing I want is to be your mother." She could feel the heat rise at the suggestion her words gave.

"I couldn't agree with you more." His husky voice sent her nerves on a dance all their own. She glanced ahead to where he instructed her to turn. The car rolled to a stop in front of a large, rambling, two-story log home with a covered, wraparound porch.

A log home such as she'd never seen. Large windows allowed her to see the uniqueness beyond the highly-polished log walls. She'd traveled many places but this was everything she'd ever seen, wrapped in one neat package; striking but not showy, luxurious yet homey. She was in awe.

"Come on." He raced up the wide steps onto the porch and opened the ornate glass door that was etched with detailed wild life scenes.

"Is your mother home?"

"No. She's away for the day. Make yourself at home. I'm going to take a quick shower." He took the half log steps two at a time.

Paige glanced around. To her left was the kitchen with a long, gray granite counter top, a sink with a waterfall faucet and a built-in cooking range with a massive grill. Off the formal dining room was a glass solarium with a rustic table and chairs. It looked as if the house just melted into the out of doors, becoming one with nature.

She walked along the wall separating the kitchen from the hall and came to the great room, which boasted a full wall of windows. Paige gazed out at a small, pristine lake. The sun glistened across the water, both asking to be used.

Hanging high above in the cathedral ceiling was a birch-bark canoe. It looked old, antique even. The room was decorated tastefully with Native American artifacts, beautifully crafted pottery and paintings depicting the heritage of the earliest North American settlers.

"Ready?" Linc's voice sounded behind her.

She turned to meet his warm smile. Spreading her arms to encompass the room, she asked, "Did you hire a decorator? Everything's so well put together." She returned her gaze to the room.

"I take it you like it?"

"What's not to like. It's exquisite. You must like Native American culture." Her eyes swept over the painting of a young Indian maiden sitting with a wolf. The eyes carried the same intense, dark depths as Linc's.

He proudly strode into the room and stopped to straighten the colorful, hand-woven blanket that graced the back of the heavy white pine, cushioned sofa. He looked at her with a story in his eyes but simply said, "I'm an avid collector, as you can see."

"Yes." Paige nodded and moved to the windows that looked across a long covered porch toward the lake. She hadn't missed his hesitation. What was it he was going to say? If she asked, she would be committing herself to too much personal interest. She left it hanging in the air.

"Come look at the pond. It's stocked with trout so I can have fresh fish daily if I want." He pulled open the French doors and stood back for her to go ahead.

Paige walked beside him onto the wooden deck, down the steps and across the lawn. Her fingers were aching to curl around the large hand that brushed hers accidentally. Everything about him compelled her body to action. She put a little space between them. Just because her body was going crazy didn't mean her mind had to. From the house, the ringing of the phone disturbed the quiet morning.

Linc glanced at his watch. "I'd better take that. Have a look around. I'll be right back." He turned and made his way back to the house.

She breathed a sigh of relief. Saved by the bell, she thought, as she stepped onto the small, wooden dock jutting out over the water. His very presence kept her off balance. She strolled aimlessly down the dock, noting a heavy dew on the planks.

Out of the corner of her eye she saw a bird in flight. She craned her neck, not believing what she saw. A bald eagle soared gracefully over the lake. "My God," she whispered, "I've never seen a real bald eagle before." She turned her head quickly to catch the last glimpse of the graceful flight and when she did, she felt herself slip. Unable to catch her balance, she rapidly slid along the slippery planks into the icy water.

Paige shrieked as her warm body met the frigid liquid. She could gracefully walk down any runway in the world in three-inch heels. But she couldn't stand on a dock alone for a few minutes without making a clumsy fool of herself. Silently she cursed. She gasped for breath and forced herself to swim to the dock.

Linc heard the scream. He dropped the phone and ran toward Paige who was grasping at the slippery dock and then sliding into the water again. He quickly covered the space between them. Crouching, he grabbed her and easily lifted her from the water.

"Relax. It's all right, I've got you." He pulled her statuesque frame to him. Gathering her into his arms, he led her shivering body back to the house.

Her hair hung in a wet tangle down her back, dark tendrils pasted to her face. Her full lips were violet from the cold and her dark complexion had paled.

Desperate to help, Linc unzipped her jacket, revealing hardened, dark chocolate nipples pressed against a white lace bra.

She timidly pulled the jacket closed. Their eyes met and locked. No words had to be said but both knew they were both feeling the same passionate throb.

He could have kicked himself for being so forward, but it seemed the natural thing to do. He cleared his throat. "You have to get out of those things before you catch your death of cold." He spoke firmly but with great gentleness.

"I can do it." Her shaking fingers finished unzipping.

"Here. Wrap up in this blanket. I'll start a fire in the fireplace. I'll keep my back turned, I promise." She's modest, he thought. He couldn't help admiring a woman with old-fashioned values.

He laid several small pieces of wood over the kindling. He lit the paper under the grate and watched as the yellow-orange flames came to life, licking the wood.

From the corner of his eye he saw the motion of her removing her clothes. He sat hunched before the fire, but his mind was on the satiny mocha complexion under the jacket and the shadow of the brown nipples tucked in the lace bra. He wanted her. The strong physical and even mental pull was there. Slow up, ole man, don't scare her away, he cautioned himself.

He waited a decent interval and then asked, "Can I turn around now?"

"Yes."

Slowly he rotated on his heels. "At the top of the stairs is the guest bath. If you'd like, you could take a shower to warm yourself and wash the lake out of your hair." He stood transfixed by her beauty.

She nodded. "Thank you. I will."

"I'll just put your clothes in the dryer."

He watched her move self-consciously up the wooden steps. She had set his blood to boil and didn't even know it. Glancing down at the pile on the floor, he picked up the lace bra and panties. Linc fought with himself not to think of her naked body beneath that blanket. He took a deep breath trying to throttle the raging current racing through him. Quickly he gathered the clothing into his arms and deposited them in the dryer.

He sat in the living room, poking at the fire to keep it roaring and his mind off her nude body. She came down with his bathrobe wrapped tightly around her.

"I hope you don't mind—the blanket was cold and wet."

He swallowed hard. He'd never seen his robe look better. She held his brush in her hand, "Is it all right if I use this?"

"Of course. Use whatever you need," he choked out. "Sit on the hearth so you'll stay warm until your clothes dry." He rose so she could sit on the warm stone.

He stared mesmerized as she tipped her head upside down and began pulling her fingers through the long tresses, something his fingers ached to do. After a short time she flipped her hair back. Deep golden eyes shyly gazed into his soul. She turned her head to the side, letting her hair fall over her shoulder while she brushed a sheen into the long waves.

She enchanted him. She did things to his emotions he'd never felt before...at least not this soon...no, never, not like this.

"I'm sorry." Her voice broke into his roaring mind.

"For what?" he choked.

"For causing such a mess." She offered him an apologetic smile.

"Don't think about it. Accidents happen."

"I feel so foolish. I should have been more careful."

He shook his head. "I should have warned you. The wet planks are very slippery."

She laughed softly and tilted her head. "Well, now I know. It wasn't as much the slippery wood as it was me gawking at the eagle that soared through the sky."

"An eagle?" He stared in disbelief. Now he knew without a doubt she was his destiny, just as his grandfather had predicted.

"Linc?" Her voice wore a smile. "Maybe we should go."

His eyes traveled the full length of her robed body. "I'll get your clothes." As he was leaving, he noted her cheeks were full of wine-colored roses.

She dressed and worked at pushing away her spiraling desire. They'd hardly known each other a day. What was she thinking? She zipped her windsuit all the way to her neck. You have other things to think about, she scolded herself. Her descent down the log stairs gave her time to bring her emotions partially under control. She glanced at Linc staring into the fire. This is not going to be easy, she thought. Her eyes moved over his well-muscled body, not easy at all.

Linc pivoted in her direction as if propelled by her presence. "Are you still hungry?"

"Ravenous."

He led the way to the front door. "We have to get out of here while you are still untouched." He was teasing but his storm-tossed eyes said he was serious.

"Why Mr. Cross, whatever do you mean?"

He hesitated, then pulled the door tightly shut behind them. "I think I'm hungry too."

Paige knew he wasn't talking about food. His intense stare was drawing her in, past the point of no return. Quickly she looked around for something to fix her mind on. Her eyes fell on a glass house. She pointed in its direction. "What's that?"

He smiled widely, glad to have the unspoken subject changed. "It's my greenhouse. Gardening keeps me in touch with the earth."

"My father used to grow a garden. It was his relaxation." Her mind gathered distant memories, trying to see them clearly. Absently she followed him to his truck.

"I find it's a good way to work out problems and grow great vegetables." He smiled down at her as he opened the truck door.

She jumped in and waited for him to join her. "I love fresh tomatoes." She wanted to keep the conversation on vegetables.

"I'll bring you some when they're ripe." This was more a question than a statement. He glanced at her as he turned the truck around.

"I'd like that."

"It'll be a couple of months."

"I know." She warmed under the heat of his stare.

Linc put the truck in gear and sped off towards the main road. "All this talk of food is making me hungry."

Their breakfast conversation had crawled back to lighter dialogue. When they were finished and were leaving the restaurant, Linc offered, "Do you want to check on your luggage?"

She reached in her purse and pulled out her phone. "That's a good idea." After a brief conversation with the airport, she looked at Linc, "It's there. Can we go get it?"

"Sure. And while we are at it, I'll show you around. Things have changed quite a bit since you lived here."

Paige stole a glimpse. There was an invitation in the smoldering depths of his eyes, an invitation she was going to hold off as long as she could.

Jack came out of the inn as she drove up after spending the entire day with Linc.

"Are you all right?" A concerned look crossed his face.

Paige turned toward him. "I beg your pardon? All right?"

"Emma looked in on you and found you gone. When you didn't return, she called me. I even went to your place and found your car gone. We were concerned."

He was acting concerned but somehow she felt he didn't mean it. She fought the urge to snap. After all it wasn't any of his business where she had been. But then he had gone out of his way for her yesterday. "I'm sorry if I put anyone out."

The frown on his face deepened. "She thought she saw you leave with Lincoln Cross."

"She did."

A momentary look of discomfort crossed his face.

"What's wrong?" she asked.

He cleared his throat. "This is a small community. You have to be careful who you befriend."

"Are you warning me against Linc?"

Jack shook his head. "No." He moved to the door.

"You and Linc don't care much for each other, do you?" she said without thinking. Don't, she warned herself. Don't get involved.

His hand stilled on the brass knob and he turned toward her. "It's a long story . . . one that stretches over a lifetime."

This confirmed her earlier observations. She knew she shouldn't become involved. Her curiosity, though, was piqued. What were the differences that made them dislike each other? Whatever it was, she wouldn't ask any more questions.

"I'm sorry you and Linc have differences. But it has nothing to do with me."

His face colored slightly. "I'm sorry. I didn't mean to involve you. I only sought to warn you. Somehow I was feeling responsible for your safety. I mean, you are our guest and our neighbor."

Her face softened into a relaxed smile, "Of course, Jack. I'll be careful. I promise." But she knew it was too late to forget about Linc.

He returned her smile. "Good. Here, let me help you with those." He lifted the largest of the bags and followed her into the house. It took three trips for him to carry her luggage to the Princess Room.

"Thank you," she said, looking down at the mounded luggage. "I didn't realize I'd brought so much."

"Oh, by the way..." He fumbled in his jacket pocket. "This message was left while you were gone." He handed her the pink telephone message slip.

She quickly read the message from Mara. Glancing up, she raised her eyebrows questioningly to Jack.

He cleared his throat and asked, "How about dinner this evening. I can show you a little of our north country."

"Oh, Jack, thank you, that sounds like fun...but I've already made plans."

His face went grim. "Cross?"

"Yes." There it was again. She felt as if he were accusing her of treason.

"Oh." He shrugged his shoulders.

To Paige's relief, he kept his comments to himself.

"Maybe another time, then. I'll leave you to unpack."

Alone, Paige lifted the pullman to the bed. But before she got involved finding a place for everything, she returned Mara's call.

"Hi. It's me." Paige lay back on the bed beside the open suitcase.

"I'm glad you finally called. There's been a cancellation. I leave first thing in the morning. I should be in Pellston around four in the afternoon."

"Great." Paige heaved a deep sigh. "I need a friend right now."

"I knew it! I had a premonition. What's wrong?" Mara asked.

Paige's brows knit together. Mara's clairvoyance always unnerved her because she was usually right. But this time it was too late, her house had already burned. Yet she still had one problem, she answered simply, "Men."

"Men? You?" Mara's burst of laughter reverberated along the telephone lines, all the way from New York City. "I can't believe it. You, the queen of holding off men?"

"My crown is slipping. And to top it off there are two of them."

"Two? Hold the runway, girlfriend. I'm on my way. I'm sure I can take one of them off your hands for a little diversion of my own."

Paige closed her eyes and smiled. She needed some-one right now and Mara had the best listening ear she'd ever talked to.

"Hey, you still there?"

"I'm here."

"This is more serious than I thought. I'll be there as soon as I can."

"See you tomorrow." She flipped the cell phone closed and stared at the ceiling. This thing with Linc wasn't seri-ous, it couldn't be. She'd made herself a promise . . . but that was before Linc appeared.

Three

Paige wakened with a start, her brain foggy, her eyelids heavy. She glanced around the strange room. Stress and lack of sleep had made her extremely weary. Slowly she became aware that it was still the same day. She shook her head to remove the fog.

After the phone conversation with Mara, she must have fallen asleep. She popped up as the last two days reassembled in her mind. Glancing at the clock, she gasped, "My God, Linc will be here in fifteen minutes." She glanced out the open windows. The evening promised nice weather with a tawny, golden sun hanging low in the West, melting like liquid gold into the still waters of Lake Michigan.

She showered and concentrated on what to wear. Throwing on her charcoal Italian viscose stripe pants suit, she couldn't help comparing the last couple of days with her harried modeling career. And all she had wanted was a simple, relaxing vacation. She might as well have stayed at work, she thought.

She glanced in the mirror. Something was missing. She dug through her accessories bag and pulled out a lime-colored scarf, the one that was supposed to go with the vest. She never would have put a chartreuse vest under this suit, but the designer did and it was great. Guess that's why I'm the model, she thought.

Hurriedly, she pulled her hair high on her head, banded it and let it fall. Thankfully she had paid attention when the hair and make-up artists did her quickly. She was sure Linc was the kind of person to be punctual and she hated being late. It was just a few minutes before seven.

The warm rays of the evening sun fell and flashed off the black Lincoln Navigator pulling into the drive.

Through the window, she watched as Linc easily slid from behind the wheel and strode to the house. Damn, he looked hot.

A laugh fell from Paige's lips. As much as she warned herself not to become involved, all it took was one look at him and she was lost again. She threw a light coat over her arm and ran down to greet him at the front door.

Amusement flickered in the dark eyes that met hers when she jerked the door open. "I'm pleased you're in a hurry to see me." He cocked his head to one side and chuckled.

Paige joined him in his laughter. "I just don't like to be late."

"Oh." His mouth quirked with humor. He held out his arm, and she accepted. "I've been thinking about this evening ever since I left you today."

"I took a nap," she said nonchalantly. It was good to keep a man guessing.

Linc opened the door of his sports utility vehicle for her. "I think napping alone is a waste of time."

She giggled. "Not if you need some rest." She slipped onto the leather bucket seat and inhaled the new smell of the vehicle. He slid under the steering wheel and fastened his seat belt. Glancing her way, his eyes slid over her. "You look well rested and very beautiful tonight."

Paige pulled the seatbelt around her. She felt warmth fill her cheeks. "Thank you. You don't look so bad your-self." She appraised his jeans that smoothly covered his well-muscled thighs and the khaki sport jacket that only improved his broad shoulders. Her gaze shifted to the white Henley shirt that contrasted with his richly-tanned skin. No, he didn't look so bad. He looked downright inviting.

The short drive around the lake brought them to the picturesque Stafford Inn. It was elegant in every aspect of its late nineteenth century appearance.

"I hope you like it here." He helped her from the vehicle.

She glanced up at the white structure with green shutters. "It's charming. I'm sure I'll love it." She climbed the steps of the porch. Linc opened the French door and allowed her to pass in front of him. Paige hesitated as her eyes adjusted to the dimly lit entrance.

A woman bumped into her and then moved swiftly toward the exit. For a moment, Paige could have sworn the woman was her stepmother. She hadn't seen her face but she'd felt her presence and the aroma of the sickening sweet perfume from the past. Just the thought of Ada being near made her edgy, insignificant. She glanced toward the exit and then chided herself. It couldn't be. Ada hated Michigan and would never leave New York. Don't let the phantoms of the past ruin this evening, she thought.

"Good evening, Mr. Cross, your table is ready. The hostess led the way across the dining room to a quiet spot and seated them. "By the windows, as you requested."

The table was covered with an Irish linen cloth. A single red rose in a crystal bud vase was its only dressing. And outside, Little Traverse Bay was aglow with the setting sun.

"This is really nice." Paige gazed out the windows at the bay. It reminded her of her past and the home where she had grown up.

"I've always liked it here," he said, motioning to the waiter. "Would you care for a little wine or a mixed drink?"

She shook her head. "No, but I would like a Perrier with a lime twist."

He ordered and turned his attention to her. "I know you're on vacation, but from what and where?"

"I live and work in New York City," she answered, deliberately vague. She tried to keep personal information close to her chest.

He raised a dark brow. "That's a big place for a girl alone."

"I'm not alone. I share an apartment with my friend Mara. In fact, she'll be here tomorrow."

She hoped he wouldn't ask any more questions. She certainly didn't want to tell him she was a model. But she didn't want to lie either. Before she became a well-established model, men had never taken much notice of her. When her face began to appear on national magazine covers, she suddenly became interesting. She wasn't going to chance that happening again. If she was going to have a relationship with Linc, and that was a big if, she wanted him to like her for herself, not her fame.

"I work in the fashion industry," she said simply.

"That explains it."

Her heart pounded. "Explains what?"

"The way you dress, you always look well put together."

She flushed at his compliment but was relieved he didn't recognize her.

"Have you ever designed anything?" he asked.

"I've tried my hand at it a time or two. Maybe in time I'll design something that makes its mark on the world." Funny she didn't want him to know she was a model, but it irked her that he assumed she wasn't. She craftily turned the subject from herself to him. "What do you do, besides fighting fires?"

"I'm an architect."

"Really." She leaned back while the waiter placed their drinks on the table. "Would you be interested in drafting the blueprints for my house?"

"I'd be glad to. What do you have in mind?" He sipped the light beer he'd ordered and peered intently at Paige.

"I want it exactly as it was."

"That shouldn't be a problem. I've always admired the design of your house. And with the pictures at the library and in your album, we should be able to duplicate it."

The waiter slipped the small tray under his arm and waited to take their order. After they ordered, he disappeared into the shadows.

Paige smiled warmly at her dinner companion. "Then we have a deal." She held out her hand to seal the contract. "Please begin as soon as possible."

He accepted the proffered hand and then cupped it between his. His gaze traveled over her face and searched her eyes. "Consider it done."

The pianist softly played a medley of love songs. Paige wanted to retrieve her hand but she also wanted the moment to go on forever. A vague, sensuous awareness passed between them, growing stronger by the moment. She wanted to look away but was transfixed by his gaze, held in those dark, hypnotic pools that led to his soul.

A mischievous grin spread across Linc's face. He scraped his chair back and gripped the hand he held. "Come with me."

She followed, loving the electricity that passed between them as his grip tightened. "Where are we going?" she whispered.

"Out here." He gently led her through the patio doors onto the veranda. He gathered her into his arms and began gliding across the deck.

She glanced around. "No one else is dancing. I don't think they dance here."

He pulled her close and whispered hot breath into her hair. "We do."

What was the name of that song? Her mind tried to concentrate on the music instead of the strong, muscular arms that held her against the hard length of his body. "Unchained Melody!" That was it.

His mouth moved away from her ear, down her face, seeking her mouth. Paige knew what was coming. She knew she should resist and warned herself to back away, but somewhere in the back of her mind she knew she wouldn't.

Hot lips lightly touched hers. He slowly pulled back, his eyes darkening in desire. His fingers caressed the back of her neck, causing sparks of electricity to spiral down her spine. His lips scorched a trail along her jaw, his breath hot against her skin.

She pulled back and shook her head. "We shouldn't," she hoarsely whispered.

"Don't you feel it?" he asked.

"What?" God, what a stupid question. What, indeed? The fire, the passion, the molten lava that threatened to erupt between them? Of course she felt it, how could she not feel what was consuming her whole body?

"The sparks. They were there the first time we laid eyes on each other. Neither of us can deny it." His hold tightened.

"But we've only just met," she protested.

"Ummm, his hot tongue tasted her cheek and ran along her lips. "You're delicious."

Flames spread hotly along her veins and settled in her deepest parts. She had to admit she'd never wanted any man the way she wanted Linc. Oh, God, she didn't just want him, she needed him. Please, God, give me the strength to back away now, she prayed. When and if she ever made love with Linc, she would have to know it was right.

He whispered foreign words against her mouth that made her tremble, sounds of promises that made her ache. Words she felt, rather than knew, were of his heritage.

Linc slowly raised his head and looked deep into her eyes. "I know you think this is too soon. And maybe you're right." His voice was a husky whisper as his finger ran down her cheek and tenderly traced her lips.

They stared at each other, neither speaking, neither paying any attention to the light breeze feathering her hair around her face. Neither saw nor heard the gulls circling above the water, cawing and diving into the gentle swells that lapped the shore.

Paige flipped through the pages of *Mode* magazine, but she saw nothing. As she waited for Mara's flight, her mind was on her unsettling but exciting evening with Linc.

Closing her eyes, she relived the feel of his lips on hers, his strong arms encircling her body. Having already spent the day thinking about him, she came to only one conclusion: If he tried to seduce her again, she'd be willing.

What a quandary. Images of making love with Linc consumed her. She had said no but had meant yes. Damn it, yes. They were both consenting adults. What would it hurt? She knew the answer to that; she'd been hurt before. She'd made herself a promise . . . never again. The next time it would be right, the next time it would be forever.

She squeezed her eyes tight. Just thinking about Linc caused a fever to rise in her blood. The memory of skin against skin caused hers to become hot and damp. And aching.

There was a peaceful yet primitive wildness about him that thrilled and excited her. If she allowed, he would remove her carefully placed barriers and show her ecstasy as no man ever had. He would release that wild, untamed thing within her that could only match his own. He was what she had waited for all her life. And she'd said no.

"Paige, are you sleeping?" Mara's voice penetrated her passion-drugged mind.

"What?" Paige started and then stared at Mara. Her friend looked as if she had just come from the "What's Hot" shoot. Her peaches and cream complexion was complemented by a brown-crocheted tunic with a colored body suit the color of her skin. The top had an embroidered hem with wooden charms sewn to the bottom. Wood and golden jewelry hung from her ears, neck and wrist. Her long golden blond hair was pulled back away from her face, making her green-blue eyes even more prominent.

"Hey, girl, are you not feeling well?" Mara surveyed her friend, concern on her face.

Paige jumped up and threw her arms around the newcomer. "It's so good to see you."

Mara gave a throaty laugh and held her friend back to look at her. "Is everything all right?"

"Of course. I'm just tired."

Mara stared at her for a moment and then asked, "Who's the guy?"

"What guy?" Paige feigned innocence. What guy indeed! She'd thought of nothing else since her dinner with Linc. He was consuming her.

"Come on. It's written all over you. He must have given you one hell of a roll in the hay for you to look so dazed," she teased, her heavy New York accent deepened.

"Mara!" Paige gasped, glancing around to make sure no one else could hear her.

"Hey. I calls 'em as I sees 'em and your face says it all, honey." Mara patted Paige's cheek with a tissue. "Maybe it's just a little hot here."

Paige brushed Mara's hand away and slipped her purse strap over her shoulder. "Let's get your luggage before you have me a model turned hooker." She wanted to quickly terminate this conversation. She turned to her friend. "It arrived with you, didn't it?"

"Yeah, why?"

"Good. Mine went to Chicago. Thankfully, I had packed extra necessities in my carry-on."

Mara laughed. "That must have been beastly. Remember when we arrived in Milan and all our suitcases were delayed for five days?"

"I remember. This time wasn't that bad, thank God. They came in the day after I arrived here."

Together they pulled the familiar hot pink luggage from the conveyor and placed it on a cart. Paige gasped as she placed the last bag high on the pile. "You brought about as much as I did, and I'm staying all summer."

"Everything is absolutely essential." Mara glanced at the cart. They laughed. Both women were accustomed to living out of suitcases and they did it well.

"Would you like help with those?" A young man stood by the cart waiting for them to answer.

"Sure, why not." Mara looped her arm through Paige's. "Lead the way."

Mara placed a substantial tip in the young man's hand after he had managed to stuff all the luggage in Paige's little rental.

His face brightened as he stared at the bill she'd given him. "Thank you!"

The friends chatted lightly for a couple of miles. Finally Mara reached over and turned down the music on the radio. "Okay, come clean. What's bothering ya? Tell me about this guy."

"What guy?"

Mara heaved an exasperated sigh. "If memory serves me right, you were telling me about two guys when we spoke on the phone. Now it's, What guy? This is Mara, remember." She tapped her chest with the long, polished nails of her ringed fingers.

Paige smiled sheepishly. She had never been able to keep anything from her friend. Did she really want to? As she turned her car from the airport drive to the highway, she said, "I think I've found Mr. Right. I'm not sure if it will go anywhere but it scares me to take the chance."

"What in the hell does that mean?"

"It means I can't get involved with anyone, not yet." Paige came to a stop at the light.

"Why don't you start at the beginning of this story. I feel like I've come in during the second act."

Paige took a deep breath and told her about the fire, Linc and Jack. Then she told about dinner with Linc the previous evening . . . and about feeling her stepmother's presence even though she wasn't here.

"Whoa! In just a few short days, you've managed to pack a lot of living into your life."

"More than I want, I can tell you that."

Mara laid her hand on Paige's arm. "Why? We all hope to fall in love one day. So you did it sooner than you expected, that's all. And as for your stepmother, she's tucked safely away in New York somewhere."

Paige threw her a determined frown. "I'm not in love, and as for Ada, you're right. She wouldn't come to Michigan on a bet."

"Right. But about this love thing."

Paige shook her head. "It's not love, not yet. It's lust, that's all. And then there's Jack..."

"Are you telling me you're in love with both guys?"

Now Paige did shoot her a withering look. "No, definitely not! I don't feel anything for Jack, except gratitude for his helping me when I needed it. But Linc is different. And I'm not ready. I have a lot of things I want to do before I finally settle down." She thought for a minute. "Who knows, maybe he isn't ready. Maybe he isn't thinking the same way I am."

"Maybe, maybe not. Haven't you ever heard of love at first sight?"

"Not me." Paige turned on the crossroad that connected with her property. "It's just plain old lust and raging hormones."

"I don't think so. I've known you for eight years and I've never seen you like this. You're in love, girlfriend."

Paige laughed. "No..." But was she being honest with her friend, let alone herself?

"Listen," Mara interrupted her thoughts. "I know love when I see it, and you're in a bad way." She settled back in her seat. "Now, tell me about this Jack. He sounds interesting. I'll take him off your hands for you."

"He's not on my hands. He owns the bed and breakfast where I'm staying. It's down the road from my place. A quaint little inn, but it's not home. Know what I mean?"

Mara nodded. "Too bad about the fire. What are you going to do with the place now?"

"Rebuild."

"Makes sense." Mara glanced out the window at the rolling hills and passing stand of white pine. "It's really nice here. I see why you like it so much."

"It's always been home, you know." Paige paused for several seconds. "Linc is an architect. He's going to draw up the blueprints for me. I want it just as it was. And someday when I retire, I'm going to settle right here."

"Mmm. Sounds like you've really got things worked out. You don't need me."

Paige turned to her friend. "You're wrong. I do need you to keep me on the straight and narrow. I can't go falling in love right now. I'm at the top of the ladder. There's no room for love."

"Love doesn't wait. It strikes when it's hot and by the sound of this Linc of yours, he's definitely hot."

Paige flushed. "He's hot all right. Too hot."

Mara shrugged and threw up her hands. "So, what's the problem. Que sera, sera."

"Right. And let a great career just fly out the window. You know how long it takes to get where we are. It was harder for me, being black, and I'm not going to give it all up for a man."

"Who's asking you to?" Mara grimaced.

Paige frowned thoughtfully. "Actually, no one. It's just that Linc is so intense. I can't see juggling being a wife and handling a career at the same time. Not that he has asked or will, but being with him has made me think about that kind of life."

"Don't give me that. We can do anything. It's the new millennium, for crying out loud."

Paige pulled into the drive of the bed and breakfast. "Mara, you slay me sometimes."

"A lot of people tell me that." Mara studied the rambling, white Victorian. "Now, this is my idea of a vacation spot." She slipped from the car, removed her sunglasses and gazed at the house.

"Nice, isn't it?" Paige opened the trunk and began taking the bags out. "Oh, by the way. I haven't told anyone about being a model. I don't want my career to get in the way of any friendships I make."

Mara laughed. "Do you think you can keep it a secret for long? God, your face has been on most of the magazines on the shelves."

"I know," Paige agreed. "But let's keep it a secret for as long as we can. Okay?"

"Sure, no problem. You know me, I'm always ready for a little healthy deception."

"Let me help." Jack's voice interrupted them as he bounded down the steps. He spoke to Paige, but his eyes were gliding over Mara.

"Jack, this is my friend, Mara Matere, from New York. Mara, this is Jack Devlin."

Mara's smile spread across her face and into her greenish blue eyes. "Hi, how 'wa ya." She held out her hand. The gold on the wooden bracelets sparkled as they caught the bright, afternoon sun.

"My pleasure." He took her hand in his, holding it longer than he needed. When she pulled her hand free, he chuckled softly and bent to lift the suitcases. "Will you be sharing the Princess Room with Paige?"

Mara threw Paige a jesting glance. "Princess Room, eh? No, I'll have a room of my own. There's no way we could both fit in one room. She glanced at her luggage and then back at Jack. "Thanks anyway."

After thoroughly looking all the rooms over, Mara decided on the Captain's Room with the small balcony jutting over the front porch with a generous view of Lake Michigan.

Almost reluctantly, Jack pulled a piece of paper from his pocket and handed it to Paige. "You had a message while you were out."

Paige read it and shoved the paper in her pocket. "If you'll excuse me, I'll be back after I make this call."

"Sure." Mara began unpacking and chatting easily with Jack as if they were long-lost friends.

Paige heard Mara ask Jack, "So you own this place and double as bellboy, message taker and whatever?" Paige laughed as she left the room. It was just like Mara to get to the crux of the matter without preliminaries.

She pulled the cell phone from her purse and punched in the numbers. "Linc? Paige here. You called?" She tried to quell the pounding of her heart by being professional.

"Yes. Did you think I wouldn't?" There was a slight tinge of wonder in his voice.

She didn't know how to answer this. Of course she knew he would phone but she also knew how to be coy. "You never know." She could hardly lift her voice above a whisper.

"You can't get rid of me that easy."

She swallowed hard, trying to push down the knot in her throat. "I wasn't trying to."

"Paige, I have to see you. Is it a good time to come over?"

Paige smiled. She had to see him too, but she wasn't sure it was for the same reason. "Why?"

"I need to discuss something with you . . . about your house."

"Architects work faster than I thought."

"This one does, but it's not about the plans." He spoke in an odd tone, almost as if he were hiding something.

"I...well, I was about to take Mara to my place."

There was a slight hesitation and then, "That's right, your friend came in today. Okay, I'll meet you there. How long?"

She could sense an urgency. "Is anything wrong?"

"Half an hour?" he asked without answering her question.

"Okay." What was wrong? He seemed strange. Maybe he had thought better of their budding relationship. Oh, well, perhaps it was for the best. If that were so, why did she feel so empty all of a sudden?

As she entered Mara's open door she saw Jack was still there.

"Jack, do you have any spring water here?" Mara's silky voice draped each word in honey.

"Hey, all our water is spring water. We just don't bottle it." He chuckled.

Mara pursed her lips sensuously and tilted her head in a pleading manner. "Do you suppose I could have a glass over ice with a twist of lemon?"

"No problem. I'll get it for you."

"Thanks. You're a peach."

Jack gave Paige a quick glance as he rushed past her.

"Hey, what did you do to him. You've got him eating out of your hand and you haven't been here fifteen minutes."

Mara smiled at Paige as she hung the last of her clothes in the closet. "Isn't he the sweetest?" She snapped close the large pullman and shoved it to the back of the huge closet.

"You know me. When I see a good looking, unattached male, I grab on." She laughed. "And then I usually throw 'em back." She pulled the crocheted outfit over her head and shinnied out of the bodysuit. "I think I'll change into something a little more country." She eyed her friend, "I could tell you weren't crazy about my New York look."

"I didn't say I didn't like it." Paige gave her that knowing look. "It's just a little ostentatious for northern Michigan, that's all."

Mara stood in her flesh-colored lace bra and panties, tapping her finger on her chin. She opened the second drawer of the tall dresser. "I have a couple pair of designer jeans for just such an occasion." She held up the classy denim jeans. "And how about this blue silk shantung madras plaid shirt and this leather belt? Country enough for ya?" She pranced in a circle with the clothes in front of her.

Paige laughed and cocked her head. "You sound like you're still on the runway. But I doubt very many gals around here would spend what that outfit cost for casual wear."

"Hey, I gotta look good, even if I'm in the country, don't I?" Mara quickly transformed herself as if she were the next one to go on the catwalk. "Did you call your Linc?"

Paige closed the door and wrinkled her nose at her friend. "First of all, he isn't my Linc. And yes, I talked to him."

"Do I get to meet him?" She pulled her long golden hair back and braided it in one long tail.

"He's going to be at my property in half an hour."

"Great." Mara rolled up the long sleeves of the shirt, fastened the belt and slipped into matching denim and leather loafers. She twirled around just as she might at a shoot. "Well?"

"Perfect." Paige opened the door just as Jack was poised to knock.

"My water." Mara rushed forward. "Thanks." She accepted the glass with great panache, took a sip and sat it on the dresser.

"What are you ladies up to this afternoon?" Jack asked.

"Paige is taking me to see what's left of her house. Wanna come along?"

He shook his head. "I can't. I have some calls to make. I'll catch up with you later."

Paige noticed a look that resembled disappointment cross his face. Could he be interested in Mara? It would be no surprise. Most men were intrigued by her glamour and beauty. But he could also be in shock. Not many people came here looking as Mara did earlier.

"Well, let's go." Paige descended the stairs with Mara closely following.

"Would you like to walk? It's only a mile down the road."

"Sure," Mara answered, waving at Jack who stood on the porch watching them.

"What do people around here do for excitement?" Mara asked.

Paige laughed and shrugged. "You know, I don't remember. I was only a kid when we left. But most of my happiest memories are here. I guess because my parents were here."

"It seems so...so..., I don't know. Sorta laid back."

"That's the point. It is laid back. That's what makes it the perfect vacation spot for people like us," Paige said. "I've been reading the resort magazine and there seems to be a lot to do."

Mara kicked a stone at the side of the road. "I'd like to drive around and see what's here."

"You know what we could do?" Paige was suddenly excited.

"What?"

"We could drive to Harbor Springs and gape at the celebrities and sport figures that have homes over there."

Mara tilted her head. "You know how we hate the paparazzi. Why would we do the same thing to others?" She looked at her friend slyly. "That was the nice Mara talking, you know."

"No, you're absolutely right. We do hate being followed by cameras and reporters. We'll find something else to do. Until then, you can use Jack for your entertainment.

"He's going to be a very nice diversion." Mara tossed her head and ran her tongue over her rosy lips. She walked with a springy bounce toward the tall pines of Paige's property.

"Well, that's all that's left of my place." Paige stopped and stared at the blackened mound. Slowly, she led the way.

"Wow. You really meant it when you said it burned to the ground."

Paige lifted a piece of burned wood that hung on another piece. It crumbled in two and fell to the ground. "I'm going to rebuild it just as it was." Sadness welled up inside her. "The only thing is, I've lost all my family keepsakes." Warmth flowed through her when she thought of Linc bringing her the album. "I do have the picture album Linc saved for me, though."

"Linc seems to be everywhere." Mara pulled a face. "How much of your savings is rebuilding going to dig into?"

"Not much." Paige shook her head. "I've kept the insurance up."

"That's good. You don't want to touch your savings. Remember, our plan is to have enough to retire by the time we're thirty," Mara reminded her.

Paige smiled at her. "How could I forget? We've been planning this for a long time. And that's another reason why I can't get involved right now."

Their conversation ceased as they watched a pickup pull into the driveway. Linc emerged from the large red truck. "Did you walk?" he asked as he approached.

Her heart stalled as she watched the tall, dark man move in their direction. It was difficult to answer calmly when her hormones were raging out of control. "It's so nice out, we couldn't resist." She turned to Mara. "Mara, this is Lincoln Cross. Linc, this is my best friend, Mara Matere."

Mara held out her hand. "Hi, how 'wa ya? Paige has told me all about you."

Linc lifted a questioning brow in Paige's direction.

"All good, I give you my word," Mara interjected.

"What did you want to speak to me about?" Paige asked.

"It's kind of personal."

Paige glanced at Mara, a smile touching her lips. "Mara and I don't have secrets from each other."

"Okay." Linc raked his fingers through his dark hair. "I heard from the fire chief today. The authorities suspect the fire was not accidental. They think someone deliberately set it."

Paige felt as if someone had knocked the air from her lungs. "What? Who would do a thing like that? Why would they?"

"Are you sure?" Mara asked.

Linc nodded. "That's what I've been told. Of course they haven't completed the investigation. This is only their preliminary finding."

"I can't believe it." Paige exclaimed. "Who would want to burn my home? I don't know anyone around here.

It doesn't make any sense." She stared at the pile of rubble.

"What made them think the fire was deliberate?" Mara asked.

"They found several gasoline cans discarded near the fire. They will be able to tell after analysis of the ashes."

"Yeah?" Mara continued, "And then what? What if someone did burn the house?"

"Then they will do a criminal investigation to try and find the arsonist."

A wave of apprehension swept through Paige. "How long will all this take?"

Linc shook his head. "You never know. If the ashes prove negative, then it's over. If they find an accelerator, then it could take a while."

Paige groaned. "This is just what I need. This whole vacation has been one nightmare from the start. I never should have come back."

"Hey, it's all right." Mara put her arm around her friend.

Jack pulled his pickup to a stop up beside Linc's, jumped out and sauntered toward them. "I finished my calls." He glanced at the solemn group. "Is anything wrong?" He glared at Linc and then turned his attention to Mara with her arm protectively around Paige.

Mara spoke for her friend. "The authorities suspect arson."

"Here?" Jack gestured to what used to be a house.

Linc eyed Jack. "Chief Stanton called and asked me to let Paige know. The preliminary investigation certainly suggests it," he answered.

"What made them suspect anything?" Jack asked.

"Gasoline cans in the field behind the house."

"Ouch." Jack grimaced. "Not good. Not good." He shook his head.

Paige and Linc turned toward the rubble at the same time and stared at the remains, as if studying it for answers.

Mara slipped her arm through Jack's and guided him away from the thoughtful couple. "Why don't you tell me what people do for entertainment around here."

Linc spoke quietly. "There's nothing we can do here. Why don't I give you a lift back to the inn?"

Paige nodded but didn't move. "You're right, of course. It's just an awful feeling to think someone would want to burn my home. I just can't imagine . . ." Her voice trailed off, wondering who hated her enough to hurt her.

Linc gently took her hand in his and tugged her away from the pile of debris. "Come on, I'll take you back."

Paige was glad he was there to make things better. She couldn't think and she didn't really want to. She could see Mara spinning her web around Jack and it made her smile to herself. Her friend's presence made her feel normal. "Mara, Linc has offered to give us a ride back."

Mara glanced at Jack and then back at the approaching couple. "Uh...Jack has asked me to go to dinner with him tonight. Maybe the four of us could go together. That is, unless you would rather do something alone tonight, just you and me." Her warm, infectious smile spread over the small group.

Linc and Jack exchanged looks. The atmosphere was anything but congenial.

Paige didn't miss the unspoken dialogue between the men. The lifetime of difficulties stood as a solid barrier between them. She did want to spend time with Mara but she didn't want to foil her friend's first night of vacation. There was no need to encumber Mara. "You know, I really could use an evening to relax and get a good night's sleep. Tomorrow will be time enough for us to get caught up."

Mara hugged her friend. "Jack wants to show me some of the sights and then we're going to dinner." She held her friend back and looked into her eyes. "Are you sure you are all right with this?"

Paige smiled widely. "Absolutely. You run along and have a good time. I wouldn't be good company tonight anyway." She watched as Jack opened the door and Mara climbed into the truck. She knew by the time they returned, Jack would not see Mara's five-foot, eleven inch large frame, he'd see only her spirited soul and the beauty she carried inside and out.

Linc tugged on the hand he had not released and looked her over seductively. "Let's go. I'm sure we can find something to entertain us this evening."

Paige loved his easy camaraderie, his subtle wit and his ability to make her feel special. She returned his gaze and flashed a bantering smile, "Are the museums open in the evening?"

Linc's laughter was a full-hearted sound. "If they aren't, I'll knock on doors until someone opens them for you."

Four

Jack and Mara drove away, leaving Paige and Linc alone. "So? Is there anything special you would like to see before we go to dinner?"

Mara shrugged. "I don't know. Why don't we just drive. It's such a beautiful day."

Jack glanced at his companion. The wild hair she had tried to tame with a braid was escaping and wisping around her face. If she wasn't so big, she would be one beautiful woman. Then he amended his thoughts, she's beautiful no matter how you look at it.

He pulled his pickup onto the Harbor-Petoskey Road.

His gaze slid over her western-clad frame. "Do you like to line dance?"

"Sure, who doesn't?" She fiddled with the radio stations until she found one that played country.

His lusty laugh filled the cab. "I can think of about a dozen people I know who think it's silly."

"Their loss." She gazed out the window as they pulled into a small town that looked as if it came straight off the New England Coast. The road dipped into a valley with Lake Michigan to the left and steep cliffs to the right. He slowed by a large fenced-in area. "This is the deer park."

Mara leaned forward. "Oh?" This guy is really a country bumpkin, she thought. A zoo, for crying out loud. She pushed the door open and climbed from the truck. She did love animals, maybe it wouldn't be so bad. The deer came to the fence expectantly. "They act like they want something."

Jack deposited a couple of quarters in a feed machine and gave the cup of grain to Mara. "Here. The deer are used to tourists feeding them."

Mara glanced in his direction. He didn't seem interested in the deer or anything to do with the wildlife preserve. She grimaced to herself. *He is treating me as he would any tourist.*

This thought didn't make her happy. But she knew she could play any game he chose and play it better. She held her hand out to the deer.

"Come on. I've got something good for you." One large doe moved forward and nibbled the feed from her hand. It was followed by several more nudging one another for the food.

Jack leaned on the fence beside her. "This isn't what you'd call exciting, is it?"

Mara flashed him a big smile. "There's plenty of time for excitement. I love animals. I just don't have time in my busy schedule to have pets." She scratched the deer's ears.

"Don't tell me. You'd be the woman with a dozen dogs and cats, right?"

"Sure. Maybe more."

"Why don't you? What kind of job do you have that keeps you from having pets?"

Paige had warned her about this topic. "I work in the fashion industry. But it's not my job that keeps me from having pets, it's the rules in my apartment building."

"What do you do for the fashion industry?"

Mara smiled, *he wouldn't believe it if she told him.* He was probably one of those guys who thought of models as the anorexic type. "A little of this and a little of that. I do help the models get dressed sometimes." *Half-truths worked very well here.*

Jack raised a brow. "A girl Friday, huh?"

"Yeah, something like that." *It was obvious this man hadn't been by a magazine rack in the past few months. And her bra ad was on television every hour. Maybe I* should take my shirt off and strike a pose. The thought made her giggle inside.

"Have you lived in New York long or did you go there to work in fashion?"

"Since I was born." She wanted to divert the subject from fashion before she told him the truth. She knew some people were having a difficult time grasping the concept of drop dead gorgeous women who weren't starving to death and she didn't want to get into that. Besides, Paige had asked her not to say anything. "Tell me about this bed and breakfast of yours. How did it get started?" she asked sweetly.

He shrugged. "It's not as glamorous as fashion, but the house belonged to my great-grandparents. My great-grandfather was one of the first doctors to come to Petoskey. He was from Boston and Grandmother wouldn't come unless she had a home equal to what she had to give up back East."

"Makes sense." Mara fed the last of the feed to the deer and brushed the crumbs from her hands.

"No one in the family wanted it because it's impractical to live in year around. No one has big families anymore. My grandmother used to rent rooms before she died. Emma worked for her. After college I got the idea to open it as a bed and breakfast. It's been very successful. Now I want to expand."

"Oh? How so?"

"I've already built small Victorian-style cottages on the back of the property and I want to put in a golf course."

"Will you be building it close to your resort?"

Jack didn't want her to know he was interested in the Turner land, but he was anxious to find out what the plans were. "Depends."

"On what?"

"I've got my eye on a nice piece near the resort. If it goes up for sale, I'll make a bid on it." He took her by the arm and led her to the truck. "Let's find something fun to do. I'm sure there are many things you'd rather do on a beautiful evening like this."

Mara shook her head. Actually she had discovered she was enjoying doing nothing. Her career had every minute of every day blocked out. "This is actually a nice change." Even if she did think he was being a tourist guide, at least he was a handsome one.

"See that strip of land out there?"

"Yeah." She followed his gaze to the finger of land with large, Victorian mansions edging the shore. What did he have in mind now, a real estate tour?

"That's Harbor Point. Only the very rich have summer homes there."

"Really." She yawned, bored.

"It's an association of sorts. You know, a person has to be worth so much to own property there."

"Emm. . . Sounds a little rich for my blood." She might have enough money for it but she didn't want to live where people drove by and envied her.

Jack laughed again. "That's why I'm gearing my resort to the middle income population. They like nice stuff and generally are nicer people." He drove past the entrance to the point, continued through town and up a steep incline to the other side. "This is Scenic Shore Drive. You ought to see it in the fall."

"Do you have a lot of foliage color in October and November?" That was something she did enjoy. Perhaps she'd take a little time off this fall and tour the Catskills. Maybe she could find a tour guide who thought he was a man and she was a woman.

"An understatement. This little strip of shoreline has been photographed by the best and has been in many travel magazines."

"Interesting." She slid closer to him. "Now, tell me what you do for entertainment, besides dancing and feeding deer, of course." Mara knew what she was doing. She'd done it a hundred times before. Before the night was over, Jack would wonder what had hit him.

He glanced at her, his eyes appraising her frankly. "Do you want the truth or..."

"The truth will be fine."

"I don't have much time for entertainment. I have my resort and as I've already said, I want to expand it."

She reached out and ran her finger over his ear. "You know what they say, don't you?"

"No, tell me," his voice suddenly husky.

"All work and no play makes Jack a dull boy." She leaned closer. "Now we can't have that, can we?"

He laughed. "And I suppose you have the remedy?"

"You can count on it." She rested her arm on his shoulder and ran her index finger around the outside of his ear.

He opened his window slightly.

Mara laughed. "Getting too hot in here for you?"

"Something like that." He made several turns and finally pulled the truck to the side of the road. "Ever heard of the Big Mac Bridge?"

"Bridge?" God, this guy was going to be tough. What was with him anyway?

"There." He pointed. "It's five miles long and spans the upper and lower peninsulas of Michigan."

Her eyes were on him, not the bridge. She'd seen a thousand bridges in her travels, but right now Jack was much more interesting. Well he could be if he let himself go. "Interesting," she purred.

He turned to gaze into her aqua eyes. "You don't seem interested."

"Not in the bridge, but I'm definitely interested." Yes, she thought. He wasn't so sure of himself now, not sure at all.

Jack shook his head. "Lady, you're something else."

A sly, calculating smile crossed Mara's face. "So I've been told."

Jack pulled back onto the highway. "I think we'd better find someplace to get a cool drink."

"Where are we?" she asked, teasing his dusky blond hair that was a tad long at his nape.

He cleared his throat. "This is Mackinaw City."

"Another tourist trap?"

"But a nice one. A casino is going in here soon."

"Gambling?"

"There are a couple of casinos across the bridge in the upper peninsula."

"All right! That's what I call entertainment. I'll have to go there before my vacation is over."

"If I didn't have early plans in the morning, I'd take you tonight. Another night?"

"Sure." She fell back in her seat. Mara wasn't sure she wanted to spend another night with the tourist guide/real estate agent. She glanced down the hotel-lined streets. This would make a wonderful place for a photo shoot. There, it was her turn. This was a vacation and she was thinking of work.

His voice broke into her thoughts. "That's Mackinac Island over there. Maybe one day we should go. A lot of history and romance there."

"Romance!" She picked up on the word. "Now I can relate to that."

"I'll bet you can." He turned the truck onto I-75 and raced at high speed down the interstate.

"I'm not complaining, but aren't you afraid of getting a ticket?"

He threw her a crafty grin. "You want to go dancing, don't you?"

"Sure."

"Then let me worry about tickets. Besides, I have a special place in mind. Dinner and dancing all wrapped up in one nice package."

"Line dancing?"

"It's called the Country Dance Club. You'll like it."

Mara settled against her seat. Maybe she would, but she'd be happier if he would show a little more interest in her. He was good looking, potentially fun, and had money. A good start, even if he was a little stuffy. This one was going to be a little tougher than usual but she loved a challenge. And he was definitely that.

Her companion seemed to be completely involved with his driving. Mara pointed to his car phone, "Do you mind? I think I should check on Paige." Using his was easier than digging into her bag for hers.

Jack handed her the phone.

Mara dialed her friend's cell phone and tapped her long fingernails on the dash to the music on the radio. "I'm sorry the cell customer you are trying to reach is unavailable or out of the region." Mara sat the phone back in its cradle. "Wonder where she is?"

Jack shrugged his shoulders. "She probably went to bed early and turned the phone off. She said she was tired."

Mara was feeling guilty for having left Paige when she felt so bad. "Maybe I should go back and check on her? She's had a rough couple of days with the fire and now the arson."

"I'm sure she'll be fine. But if you want, we could grab a quick bite and then go back," Jack offered.

Mara tried the phone again. This time Paige answered. "Hi, Mara."

"How did you know it was me." Mara laughed.

"Right about now you're feeling bad for leaving. You called so that I could tell you that you don't have to feel guilty."

Mara could hear the smile in her friend's voice. "Are you absolving me of my guilt?"

Now Paige giggled out loud. "Of course I am. Linc and I are talking. I'm fine."

"I thought you were going to bed? I got a recording when I tried to call you the first time . . . out of region."

"I forgot to turn it on, and I am going to bed."

"Alone?"

"Yes, alone, smarty-pants. I'll see you in the morning for breakfast. We'll get caught up then." There was a slight pause, "Have a good time this evening."

Mara said her goodbye and then replaced the phone. "She's fine. She and Linc are talking."

"He's a smooth operator." Jack snorted. He glanced in Mara's direction as her eyebrows shot up. "So, what is Paige going to do with her property?"

Mara wondered what he meant about Linc but she didn't want to get into that. "She's going to rebuild. Linc is drafting the blueprints to return the house to exactly what it was."

"He's smoother than I thought. Wine and dine her and then land a good contract."

Mara shook her head. "I don't think it's like that at all. But whatever it is, they're adults and can take care of their own business." She studied his profile. His jaw was clenched and the muscle along the jaw line flexed. He had a real problem with Linc and she would find out what it was.

"Is there something Paige should know about Linc?"

Jack shrugged his shoulders. "Like you say, they're adults." His strong arm flexed as he turned the wheel to exit the highway. He flashed her a brilliant smile. "And we're adults, so let's do what adults do." The truck slowed and he turned into a parking lot.

Mara glanced up to see a sign with a dancing couple in lights. She laughed a throaty laugh, "Oh, I thought you had something more intimate in mind."

Jack helped her from the truck and whispered into her ear. "This is the appetizer. We'll get to the other adult stuff later."

"Well, things are beginning to look up." Country-western music filled the evening outside the large barn shaped building. Willingly, she allowed Jack to lead her inside. Couples of every age were dancing in line on a hardwood floor. Most were dressed in western garb, and a few men wore cowboy hats.

Mara and Jack were weaving their way through the crowd when a happy cowboy grabbed her and pulled her toward the floor.

"You alone?" he yelled over the crowd noise.

She glanced at Jack who had stopped to let her catch up. "I may as well be," she laughed as the cowboy tugged her away. They joined a line of dancers doing the cowboy hustle. Mara threw her head back and shook her hair loose. She felt free. She glanced toward the tables and saw Jack sitting in the shadows. It was clear he wasn't happy with his solitary status. The cowboy picked Mara up and whirled her around. When he sat her down, they were very near Jack. "Little lady, anytime you want to dance you just stand and holler 'Sawyer', and I'll be here before the music starts." He squeezed her shoulders and planted a kiss on her cheek.

Mara turned a mildly red face to Jack. "Guess it isn't safe to leave anything unattended here." She smiled sweetly.

"I guess not." Jack retorted.

Mara could see Mr. Stuffy was losing some of his stuffing. She fanned herself with the menu. "I do like the bright lights." Mara closed her eyes and swayed to the music that had changed to a slow ballad.

Jack took Mara in his arms and roughly whispered, "I think it's time for the girl who thinks she's alone to discover she's leaving with the same guy she came with."

A satiny giggle escaped her lips as she leaned into his chest and was swept onto the floor.

"I'm glad Mara called. You told her we were talking, but you didn't tell her you were trying to send me home." He paused to look at the road sign and then continued. "If she hadn't, you might have spent the evening alone with your problems." Linc spoke softly to Paige as he turned the truck down a dark road.

Paige stared at his handsome profile as he maneuvered the vehicle. He had been right. If she had stayed alone in her room, she would have just moped around until Mara came in. After she had called, Paige decided to accept Linc's offer of an evening out. She sighed heavily.

"I'm not good company tonight. You'd have been better off to leave me at the Inn." She was struggling with why someone would burn her house.

"Why? So you could brood about what's happening? No, you don't need that. Look at the sunset. Have you ever seen a grander one?"

Paige's gaze turned to the burning sky streaked with tones of graying purple. The red-gold sun had already dipped low into the horizon, reflecting a path to shore, a path so golden it made her feel as if she could walk on water.

"Wait just a minute." Linc stopped at a small, ranch style house, jumped from the truck and ran up to the door. He talked for several minutes with a man and then returned.

"Let's go." He slid under the steering wheel, turned the key and eased the vehicle back onto the road.

"Have you ever thought about moving back...permanently, I mean?" he asked.

"To Michigan? Yes." It was her dream. It was what she was working so hard for. "I plan to return in about five years, give or take a year."

"No sooner?"

"I don't think so. I have some things I want to do, ends of my life I want to tie up and then I'm coming home for good, at least those were my plans until the house burned."

He kept his eyes straight ahead. "You still can. It won't take long to rebuild."

"I hope not. I've always thought of this as home. I can't tell you how much I've missed it." She gazed out the window at the passing countryside.

He nodded. "I think I know how you feel. I'm from here too, remember?"

He pulled into a park situated on a steep cliff overlooking Little Traverse Bay and shut off the engine. "How many views have you seen like this?"

"Not many." The lake water was unusually smooth. The setting sun was orange-gold satin spread across the bay. A few small fishing boats dotted the surface of the water. Next to the smaller boats stood the yachts of the more affluent. Nature and man living harmoniously. Her heart ached. The longer she stayed, the more homesick she became and she knew when the time came it would be hard to leave.

"When you do return, what are your plans?"

She shrugged. "I don't know exactly. I've thought about doing a lot of things. Take art lessons, write a book or maybe open a small gift shop. I'll know when the time comes. How about you? What dreams do you have, or have you achieved them already?"

A crafty smile touched his lips. "Being an architect has always been my dream, but there's more to one's dreams than work."

"Oh?" She glanced at him. "Like what?"

"Like...a wife and children."

Her heart leaped in her chest. Was he thinking of her? Get serious, she told herself. He was only thinking about the future as she herself had done so many times.

He reached for the key and brought the truck to life. "I have a surprise for you." He pulled onto the highway and headed into town.

"What?" Her curiosity was piqued.

Linc smiled at her mischievously. "I'm going to give you just what you asked for." He crossed the Bear River and pulled into a parking lot behind a large building.

"Where are we?" She squinted to make out the dimly lit sign over the door.

"Come on." He raced around and opened her door.

Paige studied the darkened building. "But it's closed."

"Follow me." He held out his hand and she slipped hers into it.

"Hi, Bill." Linc called to a fellow who opened the door and held it for them to enter.

"Bill, this is my friend, Paige Turner. Paige, this is Bill Winters."

After the introductions were made and Bill turned on the museum lights, Linc and Paige entered the large room to the right.

Paige smiled broadly. "Next time I'll be careful what I ask for." Her face felt hot as she thought of his body tight against hers. Because she would certainly ask for that if she could do it without a commitment.

Linc didn't notice her flushed cheeks. His mind was on another situation, something he knew he had to tell her soon. He took her hand. "There's something I want to show you." He led her to the Native American section of the museum."

Paige admired the fine basket weaving and leaned over the glass case to admire the beadwork. "Some of these look like your collection. They're beautiful."

"My mother does a lot of this type of work. That beaded belt? That's hers."

Paige turned to Linc. "You're Native American, aren't you?" The question hung in the air. She should've known by just looking at him. His raven hair was soft and straight and his tan wasn't a tan but his natural coloring. She gazed into his jet black eyes waiting for him to answer. But she already knew.

"Half." His voice turned bitter. "My father was white."

"Oh."

"Does that bother you?" he asked.

She raised a shapely brow. She couldn't believe he'd asked. A light giggle escaped her lips as she gazed up into

his face. "Well I do prefer my men a little taller, but..."
She laughed lightly.

He smiled. "You know what I mean...ah, some..."

His usually calm demeanor changed into a challenging
stance. Paige stood on her tiptoes and kissed his cheek.
"Don't be silly. I've spent my whole life fighting my
weight and color. If I'm not being judged for one, then I'm
being judged for the other. I know better than to judge
someone by the way they look or their ancestry. And you
look like a storybook prince to me."

Suddenly, the thought of her stepmother flashed
through her mind. Ada who tried so hard to pass for white
to the point of dying her hair red and moving back to New
York where no one knew her. Ada had been the source of
great confusion in her life but now Paige knew who she
was and was beginning to truly like herself.

Linc pulled her into his arms. "You're not overweight.
You are exceptionally beautiful the way you are."

Paige inhaled deeply of the male odor she had grown
to know and love in such a short time. She spoke into his
chest. "And you're not a mixed race in a racist society.
You're beautiful the way you are."

Linc lifted her chin and stared into her eyes. "Flirting is
my job. I think you've stepped into untried territory.
You'd better be careful or I'll misinterpret your signals."

His smile covered his face but his eyes carried a sincerity that worried her. A casual relationship was all she
would allow herself at this time no matter how tempting
this virile man was.

She unwillingly pulled from his embrace and moved
along the glass case that held everything from quill and
bead jewelry to knives with carved elk horn handles.
"Now that I am here, I want to look."

She wondered at the bitterness in his voice when he spoke of his father. Maybe she was wrong, but she had the feeling it was best to stay away from that subject.

"Look all you want. That's why I brought you here." His smile was warm, infectious.

She returned his smile and then moved into another room. A large portrait loomed over the display. A portrait that reminded her of Jack. She read the information on display. "Dr. Devlin—is this a relative of Jack's?"

Linc's eyes narrowed and his brows drew together. "Yeah. His family is quite prominent in Petoskey's history."

There it was again. These guys really didn't like each other. She gazed into his ebony eyes. She could feel his displeasure growing and searched her mind to say something positive. "I bet your family was here first." Was this it? Had race caused the animosity between Linc and Jack? It was too soon to ask such personal questions. If he wanted to talk about it, he would, and she would listen.

"I'm sure we were, for whatever that means. My people struggle with an everyday existence, too busy to worry about their proud heritage." He glanced around the room. "Someday I plan to build a museum and fill it with Native American artifacts that will tell our story."

"Linc, that would be wonderful. You could start by donating most of your household items." She giggled when his gaze caught hers.

"My mother holds on to the old ways the best she can. And so do I. Sometimes she makes me feel guilty that I have made a life in both worlds."

Paige pulled a frown. "I think you are really lucky to have more than one world. You should be very proud of both."

He laughed. "My mother doesn't see it that way. The People, as she calls us, were the first created by the Great Spirit to care for and preserve Mother Earth."

"Your mother may be right. Who knows?"

"She's from the old school. She fights for Native American rights and tries to teach the younger generations their obligations to their heritage." He paused and reflectively looked around.

She followed his gaze and knew he was comparing the opulent display of the Devlin family to the handcrafted treasures of the Ottawa/Chippewa Tribe. She thought of her struggle to be accepted as a large black woman in a thin white world and felt a kinship with Linc's people.

"My people have had to work hard to restore some of their culture. We too have a proud and beautiful heritage that was almost lost to us. But we'll keep working, just as you and your mother have, to preserve it."

Paige placed her hand on his hard-muscled forearm and waited for his stormy eyes to partially clear. His gaze pulled back to her. She spoke softly. "It's good that your mother follows her heart. We should never give up a fight while the war rages on."

The turbulent eyes shifted to molten lava as he gazed at her. Linc pulled her close. "I couldn't agree with you more."

Paige knew his thinking had switched from his mother to more intimate thoughts. She melted into his warm chest and let go of the whole day. The pain of the fire and the possible arson lifted as she snuggled against his muscular body.

She didn't resist as his hungry mouth sought hers and devoured her lips. Hers parted as his tongue tenderly explored.

Linc gently slid his hands down her back and then slipped his fingers under her knit shirt. As his hands moved up her ribs and cupped her fully aroused breast, Paige fought to return from her passionate daze.

She wanted him. Yet she knew, like her, if he physically committed it would be for a lifetime—and she wasn't ready. She had to be sure this time. She had to be sure it wasn't just physical. She had to be sure she would be willing to change her life. A life that was hectic—but one she loved. Gently she placed her hands on his chest and pushed him away. "Linc, I'm...I can't...I'm not ready for a deeper relationship, not yet."

Her breathless words hung in the still of the night.

Linc dropped his hands from her shoulders and stepped back. Her words had the same effect on him as being doused with the icy cold waters of Lake Superior. He closed his eyes for a moment, and an eagle in flight flashed through his mind. The graceful bird soared through the vapor of the brilliant full moon; a golden moon reminding him of the deep golden flecks in her eyes. He blinked and then met her gaze. "Please forgive me. I can't seem to control myself when I am with you." A hint of a smile turned the corners of his mouth.

She flushed, thinking of her own lost control. "I know what you mean." She laughed softly. "Maybe we should leave and visit when there are more people here."

"I think that's a good idea." He grabbed her hand and tugged her back through the museum to the door where they had entered. Linc placed money in Bill's hand and wrapped the older man's weather-worn fingers around it.

The proud man shook his head. "I can't take this."

Linc patted the hand he had placed the money in. "This isn't for you. It's for the kids." He pulled on Paige's hand as he pushed open the door. "Thanks for opening for us." Paige echoed the thank you.

Linc drove along the bay for a few miles. Neither spoke. He chanced a glance at his silent companion. Her beautiful heart-shaped face was bathed in moonlight. He groaned inside. How long did she want this "casual relationship"? For him three days seemed like three years, no, a lifetime. He had known her a lifetime. He patted her knee. "Want to grab something to eat?"

She turned a golden gaze in his direction. "I think that would be a good idea."

He felt her gaze drift over him. The urge to fulfill his immediate physical need was replaced with the need to make this woman his lifetime partner. He could wait. He'd have to. Linc smiled to himself. He would get used to cold showers, until she was ready.

Paige tiptoed through the hall at the inn. She placed her hand on the newel post of the staircase. She could smell the pleasant aroma of fresh coffee. That's what I need; Emma's chatter will help me unwind. In the few days she had known the older woman she had grown to enjoy their brief chats. As she neared the kitchen she heard Jack and Emma's voices, and she stopped. She didn't want to interrupt.

"Emma, don't worry. Mara is a big girl, she can take care of herself." Paige held her breath. She normally would never eavesdrop but this concerned her best friend.

"Young man," Emma scolded, "just a few nights ago you didn't want to date a girl with a large stature and now you're dating one who is even larger. Don't be toying with that girl's heart if you don't mean it."

"I told you I want to buy the Turner property, and Mara gives me the inside track. Maybe in time she will convince Paige to sell." Jack's voice was light and carefree.

Paige's hand flew to her mouth as she leaned against the wall for support. My God, he's using her. How will I tell her? She turned to leave and then stopped, compelled to listen.

"I thought you said Paige was going to rebuild." Emma's voice was harsh with recriminations.

Jack's voice grew farther away. Paige heard the back door open. "People change their plans every day." A long pause followed. Paige could imagine Emma's scornful face. "Don't worry," he continued. "I won't do anything illegal—maybe a little immoral..." Paige heard a light gasp from Emma and then a laugh from Jack as the door closed.

She inched her way to her room. What would she do? Why on earth did Jack want her property so badly? How could she tell Mara? Her wonderful friend had come to help her and now someone was trying to hurt her. The last few days were like one long nightmare. Nothing was right. "Oh my God." She spoke the words to her reflection in the vanity mirror. "What if Jack is the arsonist?"

Five

Fog born of a still, northern morning crept along the low-lands from Lake Michigan. Of course, it wouldn't last long, would easily be burned off by the sun before ten.

Paige did her morning stretches in front of the open window, enjoying the cool breezes off the lake. Had it really been two weeks since she'd arrived? So much had happened. Her house had burned, she'd met Linc and begun the kind of relationship she'd hoped would wait until she was ready to retire from her modeling career. And Mara was still here after canceling her European shoot. Things had a habit of changing.

She sat on the floor and pulled her knees tightly beneath her chin. Where was her life going? She was confused, especially about Linc.

He was kind and gentle, intelligent and strong. Still, was she ready to make a lifetime commitment? A woman was lucky to have a man like Linc come into her life at all, much less question if the time was right, she told herself. God, what was wrong with her?

Then there were Mara and Jack. After she had over-heard Jack's conversation with Emma, she had tried to warn her friend but Mara wouldn't hear it. She had told Paige that she knew how to take care of herself. Paige could only hope Mara was right. And if she wasn't, Paige would be there to pick up the pieces. "Damn you Jack! The more I think of it, the more I think you are the only one with a motive for burning my house," she whispered into the empty air.

Paige shuddered. She wouldn't allow Jack to lead Mara down any wrong path. She'd keep a close eye on that situation. Before she could ruminate further, the telephone rang. Scrambling from the floor, Paige grabbed the phone and plopped on the bed.

"Linc, I was hoping you'd call."

"Did I wake you?" he asked.

"No, I was just finishing my exercises, and then I'm going to take a shower."

"It saves water if you shower with someone and I haven't had time yet this morning."

Paige laughed softly. The thought of his naked wet body next to hers in the shower caused her innards to contract. "I think in this case showering alone is the best idea. I don't care for cold showers."

"You just might pay for that one." His voice deepened. "But I was trying to save the environment. Someday when the water is gone people will look at us with disdain because we were so thoughtless."

Her laugher tinkled through the phone. "I'll have to take my chances." She paused for a moment. "I'm sure you didn't call about showering with me, so what did you want to talk about?"

"Maybe I didn't call about showering with you, but I really think it's a good idea." He chuckled. "The truth is, we have an invitation from my mother."

"Yes?" She'd wanted to meet his mother but worried that his mother wouldn't like the fact that she wasn't Native American. She was glad his mother had been out of town caring for her sick sister. Yet she truly cared for Linc, so she would go. It probably wouldn't be as bad as she thought.

"She would like to meet the woman who is taking up all her son's time."

Paige pulled her legs in and sat cross-legged on the bed. "She's home then?" The woman who was taking up all his time? What had his mother meant by that? A dark warning flashed before her eyes. Was someone trying to tell her something?

"Yes, she arrived just this morning."

"And how is your aunt?" Paige asked.

"Doing well now. She will have to have another surgery, but for now she's stable enough for Mom to come home for a while."

"That's good." She wondered how this wise woman who lived by the old ways was going take to her son dating a modern woman who wasn't the right race. She shoved the dark thoughts away. She envied him his mother. "You said something about an invitation?"

"Mom would like you to come to dinner tonight."

"Tonight?" Paige exclaimed. "Is she up to it? I mean, she's only just returned."

Linc's throaty laugh echoed through the phone lines. "You don't know my mother. Work is her middle name. She wants to have you for dinner and she won't take no for an answer."

Paige's laughter matched his own. "Never let it be said I turned down a home-cooked meal. What time?"

"We eat around seven."

"Fine. Shall I drive over?"

Again Linc laughed. "No. If I pick you up, I have an excuse to see you alone."

Warmth rose to her face. Being with Linc, just thinking about being with him, made her skin tingle.

"Linc?"

"Hmm?"

"Have you heard anything about the investigation yet?"

"Not a word. I was just thinking it was taking a long time to wrap this up."

Anxiety wrapped around her. "What could be wrong?" She pulled the decorative pillow into her lap and fiddled with the lace.

"I don't think it's anything to worry about," he assured in a calm voice. "But I'll ask Stanton. Oh, by the way. I have the prints of your house ready for your approval. You can see them tonight."

"Great. As soon as the investigation is settled and the insurance is cleared we can get started."

"The sooner the better. I have to get ready for work. I'll pick you up about quarter of seven."

"I'll be ready." She closed the phone and stared at it, imagining his smiling face, warm eyes and shiny black hair. His face was constantly in her mind.

Was he Mr. Right? She and Linc had spent a lot of time together these past two weeks. The more time she spent with him, the more she wanted him. It was like dismembering her own body each time they parted.

She rose from the bed and straightened the comforter. Would she and Linc someday share a bed? Her whole body was blanketed with a warm feeling. Would he be the lover she imagined? She shook her head. Get your head on straight, she admonished herself. You're acting like a love-sick teenager.

She showered and smiled as she let the hot water pelt her body. Maybe she should be taking a cold shower to cool her thoughts. Then she wondered if Linc was showering in cold water. Rivulets of water rushing over his sinewy, buckskin-colored body. Droplets hanging from the mat of hair on his chest and . . . she shook her head to erase her wandering thoughts.

She threw on jeans and a white, big shirt tied at her waist. She pulled her hair back and clasped it at her nape. All the while she thought about Linc, what he was doing, whether he was in his truck on the way to his office or with a client.

A soft knock sounded at the door, interrupting her musing. Paige found Mara leaning against the doorway.

"Breakfast is ready."

"I'm not very hungry." Paige stepped into the hall and closed her door.

Mara scowled and linked her arm in her friend's. "You know, if you don't watch it, you might end up being one of those emaciated models."

Paige laughed. "I don't think there's much chance of that."

"It looks like you've lost weight since you've come back. Emma has made the most wonderful smelling bacon and cheese quiche to put some meat back on your bones."

"Quiche, huh? Did you tell her that was my favorite?"

Mara pulled a face. "Now, would I do a thing like that?"

"Yes, you would."

They giggled as they raced down the highly polished, winding staircase to the first floor. "You're right, I would and I did," Mara called over her shoulder, reaching the kitchen first.

The quiche was in the middle of the breakfast bar, flanked by bowls of fruit and a breadbasket with fresh bread waiting to be served.

"Emma, you shouldn't have gone to all this trouble for me," Paige admonished.

"Nonsense." Emma gave her a mild look over the top of her glasses. "I guess I can make a special breakfast if I have a mind to. Actually this is nice. When the season opens, I have to serve a full breakfast to our guests." She gestured toward the hall, "It's either served in the breakfast nook or the dining room, depending on how many guests we have." She cut a generous slice, expertly arranging it on a plate, and handed it to Paige, and then another to Mara. "I enjoy having the two of you here. It reminds me of when my children were home." She gave off a wistful sigh for days gone past.

Mara glanced at the round kitchen clock on the wall. "Jack should be here soon. We're going to Mackinac Island."

"Sounds like fun." Paige avoided Mara's searching gaze. She held her cup for Emma to pour the coffee.

Emma removed the glasses from her face and placed them in her apron pocket. "If you girls will excuse me for a minute, I must call the grocery." She headed for the little office off the kitchen.

"I'd ask you to come, but I'm sure you wouldn't want to be a fifth wheel, if you know what I mean." Mara threw her friend a wink.

"This is getting a bit serious between you and Jack, isn't it?"

Mara shrugged. "Could be, so don't expect us back tonight."

"Mara," she gasped. Then she lowered her voice so Emma wouldn't hear. "Are you and Jack sleeping together?"

Mara shrugged. "And if we are?"

And what if they were? Was it any of her business? Mara was a big girl and had already told her she could take care of herself. Still, hadn't she heard Jack tell Emma he didn't like big women? God, he was using her best friend to get at her property. Precious good it would do him, but damn him if he hurt Mara in the process.

"Well?" Mara prodded. "Are you angry?"

Paige couldn't look at her friend for fear she would read the concern in her eyes. "It's none of my business what you do. Just be careful."

"Oh, we use protection."

"Mara, really!" Paige put her fork down. She couldn't eat after this. "When? How? I mean..."

Mara laughed. "Jack has an apartment in Petoskey. Remember those nights when I supposedly came home late?"

"You didn't!"

"I really like him," Mara whispered. "And he likes me."

"This really does surprise me. I never thought you'd get serious about him after that first date. I mean...come on, you called him a stuffed shirt and—and a country bumpkin, for Pete's sake."

Mara lowered her gaze. "Well, you know the old saying. You can't tell a book by its cover. You have to get inside to really know." She giggled. "And this country bumpkin has a lot under his stuffed shirt."

Paige didn't know whether to laugh or cry. "Then you are getting serious?"

Mara finished her coffee, slid off the stool and abruptly changed the subject. "Jack said he'd be here by nine. I have to pack a few things yet."

"Wait." Paige left her seat and raced up the stairs after her friend. "Mara, we have to talk."

Mara held up her hand. "I can tell you don't like Jack very much, but I'm having a wonderful time. Don't ruin this for me." Her voice held a warning.

Paige knew when to back off. "Hey, I was only going to ask your opinion on the dress I was thinking about wearing to meet Linc's mother tonight," Paige lied.

Mara's face relaxed and her impish smile returned. "Well, why didn't you say so? What are friends for if it isn't to help pick out clothes that will wow the boyfriend's mother."

"Come on." Paige turned toward her room. If Mara didn't want to hear anything against Jack, then so be it. Sooner or later she would see his true colors. She flung the room door open and then the closet. "What do you think about this little basic black?"

"Whoa! You go, girl!" Mara clicked her tongue. That little number screams take me home and take me...or take me right now."

Paige grimaced at the dress. "This dress talks way too much." She hung it back in the closet.

"I don't think so." Mara argued.

"Oh yes, it does. I'm trying to impress his mother, not Linc." He was already too impressed. Her insides warmed thinking of his hot embraces.

Mara shrugged. "It's up to you of course, but you gotta keep 'em panting girl. Keep 'em begging for more."

Like you and Jack. Stop! she chided herself. Mara would learn in time what a snake Jack really was. In the meantime, she'd watch for his vulnerable spot and then she'd use whatever means available to expose him. "Umm, maybe." She ran her hand over the soft black material. "I'll think about it."

A horn honked insistently. Mara rushed to the window like a giddy teenager. "Jack's here." She gave Paige a quick air kiss on each cheek. "See ya when I get back."

Paige went to the window and pulled the soft curtain back. She felt she was watching her friend rush headlong into disaster. If Mara got hurt, it would be her fault for bringing her here. She knew she should have told her about the conversation between Jack and Emma. But Mara wouldn't listen. Damn, why did Mara have to be so stubborn?

Mara rushed out to the truck, duffel bag in hand. Jack was waiting to help her in. He kissed her on the mouth and threw her bag into the back. When he straightened, Paige could see his face. There was a tenderness in his expression that would fool her if she hadn't heard his conversation with Emma. God, the man was good.

She watched them drive away. "Be careful, Mara," she whispered. "This guy is a first class vulture."

When Linc arrived, Paige had chosen a spring flowered A-line dress. Better safe than sorry. Linc's mother wouldn't be able to find fault with her clothes. But the black dress might have made her raise her eyebrows.

"Hi. You look wonderful." He gathered her into the circle of his arms and took her lips with his. "I've got a surprise for you."

"What?"

"Come and see." He urged her toward the door.

"Wait." She pulled back. "I have to get my sweater and purse." She grabbed them from the deacon's bench and followed him outside.

Inside the black Navigator he handed her a roll of white paper. "Do you know what this is?"

"Paper?" she teased.

He nodded. "Yes, but it's what's on the paper that counts."

She smiled. "My house plans?"

He turned the key and backed the vehicle out onto the highway toward his house. "I promised I'd have them ready for you tonight."

She unrolled the paper and there in print was her house. She lifted each sheet, a front and back view, and another of the floor plan. It was all there.

"How did you know exactly how the inside was laid out?"

"Trade secret."

"Really? I thought you might tell me you were psychic."

"That too." He pulled to a stop at the front of his home.

"Seriously, how did you know?" I mean it's exact, right down to the little cellar off the kitchen."

He reached out and tweaked her chin. "A lot of Victorian houses had several basic prints. Some were packages that could be purchased from a catalogue; others were just blueprints."

Her face showed surprise. "C'mon. Are you telling me my house was ordered through a catalogue?"

"The plans could have been. Some ordered just the plans and others ordered the whole package. I have several reproduction books on houses of that era. It wasn't hard to find yours."

She glanced at the plans and rolled them up, securing it with a rubber band. "Thank you. I just wish it was rebuilt so I could be living there."

He opened her door and held out his hand. "I know. It won't be long. Come inside. Mom is anxious to meet you."

When Linc opened the back door, wonderful odors of dinner wafted through the air.

"Something smells delicious."

"Mom's a very good cook." He took her sweater and purse, placing them on the wooden rack by the door. He urged her to the kitchen.

"Mom, this is Paige Turner. Paige, my mother, Nuna Cross."

A tall, thin woman with silver-black hair braided down her back turned toward her. Her eyes widened in surprise which was immediately replaced with a welcoming smile. "At last I meet you." She held out her hand.

Paige accepted the hand offered her. "I'm happy to meet you, Mrs. Cross."

"Nuna. Please call me Nuna."

Nuna turned to the stove and lowered the heat on one of the burners. "So, Linc tells me you're from New York?"

"Of late, yes. But I lived here until I was a young teen."

"Have you come home to stay?"

"Not really. Not right now. Maybe in three or four years I'll come home for good."

Nuna stirred a pot of vegetables simmering in a delicate sauce. "I keep trying to remember the Turner family, but we lived in Harbor Springs at the time. There weren't many..."

Paige smiled. "Black families back then. I know."

"Turner." Nuna mused.

"Yes, well my parents were from Detroit. When the race riots of the seventies began, they decided to get out of the city, mostly for me I think. They bought the old Clayton place and restored it. It was home until my mother died and dad remarried. His second wife didn't like it here." What was wrong with her. She was rambling off at the mouth, hardly taking a breath.

"I see," Nuna said.

Nuna checked the stove again. "I'm sorry about your house. But Linc tells me you will be rebuilding?"

"Yes, I will." She glanced around. "May I help you with something, set the table perhaps?"

Nuna smiled. "No, everything's ready. We're just wait-ing for another guest."

Linc looked at his mother. "Another guest? I didn't know you had invited someone else."

Again Nuna smiled. "Winona will be joining us."

His eyes narrowed suspiciously. "Mother? You invited Winona? You asked her here tonight?"

"Of course. I haven't seen her in weeks."

Paige watched Linc's angry expression but before he could respond, the doorbell sounded.

"Would you get that, dear?" Nuna asked Linc as she began dishing up the dinner.

"I hope you don't mind but Winona and Linc have been close since they were children."

Paige felt a flutter of apprehension flow through her. "Of course not. I'd like to meet Linc's friends."

A tremor touched Nuna's smooth, marble-like mouth that had fallen to a thin line. She turned away just as a young woman came into the kitchen.

"Hello, Nuna." A small, young woman with black hair and dark, dancing eyes entered the room, interrupting the tense moment.

"Ah, Winona, it's so good to see you, dear." Nuna rushed across the room, a bright smile replacing her cold frown. She turned to Paige. "Winona has been a member of the family since her parents and I planned hers and Linc's..." She waved her hand in the air. "That was many years ago." Her voice was wistful.

Paige forced a smile she didn't feel. If she had thought going with Mara and Jack would make her feel like a fifth-wheel, then what was this? God, what had she gotten her-self into? She had thought this meeting wasn't going to be easy, but this was worse than she'd imagined.

Linc pulled Paige toward him. "Paige, this is Winona George. Winona, this is Paige Turner."

A warm smile touched Winona's lips and echoed in her voice. "I'm very pleased to meet you."

Paige felt discomfort. Winona was clearly staring at her, as if she were studying her. She held out her hand. "Hello, Winona. I'm pleased to meet you too."

They had dinner in the solarium. The glorious sunset really couldn't be fully enjoyed because of the dense trees. Only a soft orange glow peeked through the branches.

"This is delicious." Paige took another bite of the tender dark meat. What is it?"

Nuna spoke without smiling. "Venison that Linc shot last fall. And the morel mushrooms, Winona and I picked in the early spring. Remember, dear?" She warmly glanced at Winona.

Winona nodded.

Something was happening here. Paige watched Winona look at Nuna and glance in puzzlement at Linc.

"Linc said you were a wonderful cook and he was right," Paige said trying to ease the tension.

Nuna pressed a smile onto her mouth. "Thank you for the compliment."

Paige took another bite of mushroom. "My father and I used to pick morels in the spring. I could never seem to find them, no matter how much in plain sight they were, but he found so many. We used to string and dry them."

Nuna nodded. "You have to have an eye for such things. Are you sure your father wasn't part Native American?"

A discreet cough caught Paige's attention and Nuna's. A dark scowl crossed Linc's face as he threw his mother a meaningful expression.

Paige was relieved to have the attention from her, even if it was temporary. She wondered, had Nuna thought that telling her Linc hunted would make her uncomfortable? What was this evening all about? Winona and all the little remarks that seemed innocent enough but hinted at her being an outsider. What was it that Winona and Linc's parents had decided all of those years ago? Were they hoping for an engagement?

Nuna wiped her mouth with the napkin. "I'm glad you liked the meal. A lot of my cooking comes from the old ways. I've incorporated them into usable, modern recipes."

"You should write a book. You know, share your knowledge with the world." Paige tried to keep her voice even, tried to stay on friendly terms with the woman who wanted to protect her son from this outsider.

Nuna rose and began scraping the plates. "I'll think about it. But there are some things our people don't share with others."

Now what did that mean? Linc? She wasn't about to share Linc with a black girl or any girl who wasn't one of the people?

"Let me help clean up." Winona scraped back her chair and began to gather the plates.

Nuna waved her hand. "I wouldn't hear of it. You three go along and visit. I'll take care of things here. I'll bring coffee out soon."

"You two go ahead," Winona assured them. I won't be but a minute." She disappeared into the kitchen with Nuna.

Linc's hand rested on Paige's back as he led her to the deck off the living room. She felt the warmth of his hand through the thin material of her dress, sending delicious shivers through her.

His inky eyes gazed down into hers. "Damn, we should be alone." His lips found hers, his tongue teasing and tasting.

Paige pulled back. "Linc...not now...not here." She pushed away, glancing at the door, expecting Winona or Nuna to emerge any minute. And she wasn't disappointed. The soft clicking of Winona's shoes as she crossed the hardwood flooring announced her approach.

Paige turned and leaned on the deck railing. The evening was warm. Much warmer than it had been inside the house. She certainly hadn't missed Nuna's dislike of her. Her innuendoes were subtle, but they were plainly there. You're not right for my son. That message permeated the air.

"Linc tells me you've been living in New York," Winona said in a soft, melodic voice.

"Yes. I've come home for the summer." Why couldn't she have just stayed in New York? Winona seemed like a nice enough young woman and there wasn't any animosity coming from her, but she was obviously Nuna's choice for her son. This was awkward.

"I'm sorry about your house," Winona said with sincerity. "But I understand you're going to rebuild?"

"I hope to, yes." She glanced at Linc who was staring intently at her. She offered him a weak smile.

Linc returned the smile. He patted Winona on the shoulder. "You should know that Winona is like my little sister. Our families have always been close."

Winona nodded in agreement. "Linc is the big brother I never had. I am the first-born child. In fact my name means first-born daughter." Her warm smile slid from Linc to Paige.

The telephone rang and almost immediately Nuna poked her head around the corner of the glass doors. "Linc, it's for you."

"Excuse me, ladies. I'll be back shortly."

Winona watched Linc leave. She rose and moved to look inside and came back to sit beside Paige. "Have you told them who you are?" Winona asked with suppressed excitement.

Paige stared at her in disbelief. "I don't understand. What do you mean?"

This time Winona looked her over completely. "I've seen your picture on many magazines. You're famous!!"

Paige smiled weakly. Well, that was it. The game was up. She knew it. How would Linc feel when he found out. Maybe she should have told him she was a model when they first met instead of hedging.

"No, I haven't."

Excitement flashed through Winona's dark eyes. "Why not? I mean, you're famous. You have a wonderful career. I envy you."

"I really enjoy my privacy when I am on vacation. Why would you envy me?"

"I want a career so badly, but I don't know where to start, really."

She was sincere. Paige could tell by the tone of her voice she wasn't jealous or envious in a vindictive sort of way.

"What kind of career are you looking for?"

Winona lowered her eyes and her face turned pink under her dark complexion. "Not just me alone. I have a sister who's tall and built a great deal like you, who wants so to be a model. She's beautiful, really beautiful."

"So are you," Paige said gently.

Winona shook her head. "Not like Pazi. She has what it takes to be a model...you know, the confidence—and she's so sure of herself. We just need to know where to start."

Paige leaned forward. "What about you? What do you want?"

"You'll probably think I'm silly, but I design clothes."

"So?" Paige tilted her head. "What's stopping you?"

"How can I ever get any place from here? This is northern Michigan. Oh, sure, I sell things to the gift shops but that's not going to get me anywhere."

"May I see your work?"

Winona jerked a look up. "Really? You'd really look at my work?"

"Of course I would. Someone gave me a chance when I least expected it. I'd be glad to help."

"Who helped you?" Winona asked.

Paige flushed, thinking about it. "You're not going to believe this, but I was just walking down the street and this obnoxious young man with a camera came up to me and asked if I'd ever thought of becoming a model."

"No. Really?"

Paige nodded. Just thinking about it made her want to laugh. "I still can't believe it. I tried to get rid of him but he was so insistent. He made a real nuisance of himself trying to get me to stand still so he could take my picture. He finally gave me a card and told me to call the agency he shoots for. I did and the rest is history."

Winona leaned back, her eyes reflecting deep concentration. "It sounds so easy."

Paige shook her head and laughed. "It was anything but easy, I can tell you. It was a lot of hard work to become a model, but after I got into it, I found I really wanted it, no matter how hard I had to work."

This girl was very nice. If she had talent she'd help her any way she could. "May I come and see your work?"

"Tonight? You want to come tonight?"

"Sure, unless you have something else to do?"

"No, I'd love to show you."

"Well, then. Shall we go?"

Winona glanced around. "Now? You'd leave now?"

Paige cringed and whispered, "I'd love to leave now."

"I understand," Winona said, glancing toward the kitchen. "And I'm sorry about Nuna. But I'm not sorry that I've met you."

"Leave for where?" Linc had a look of worried concern on his face.

Paige turned around. "I should really be going. I'd like to look over those prints. Besides, it's been a long day and I'm whipped." She hated lying to Linc but she couldn't stand another minute in the same house with his mother.

"I'll take you back to the inn. Why don't we have breakfast in the morning. You can tell me then what you think of the plans."

"That would be fine." She turned to Winona. "Give me your number and I'll give you a call." She winked and saw by the girl's expression she'd received her message.

After Linc dropped her off, she called Winona and got directions to her apartment. It was just outside of town in a quaint set of condominiums built in a stand of maple trees.

Winona welcomed her into their apartment. "Hi. Would you like something to drink, a Coke or iced coffee or tea?"

Paige removed her sweater. "No, I'm fine."

"Come, sit down." She ushered Paige into the spacious living room decorated in Southwestern flair.

"Pazi." Winona called.

A beautiful, exotic-looking young woman emerged from the hall. Winona had been right. Pazi had a special beauty and the graceful movements that were needed on the runway.

After the introductions were made, Pazi helped Winona show Paige her work.

"This is something I've been working on." She held up a simple top that had been delicately painted in soft earth-tones with an intricate application of beadwork.

"This is wonderful." Paige ran her hand over the tiny beads.

"It goes with this skirt and I've woven a matching belt."

Paige reached for the belt and lifted the round charm that hung near the buckle with a silver threaded web and a silver eagle's feather attached. "What's this?"

"It's a dream catcher. We believe it will help catch our bad dreams and let the good ones pass through. It helps us to realize our good dreams and it holds the bad ones until they dissipate in the light of day."

"You have a wonderful talent." She turned the dream catcher over in her hand. "I could really use one of these right now," Paige said wistfully.

Winona reached behind her and brought out a large feathered dream catcher. "I would be honored if you would accept this gift of protection from us."

Paige stared at the gift and then at the giver. "I am the one who is honored. Thank you."

"Look at this." Pazi stepped to the bookshelf and took down a large black book. "She draws all the time."

Paige opened the sketch pad. Inside were hundreds of sketches of fashions. They were original, styles that had a Native American flair but would easily cross over to the general population. The sketches would be sure to catch some designer's eye.

"You should be in New York!" Paige flipped through the pages. "You're good. Really good."

"Do you really think so?"

"I know so." Paige was astounded by this untapped talent. "I'm going to call my agent in the morning." She searched through her purse and pulled out a card. "Here's her address. I want you to send her a portfolio of your work."

Winona gasped. "This is wonderful. I never thought...how can I ever thank you?"

"By making your dream come true." Paige handed her the book. "Pick out your favorite sketches and have some pieces that are finished."

"Could I impose on you for one more thing?"

"Sure."

"Could we send Pazi's pictures to your agent too? I would really like her to have a chance."

Pazi shook her head and placed a hand on her sister's arm. "Worry about yourself. Make your own dreams come true."

"But..."

"There are no buts. I will help you and then you can help me."

Paige admired the sacrificial love between the sisters. The closest thing to it she had ever had was Mara. Mara. Her sister. She worried about her and this thing with Jack. She knew she had to stop it even if it meant returning to New York before her vacation was over.

"Of course you can send along pictures to my agent. I think you will both find your dream." She reached for her sweater.

"Thank you. It's easy to see why Linc thinks so much of you."

She glanced from one set of dark, bright eyes to the other. "You will both do well. I'll call my agent in the morning and tell her you are sending her a package." She smiled at Pazi. "You will make a beautiful model. Send my agent some photographs."

"I will, and thank you." Winona and Pazi clasped Paige's hands in theirs.

Paige left the young women in excited chatter. She drove to the outskirts of town. Instead of returning to the inn, she took a turn that led her to Sunset Park where she and Linc had watched the sun go down. It was quiet and serene in the near darkness.

She sat there for a long time, thinking. Then she opened the door and got out and stood by the car as the evening breeze played with the dark, wispy tendrils framing her face. The moon was full and had a gauzy ring around it. It hung low over the horizon, almost spiritually.

The truth hit her. She had fallen in love with Linc. She felt he was in love with her too. Facing it squarely, finally admitting it to herself made her realize this was the most important thing in her life. But would it work out? Would the differences in their heritage and backgrounds cause a rift in their relationship? Would his mother be angry with her for helping Winona leave town?

What was the alternative? Going away and never seeing him again? Could she do that?

Paige watched the silvery streak of the moon's reflection in the slowly moving water and listened to the gentle waves as they lapped the shore. She couldn't make any decisions now. She would wait for Mara to return. Mara always made things better.

Six

What in the hell had gone on tonight? Linc thumped the heel of his hand on the steering wheel as he sat in the driveway staring at his house. If his mother had set out to scare off Paige, she couldn't have done a better job. And why had she invited Winona? She knew he wanted a get-acquainted dinner with just the three of them.

And then there was that outrageous phone call from Stanton this evening. The prosecuting attorney's office was considering charges of arson and fraud against Paige. Someone had bought several insurance policies in Paige's name. But who? He was sure she would have only one. How was he going to tell Paige they suspected her of burning her own house? All of the memorabilia she had loved had been removed from the house. Anyone would benefit from the artifacts and antiques in her house, but none would have loved them as she did. Stanton's phone call had cast shadows over his thinking.

No, he couldn't think like that. Paige loved her home. It was all she had left of her beloved parents. She didn't look like she needed money—not that bad anyway.

Where did he start for the truth? She was going to need his help and he'd be there, but right now it looked bad, real bad.

He stared at the lights shining from the windows of his home. Pulling the keys from the ignition he hauled himself from the truck.

Linc was aware of the wise one's presence, even before the owl called out to him from his nocturnal watchtower.

"I hear you, wise one." He spoke quietly into the moist night breezes. "Help me to be strong when I talk to my mother. She is a good woman. I don't want to hurt her, only to make her understand."

Over his head passed a nighthawk in ragged flight, making its way toward the stand of tall white pines. The bracing scent of night hung heavily, yet it was warm. Nature was all around him, giving him the strength to do what he must. It wrapped him in a blanket of tranquil darkness, steeling him for his confrontation with his mother.

He glanced through the windows and saw her aging face bathed in light from the fireplace. The last thing he wanted to do was disturb her peaceful state, but it had to be done. He reached for the door then shook his head. Not yet. He wandered past the house, toward the small lake.

The path along the lake snaked through the woods. His footsteps were cushioned by last fall's carpet of brown needles and once crispy leaves. Frogs croaked and the crickets stopped their song as he approached. Nature was in complete harmony here. Why couldn't he and his mother be in tune with each other? They had been until now. The owl called out again. "It's time. It's time." The mournful call echoed in the night. Linc nodded. The wise old fella was right. He was only stalling the inevitable.

He abruptly turned and made his way to the house.

The only light came from the fire. Nuna sat in the wing-backed chair with a brightly colored native blanket on her lap.

"You're home early." She glanced at the turquoise studded clock on the mantel.

He gazed at his mother's fawn-colored face. Years of hard work and worry had creased the once perfectly chiseled features. Silver strands showed in the long braid and at her temples. "What did you expect after what you pulled tonight?" The words came out in an angry rush. He hadn't meant to sound so harsh.

She gave him a dour look. "What's wrong with you? I thought tonight went very well."

"Did you? Is that what you call chasing a guest from our home? I'll be surprised if Paige ever steps foot in here again."

"I don't know what you mean." Her eyes glittered as if the thought pleased her.

Linc's eyes darkened under furrowed brows. "I think you do and I think you deliberately set out to chase her away. Why, Mom? Because she isn't one of our people?"

Her face grew still and paled under his stern attack. "I've never seen you like this."

"And I've never seen you be so rude and inconsiderate either. I love Paige and I hope someday she'll be my wife, even if she doesn't know it yet."

Nuna gasped and her hand flew to her mouth. "Oh, Linc, no. You told me you would never make the same mistake I did. You would not marry out of your race. You promised."

"I never promised that." Linc's voice softened, knowing this subject was very painful to his mother's heart. How many times had he wanted to ask about his father? Yet could never bring himself to hurt her. But now he had to continue down this rocky path. "No, Mom. You decided I'd marry one of our people. But what you forget and try to make me forget, is I'm part white too. I'm no longer ashamed of that."

Tears glistened in her eyes. "Why are you doing this?"

"Why did you, Mother? You fell in love with my father and he was white. Did that stop you?"

"I made a mistake. I don't want you to do the same."

"Loving Paige isn't a mistake. She makes me laugh and feel alive, more than anyone I know. For God's sake, don't you want me to be happy?"

Nuna turned away. "She can't make you happy. Your father..."

"My father doesn't have anything to do with this. Paige is not like my father. She isn't going to leave me."

"How do you know that?" Her voice was pleading; years of anguish filled her face.

"I don't. But I'm willing to take the chance. It's a chance every couple takes. I don't care if they're red, white, black or purple, marriage is a chance. And I'll take it too, if she'll have me."

"Oh, Linc, you don't know what you're saying. Winona would marry you if you would only give her half a chance."

He laughed roughly. "Winona and I are like brother and sister. There never have been any romantic feelings between us. We both know that. It's you who won't accept it."

"You haven't given her a chance." She reached out in appeal.

Linc gave his head a shake. "I've known Winona since we were kids and I'll always love her as a sister. But I'm not in love with her. She's not in love with me. It's as simple as that. You, of all people, ought to remember love. You gave up your life for it...and mine."

He heaved a sigh. His mother was becoming distraught and he hated upsetting her. But she must understand how he felt. This was his life and he had to live it his way.

She turned away and whispered, "Yes, I loved your father."

"Why did he leave you?"

She pulled the Indian blanket close to her and stared into the flames that licked the charred logs. "I never wanted you to know."

"I gathered that. What happened?"

"He was already married. And his wife was expecting a child."

This wasn't what he'd expected to hear. His mother had an affair with a married man? A married white man? "Who is he? Where is he?"

"Linc, this isn't doing either of us any good. I don't..."

"Who and where is this hypocrite who drops his sperm in two women at the same time? And then cast the bastard son aside to protect his legitimate child." He ground out each word, leaving no doubt that he expected an answer.

She flinched as if she'd been hit. But her voice was even when she answered, "He's dead."

"Dead?" He hadn't considered that. He stared into his mother's eyes. "Did he know about me?"

Her eyelids shuttered down. "Oh, yes. He knew and he was proud of you."

"Proud? Of what? A son he refused to acknowledge?"

Nuna sighed. "He had a family to think of and a business to protect. At that time people were quiet about their affairs."

"Except for the woman who carried the stigma of being an unwed mother all her life. And the child of the affair. Don't you realize what that did to me at school? Do you know how many times I was called the half-breed bastard?"

"Oh, Linc, I'm sorry. You never said..." Her face reflected his pain.

"Of course I never said anything." His expression was one of pained tolerance. "I didn't want you to be hurt. I could take care of myself. You had enough problems being a single mother in two worlds."

"No." She shook her head. "I was rewarded ten-fold having you as my son. Being a single mother was a problem to society, not me. You were good at all you did. And you belonged to me." She sighed heavily. "You have made it all worthwhile."

"I was good because I was always proving myself. I suppose I should be grateful to him for making me strive harder. Maybe I wouldn't have accomplished all I did, if it hadn't been for his absence."

She gave her son an unyielding glare. "You are good because you are Grey Wolf. You are the proud, bold hunter, our mighty warrior." Her gaze traveled to her sculptured bust of Grey Wolf and then back to her son. Her voice was almost a whisper as she added, "The loyal defender and fiercely protective one of your pack and territory." She drew in a deep breath as if she needed energy to finish. "Your grandfather gave you that name because he knew you would bring the proud Native American heritage to the white world. And you have." She sat proudly in her chair, looking every bit the princess.

"Mom, I am proud to be Native American and I'm proud to be white, too. Some of my white ancestors traveled to foreign lands in search of a better way. All of that racial hatred has to be left behind with the ancestors, of both races, who spawned it. We are responsible for the present and for what we can do for our future." He wanted to go to her and hug her but he couldn't.

She stared at him as if he were a stranger.

"Mom, there is no deadline on the truth." He pushed on, ignoring her stare. "Who was my father? Why are you ashamed to tell me?" He saw the look of shock on her face.

She jerked a glance toward him. A tear spilled from its perch on her eyelid and slid down her face. "Linc, it wasn't...no, it isn't like that. There is no shame. He was a wonderful man. Your father and I made the decision to stay silent for everyone's sake. I'm sorry if our agreement hurt you, but we both loved you the best we could." She shook her tired head. "I can't tell you."

"Your father and I" rang in his head. He'd never thought of them as a couple. "You can't or won't?" he asked pointedly.

"Both I guess. I made a promise a long time ago." She closed her eyes as if to blot out the painful memory.

He wearily paced the room, raking his fingers through his hair. His father loved him? But obviously not enough to be anything more than a monetary provider. He'd never been a dad. He'd never visited him, never played with him or took him to little league. If it hadn't been for his mother's employer, he never would have been at little league games or practice. And that was only because he had to take his own son. Damn his father to hell for what he'd done.

"Don't hate him," she continued as she watched him pace. It was our mistake. We did the best we could under the circumstances."

"How can I hate what I never knew?" He stopped his pacing and stood in front of her. "You know Mom, sometimes the cruelest lies are told in silence."

She didn't look up, but said, "And sometimes silence is golden."

Linc gazed at his mother and wondered how a woman so independent and proud could have settled for so little. Not only for herself, but for her son. "He gave you crumbs and you were satisfied. How could you accept that?"

Sadness filled her face. "It was those crumbs that kept us off welfare. Did you actually think I sent you to the best schools on a secretary's pay? Did you think we lived in a house as nice as you grew up in, on what I made? Your father made our life comfortable and gave you a wonderful education so you could be the man you are today."

She looked tired and drawn. "I don't care to discuss this any more. It's over. I will keep my promise and I ask you not to question me again."

Linc knew when his mother gave her word that was the end. She would die before she broke a promise. But he would find out who his father was. Somehow he'd discover the truth.

"By the way," she changed the subject as if they'd never had words, "your grandfather is coming from Sault Saint Marie this week."

He looked at her and remembered the eagle Paige had seen. Had his grandfather somehow visioned he had met the girl he'd predicted would come into his life? After all, his grandfather hadn't been off the reservation in years.

"Grandfather? What's bringing him away from home? Did you call him?"

She shook her head. "No. He called me and said he had to come. He'll tell us when he gets here."

He knelt before her chair, taking her hand in his. This must be serious if his grandfather was leaving the reservation. He seldom left any more. "I never told you that grandfather had a vision concerning me."

"A vision?" Her eyes fixed on his.

He nodded. "Yes. A long time ago, maybe eight or nine years, when I was visiting the reservation. It was in the sweat lodge. He said my future was in the hands of the girl with golden eyes." He squeezed his mother's hand. "If you haven't noticed, Paige has golden eyes."

She leaned her head back against the chair. "My father's visions are always right. I've learned never to doubt his great wisdom." She searched her son's face, "I just hope, for your sake, hers are the right golden eyes."

He leaned forward and brushed a kiss across her dusky-brown face. "I feel good about his coming." He ignored her doubts because in his heart he knew Paige was the right woman for him.

"So do I," she murmured. "So do I."

At breakfast the next morning, Linc spread out the prints on the table in the restaurant. "What do you think? Is this what you want?" His heart warmed as the golden eyes gazed into his. The sun touched her nutmeg-black hair, causing sparks of red flames. The more he saw her, the more he loved her. How could he tell her the fire had been arson? And that they suspected her?

Paige ran her hand over the drawings and seriously studied them. "I couldn't ask for better. Now I have to find a builder. Who built your house? That's the kind of workmanship I want." She couldn't let herself believe that it was really going to happen. She glanced up from the blueprints, waiting for an answer.

He was silent. His usually animated face seemed sullen. She gazed at him as he raked his long fingers through his silky raven hair. He was too quiet, no teasing. No laughing. In fact he was acting strange this morning. Distant.

"What's wrong?" she asked. "You seem quiet this morning."

He gazed at her, his eyes dark with concern. "I had a phone call from Stanton last night and I have something to tell you."

"What?" she prodded.

"They've completed the investigation."

"And?"

"And it was arson."

Her golden eyes grew bright. "I was so hoping it was all a mistake. Do they have any idea who did it?"

He looked away and nodded. "They suspect you." he mumbled.

"Me?" Her voice rose an octave. "My God. Why me? I loved my home and everything that went with it."

He reached across the table and covered her hand with his. "Do you have any enemies? Anyone who would want to harm you for any reason?"

She shook her head. "No. No one." Her eyes darkened. "I don't understand this at all."

The dark centers of his eyes became pinpoints of anger, his nostrils flaring. "There has to be an answer. I know it wasn't you. But who?" He was talking as much to himself as he was her.

She tightened her grip on his hand. "What am I going to do? What makes them think it's me?"

He squeezed her hand. "The gasoline cans." They were purchased at a local hardware with your credit card. And then there are the insurance policies from all those different companies with you as the policyholder. Then they found your antiques and other personal belongings in a local storehouse. Your name is on that receipt too."

"Oh, God." She gasped. Her hands covered her face. "I don't have any idea what you're talking about. Gas cans, insurance policies? "I didn't do it. I swear I didn't." She reached for her purse and opened her credit card holder. They were all there. Not one was missing. She raised her gaze. "My cards are all here. But I didn't do it. I swear. I only have the one policy, the one my father took out years ago. I've kept it up."

"I know. But we have to find out who used your card."

"I don't have any idea. No one knew I was coming home except Mara. And of course she's out of the picture." She stared deeply into his eyes.

He returned the gaze. Was Mara really out of the picture? He wondered. Could they be so sure about her? Was she really the friend Paige thought she was? He wanted to blame anyone except Paige. "Yes, of course."

"Are the police going to arrest me?" she stammered.

He shrugged. "Not if I have anything to say about it." He paused for a moment. "I think it would be a good idea for you to consult a lawyer."

The buzz of breakfast customers filled the atmosphere around them, but for Paige the world had suddenly stood still. All her life she had tried to be a responsible, dependable person. She had been the helper and confidante her father needed, the friend he had leaned on after her mother's death.   When Ada convinced her father to marry, Paige's life began to crumble. Yet her father still confided in her. She hated the way the woman used him. A shiver ran through her.

And when he died, the house and property had become Paige's whether she wanted it or not. But she did want it. She'd always wanted it. It was her home, where she had roots and memories. Now someone was dumping this vicious crime in her lap. She had to learn the truth. Ada had hated her for inheriting it, she thought. Yet, she knew Ada did not want to live here. It was all too confusing.

"Are you up to it?"

Linc's words made their way through her maze of thoughts. She raised her gaze to meet his. "What?"

"The fight it's going to take to prove your innocence. Are you up to it?"

"I have to be. I am innocent."

"Well, someone has gone to great lengths to make it look like you did the arson. Someone must hate you an awful lot. Do you have any idea who it might be?"

She thought. "The only person I never got along with was my stepmother. But she isn't even here. God, she hates Michigan. She's the reason my father never came home. She wouldn't hear of returning."

"You don't think it's her then?"

"No, I don't." But she couldn't say the same for Jack Devlin. He wanted her property. Would he go to these lengths to get his hands on the land? Oh, poor Mara. It would break her heart to discover she was being used for a piece of land.

"There must be someone. Think, he urged."

She lowered her head. "There is someone."

"Who?"

She raised her gaze. "There is someone who wants my property. But I don't know if he'd take such drastic measures to get it."

"Who, who?" he asked impatiently.

"Jack Devlin."

He let out a deep sigh and leaned back in his chair. "Devlin? He wants your property? The man is never satisfied."

She nodded. "He wants to expand his resort. I overheard him telling Emma that he'd do whatever it took to get it. And now he has Mara on Mackinac Island alone. He wouldn't harm her, would he?"

Linc scoffed, "Devlin doesn't have the guts to hurt anyone physically. He's unscrupulous and I dislike him, but he wouldn't hurt anyone." His eyes held hers. "But he is the kind of guy who would use other means to gain what he wants. He knows he can use the good ol' boy network to aid in his deceit. His uncle is a judge and that's only a tiny part of the network."

Fleeting relief flashed in her eyes. She was glad Mara was physically safe but her heart ached for her friend's future emotional well being. "I wish I'd never come back."

He reached across the table and lifted her chin. "Then you'd never have met me."

"I'd probably never have met you if my house hadn't burned either."

He shrugged. "Maybe, maybe not. We'll never know because that's how we met. Now we have to get at the truth and clear your name."

The brightness from the sun dimmed and shadows took its place. Paige glanced out the window as gray clouds gathered in the sky above. Was that the sound of distant thunder? She hoped they weren't in for a storm, although she had heard someone say they needed rain badly.

A tap on the window drew her attention. She focused in and saw Winona standing outside as droplets of rain began to fall. She waved and Winona motioned that she'd like to come in. Paige nodded.

"She's sweet," Paige said. "She's asked me to help her with her work. She's very talented."

Linc's face softened. "I knew the two of you would be friends. Thanks for helping her. I think she's talented too." He watched Winona run along the sidewalk. "I think I'll leave you women alone to talk."

"It doesn't matter. I don't think...hi, Winona. Come join us." She pushed out the chair beside her.

Linc stretched as he rose from the chair. "Hi, kiddo," he said in his stretching voice. "I'm going to pick up a newspaper. I'll be right back."

Winona's face brightened. "I have a portfolio ready to go, just as you told me."

"Great." Paige smiled. "I did call my agent this morning and she said for you to send it to her. She'll be glad to look at it and tell you what she thinks."

"Thank you." Winona squeezed her hand. "I can't thank you enough."

"You don't need to thank me. Just do your best and succeed."

Winona glanced over her shoulder and then back at Paige. "I do need to thank you." She lowered her voice. "You know a favor done is a favor earned." She took another quick survey of the room. "First of all, your secret about modeling is safe with me." She leaned in close. "I went with my father to the tribal council meeting the other day and the council has their eye on your property for another casino and resort."

Paige glanced around. "Does Linc know?"

"I don't think so. But please be careful. I get an eerie feeling about your land." She looked behind her and saw Linc coming. "Thanks again. I owe you."

Linc strolled back to the table with a paper under his arm. "If you ladies have finished with your girl talk, I think we'd better be going." He held his hand out to Paige, "Are you ready to go?"

Paige took his hand and let him guide her to her feet. "Can we give you a lift?" she offered.

"No. I have a little more shopping to do before I go home." She turned toward the door. "Thanks again."

After a few well-placed phone calls, Linc found the lawyer he wanted for Paige. He was at the country club but agreed to meet with them. The attorney took the case and counseled them not to speak to the police without him present. After their meeting Paige felt like a criminal. He had questioned her as if she was guilty and warned her the police would be worse. She needed time to think, time to cleanse herself of the tainted feeling she now carried. Against Linc's protestations she insisted she had to be alone. He drove her to the inn and directed her to call him if she needed anything.

Without Paige to think about, his own problems began to nag him. The confrontation with his mother had left him disturbed. They had argued and discussed. He had learned a great deal, but not enough. He checked his watch. His mother would be in town at a luncheon for the museum. Linc rushed home to retrieve his birth certificate. He'd never really looked at it or thought about it much. He'd simply put it away with all his important papers when his mother had given it to him.

He lifted the little yellow manila envelope from the depths of the safe and pulled the certificate from its casing. Slowly, he opened it. Scanning the official form, his eyes fell on the phrase, father unknown. His mother had kept her promise.

Slowly he worked his way through the house to his mother's room. God, he felt like such a heel as he rifled through her personal property. He lifted her bankbook and stared at it. Rubbing his fingers over the tattered cover, he stared at it for a long time before shoving it into his pocket. He ran through the house like a thief trying to escape. He reached for the door handle and stopped. "How can I do this?" He stood in guilty thought, then pulled the door open. "I have to find out," he rationalized.

The argument he'd begun with himself at home continued as he drove to town. His shoulders sagged as he entered the bank. He'd never felt lower. He approached the clerk's window and responded to her smile by handing her the bankbook. "I need a list of the deposits and who made them on this account." He stared into empty space and waited for what seemed an eternity for the teller to return.

She handed him a computer printout of the account's activities. "I'm sorry, but all the deposits were made in cash. There is no record of who made them."

"Thank you. I guess I'll have to go over all of my old deposit tickets."

A warm smile flashed across her face. "If you need any help, I'd be glad to do it."

He wrapped the printout around the book and shoved it in his jacket pocket. He nodded and left.

He drove his car to the breakwater and stared out over the bay. Linc hauled himself from the car and began walking. Gravel crunched beneath his feet. He found the point where the white-blue of the sky met the blue-green of the water and fixed his gaze there. Now he could think without interruption.

His mother wouldn't tell him who his father was but she had inadvertently told him he had a sibling. He wondered if he had a sister or brother. Somewhere in this small city was another person who shared a father with him. But who? The wind whistled a message in his ears. "It is better this way. Why would you want to open a box that cannot be locked again?"

He shook his head, trying desperately to clear his thoughts. This whole thing would pass, wouldn't it? His mother had gone to a lot of trouble to hide his father's identity. Maybe he'd never know who he was. All he needed was a good run along the stony shore. He needed to run and forget everything else. No more wondering about his parentage, no thinking, nothing, just running.

He reached the end of the gravel path and stopped. He pushed his arms high in the air, reaching for the spirits of earth, wind, and fire to bring him solace. He turned in each direction, asking for peace and reconciliation. Then he struck out over the breakwater that jutted out into the bay. He didn't let up his pace. He raced along, emptying his mind. By the time he came to the end of the breakwater and returned, he was winded. He doubled over from the waist, trying to catch his breath.

Seagulls screamed overhead, fighting against the wind currents and updrafts that tugged at them. It had been one hell of a morning, Linc thought. He wanted to stop thinking. Clear his mind. He couldn't. The inner place he sought, the place of peace and harmony his grandfather had taught him, was elusive. New thoughts came rushing in as soon as he filtered others away.

"Damn my white half," he swore, and kicked a stone into the water. When he couldn't accomplish his Native American meditations, he always blamed his "white half" and today was no different. Why should all this bother him? His father evidently didn't want him to know who he was and it was a certainty his mother didn't. So why should it matter to him?

"Damn it," he cursed again, recalling the look of pain that filled his mother's face when he demanded to know who his father was. Treating her like that was no different than what his father had done. He would apologize and forget all this. He didn't need to know. Not if it was going to cause her that much pain.

He had enough to think of, worrying about Paige and her problems. He struggled with his thoughts about Jack Devlin. He was a rogue, but this seemed too well planned for him—although he could have seen the activity at her house and decided to scare her off before she settled in. But how could he have moved the furniture, taken out policies and committed the arson in such a short time? Unless somehow he knew she would be home soon. But Mara was the only one that knew. And what was this with him and Mara? He always had a petite, beautiful blond on his arm. Mara was a beautiful blond but she just didn't fit the rest of the profile.

He stopped and pulled into his lungs the cool breeze off the lake. Gentle waves rolled in and then back out again. A lot like his life he thought. The next wave washed in, cold water seeping into his shoes and socks. Even more like his life. He didn't care. He reached down and pulled icy water to his face. Again and again he rinsed his face, trying to cleanse his father from his mind. He'd put away the feelings of shame a long time ago and he wanted them to stay away. If he couldn't keep his mind straight, how could he help Paige?

Later, when he walked into his house, his mother stood waiting in the kitchen. He handed her the bankbook. "I'm sorry, Mom."

She smiled and placed thin arms around her son. "I know."

It was over and he would let it stay where it belonged. In the past—in secret silence.

Paige had crept through the house. She didn't want to take the chance of running into anyone, afraid she would break down and cry.

She had spent the day and into early evening in her room. The pieces of the puzzle just wouldn't go together. Who was trying to frame her for arson? And why? And if the tribe wanted the land to develop as casino resorts, why didn't they just come to her? She had a hundred and eighty acres. It was feasible she would part with some of it. After all, she wasn't going to farm or develop it. She just wanted her home back.

Linc called for the fifth time and again she declined his offer to go out. Tomorrow would be soon enough. Before she replaced her phone, she tried calling Mara again, and again she didn't answer. Chills traveled through her as she conjured up thoughts of what Jack might do to her friend.

The smell of coffee and freshly baked bread made her stomach growl. She was hungry. She could hear Emma humming in the kitchen as she made her way toward the aromas. "Hi. Am I too late to get a snack?"

Emma turned a loaf of bread onto a cooling rack and peeped over her glasses at the younger woman. "Of course not, dear. What would you like?"

"Just a piece of that delicious smelling bread will do."

Emma sliced a piece and placed it in front of Paige. "This is hardly enough," she said as she poured a cup of coffee for Paige too. "You left early this morning. I hope you had something to eat today. I missed you girls at breakfast."

Emma had no idea how good it made Paige feel to have a motherly figure fussing over her. "I had breakfast with Linc. He gave me the plans for rebuilding my house." She watched the older woman closely for some sign of distraction when she said she was rebuilding but saw none. "I hope to begin construction soon."

"I think that's wonderful. Your father would be proud of you." Emma wiped her forehead with the bottom of her full apron.

Paige felt she had an ally in the motherly older woman. But could she get her to talk about Jack's plans? "It seems there are a couple of parties interested in my property." She watched Emma's bright blue eyes darken. "I may have some difficulty clearing up the fire mess in order to begin."

Emma turned toward the stove and stirred a pot on the burner. "Just because someone wants your property shouldn't mean you will have a problem beginning your construction." Her voice had suddenly tightened. Paige knew she had hit a nerve.

"No." She weighed her next words carefully. "The fire was arson and they think they have a suspect." Paige saw Emma's back stiffen. Disappointment flooded through her. She knew Emma thought it was Jack and now she felt he was capable of arson too.

Paige squeezed her eyes tightly closed to avoid the tears she felt welling. Never in her life had she felt so alone. The older woman cared for her but her loyalty was with Jack.

She forced her eyes open and stared at the back of the white-haired woman who had pulled her apron up to dab at her face. Paige could tell she was dabbing at her eyes. "Emma," she said softly.

Emma's head nodded and she responded with a garbled, "Yes."

"Thank you for the snack, the bread was delicious." She slid from the stool. "I'll see you in the morning."

In hushed tones Emma uttered, "Good night, dear."

Paige inched her way back toward her room. She paused with her hand on the newel post of the stairs, considering going to Emma and telling her she was the one who was under suspicion, but decided the fewer people that knew the better. Everyone would know soon enough.

She ran the rest of the way to her room and flopped on her bed. She was so tired, yet she couldn't put the puzzle away. Would Linc try to gain her trust to get the property for the tribe? No, he wasn't like that, was he? It was probably Jack. After all he had told Emma he would stop at nothing.

She tried to call Mara again but she still wasn't answering her cell phone. Paige couldn't understand. Mara's phone went everywhere with her. Mara had always said that an outfit wasn't complete without her phone. Laying her head back on the bed pillows, she whispered to the night, "Please let her be okay."

Seven

"Twenty-one, twenty-two." Paige stopped pacing, bent down and picked up a diamond stud earring that must have fallen from Mara's ear before she left. She'd been in such a hurry to run to Jack. "Oh, Mara," she whispered aloud, clutching the earring in her hand.

Emma's reaction had sent her reeling. Here she was, alone again. She couldn't help Mara or herself. Mara had said, "Don't expect me back tonight," and that was two nights ago. "Twenty-three, twenty-four." There would be no sleeping tonight.

She wished she could call Linc and tell him her suspicions about Jack, but he would be asleep. And what if his mother answered the telephone. "Twenty-five." Now that would make an impression on Nuna Cross. Her son's crazy girlfriend calls late at night. She glanced at the clock; it was almost midnight.

Paige couldn't stay cooped up any longer. She was smothering. Maybe she would feel more like sleeping if she went for a walk.

She pulled her hooded sweatshirt over her shirt and quietly left her room. She stopped outside Mara's room and reached out, laying her hand on the raised panel door as if the simple touch would give her some sort of assurance.

She tried to shake off the feeling of foreboding but instead, it grew with each step she took. The house was dark except for occasional flashes of light from the kitchen television. Slowly she peeked her head through the kitchen door. Emma sat staring at the television. The credits were rolling and the large word appeared across the screen. Casablanca.

"I'm going out for a walk. I'll be back in about an hour."

Emma started. "Oh, I wasn't expecting...a walk at this hour?"

Paige nodded. "I can't sleep."

"I'll put on a fresh pot of coffee if you're interested."

Paige shook her head, "I don't think that would help my problem. Caffeine, you know." There was a strain between them that hadn't been there before.

"Then I'll make a cup of hot chocolate for you. That should help. She offered Paige a smile, but her eyes were void of pleasure.

Paige ran her fingers along the breakfast bar as she walked through the dimly lit kitchen to the back door. "That would be nice. If you aren't up when I return, I'll just pop it in the microwave."

Emma didn't look her way and didn't move. "I'll wait up for you."

"You don't have to do that. It's really quite late now." She opened the door.

"It's no bother. I want to finish watching this movie and it just began." She waved her hand in the air. "Enjoy your walk."

"Thank you."

Paige closed the door and stepped into the cool night breeze. Even if Emma's loyalty was to Jack, she was a good and kind woman. It felt warm and comfortable having someone waiting for her.

The moon cast heavy shadows from the trees across the road. The hoots of an owl and the swishing cry of a nighthawk sounded eerie in the semi-darkness. Crickets sang their song while distant tree toads joined in with their chirping. The midnight symphony was strangely peaceful and harmonious.

She wanted to walk forever, to keep on walking until she came to the end of time. She picked up her pace. Her heart was pounding against her ribs, her breath rasping in her lungs. She should pace herself as she usually did, but she pushed herself faster and faster, trying to run from her problems.

The trees above her were bursting with new foliage. All around her oozed the smell of wet spring earth. It was perfect here in God's country; only a serpent had entered her Garden of Eden.

She finally slowed her stride. She was in good shape but this time she had pushed beyond her limits. Longingly, she made her way to her home. Home. Her place of memories. The aroma of lilacs filled the air, yet there were only a couple of blossoms that had opened early. She ran her fingers over the bush and lightly touched the pristine blossom. The memory of her mother's soft melodious voice enveloped her.

"Oh, Mom, I need you." Hot tears rolled down her cheeks. She didn't try to stop the flood, since she was alone. She could cry. Paige lamented the loss of her parents and the loss of the home they had happily shared. Sweet familial memories enveloped her, warming her mind and body. She cried until she was spent, until her eyes were dry and there was nothing left.

She stared at the moonlit pile of rubble. How could anyone think she'd burn her own house? Why? How would it help her to lose her home and the wonderful memories that went with it?

Stepping toward the blackened wood, she pushed the questions away. Suddenly the hairs at the back of her neck prickled. She turned around to see if someone was there, if someone was watching her. Her body shivered as fear struck a chord in her heart. "No," she whispered to herself.

"Stop being foolish." Yet she could feel the presence of someone or something watching her every move.

The sense that she wasn't alone filled her with gnawing trepidation. She took a step away from the foundation. How was she going to get away if someone was lurking out there in the shadows? She had no car and there was no one to help.

Her breath came in rapid, shallow gasps and nervous perspiration formed on her skin. She listened. Nothing, only the sounds of the forest's nocturnal residents and an occasional buzzing hum of a pesky mosquito.

Off in the distance a dog barked, almost howling like a wolf. Then from the corner of her eye, she saw movement. She turned and her heart lurched. From under the darkened stand of dense trees where she'd played as a child, emerged a black bear.

"Oh, God, help me," she hurriedly prayed. She wildly jerked her gaze around for a means of escape. But hadn't she always been told not to run when a bear was near and to never look him right in the eyes? She stood frozen in place.

The bear lumbered a few steps closer and suddenly reared up on its hind legs and opened its mouth as if to roar, but nothing came out. The bear raised its front paws skyward and opened its soundless mouth again.

Paige studied it. What was happening? Suddenly, something made a thudding sound in the basement. She looked toward the blackened hole, inched toward it, and peered in. Nothing, only a black burned-out hole.

Hands touched her back. She was relieved. She wasn't alone; someone was there to help her. "Thank God," she uttered. Then the hands shoved hard against her back.

She flailed her own hands out to grab something, but only clutched at thin air. The sound of cracking wood echoed through the night as she hurtled through the air into the fire-blackened pit. Desperately she grabbed for something to stop her fall but there was nothing. Pain shot through every part of her body as she slammed into a half-burned beam that stretched across the gaping cavity. She held her breath, afraid to move and afraid to stay where she was.

Again the wood creaked as the fire-weakened beam groaned from the added burden, and she knew...

Oh, God, she was going to fall to the depths of the cellar! She clutched for something stable but there was nothing. The treacherous beam gave way and she screamed as she fell the rest of the way through the night. She hit the hard-packed cellar floor with a thud. Pain was everywhere but her mind was clear. Someone had pushed her.

Why? Paige opened her eyes and saw a blur of stars above her. Her first thought was she was going to die. Her head throbbed and she could feel a lump growing. When she attempted to raise herself, she couldn't. Her head spun and blackness reached out to envelope her.

Mara jerked awake, feeling a deep pain in her chest. Her breathing was heavy. She scrambled to her knees.

Jack rolled over and lazily looked at her. "And what brings my sleeping beauty awake so abruptly? Can't get enough of me, can you?" he teased.

Mara shook her head. "I dreamt I was falling. It was so real I could feel the wind being knocked out of me when I landed." She shivered. "Sometimes I get premonitions. Maybe I should call Paige."

Jack pulled her into his arms and smoothed her hair away from her face. "Shh. It was just a dream." He lifted her chin and brushed her lips. "It's probably because you fell so hard for me."

"Aren't you just the dreamer?" she said with a smirk. The intense feeling lessened as Jack caressed her. Paige would be fine; she was with Linc. As Mara and Jack made love, she moved to a different plateau, and left the nightmare behind. It was difficult for her to think of anything or anyone but Jack. For the first time in her life she had fallen fast and hard. She only hoped he felt the same.

They slept late into the day and then played in the pool and rode bikes around the island until dinner. On this very special island where the eighteenth century ruled, two hearts beat as one.

"You romantic, you." Mara reached out and ran her fingers over Jack's freshly shaven face. The whole day had been a dream come true and now this special candlelight dinner. She sighed. "I hate the thought of going back; it's been like a dream coming here."

"Why go back?"

She shot a questioning gaze at him. "What do you mean? We have to."

He smiled a mischievous smile. "Not right away we don't. We could stay for a few more days. In fact," he reached into his pocket and handed her a reservation confirmation. "I've reserved a room at the Grand Hotel for two days and nights."

"The Grand Hotel?" She gasped as she stared at the paper. "It says Honeymoon Suite."

He nodded. "That it does." He pulled another piece of paper from his pocket. "My uncle's a judge. He waived the three-day waiting period and those silly classes so we can get married tonight."

"Married?" she whispered. "You're asking me to marry you? But we haven't known each other very long."

"I love you, Mara. More than I ever thought possible. Time won't change that. I can't lose you. Please, say you'll marry me."

She lowered her gaze to the piece of paper that could change her life. She'd wanted him to love her as she did him but she didn't want her life to change. "I have a career and I live in New York," she whispered.

Jack nodded. "I know. I'm not asking you to give it up although I do think we should live together," he teased. "I'm only asking you to include me in the rest of your life. We can work out a compromise on the rest."

She gazed at him from across the table. "Do you think it could work . . . my working, I mean?"

"Whether you work or not doesn't make any difference to me." A frown creased his brow. "Come to think of it, you never told me exactly what your work is."

She looked away and smiled. "You won't believe me if I tell you."

"You said you worked in the fashion industry."

She felt color deepen in her cheeks. If Jack was to become her husband there should be no secrets between them. A crooked smile touched her mouth and she tilted her head to one side. "I'm a model."

"A...?"

She nodded. "Paige and I work for the Big and Beautiful Agency."

He leaned back and laughed. "Well, I'll be damned! I thought you were too glamorous to be a normal person."

"Jack," she warned as she glanced around hoping no one had heard them.

"A model. I picked a model to be my wife? Are you serious? You're really a model?"

She nodded. "I really am. If you ever picked up a fashion magazine or turned on television once in a while, you just might see me doing a bra commercial."

"You're kidding?"

She laughed lightly. "I'm serious. That's why I want to continue working for a few more years."

"I'll be damned. A model! And Paige too?"

"Yes, only Linc doesn't know."

"Why all the secrecy?" He poured her another glass of champagne.

"Because Paige has had a hard life. She wants people to like and accept her for who she is inside, not for what she is on the outside. She says guys never find her interesting until she says she is a model." She eyed him closely. "When a woman is bigger than the unreal, ultra-thin models, it's hard to tell whether a man is interested in you or your fame." Jack sat nodding. Mara continued. "Anyway, she wanted to come back here as just an average Jill and make friends on that premise. And to be honest with you, the anonymity has been nice for both of us."

"I hope you know that I love you because you are you. It's true I've never dated anything but smaller women, but that's because I hadn't met you." Jack gazed deeply into her eyes. "You haven't given me an answer yet."

He reached under the table and came out with a small, pink velvet box. Inside lay an old-fashioned, white-gold filigree ring with a beautiful one-karat solitaire diamond that sparkled blue-white as it caught the moon's light.

She gasped. "It's beautiful."

"It was my grandmother's." He took the ring from the box and took her left hand in his. "May I? Will you?"

She glanced at the ring and then at Jack. "Yes," she breathed. "Oh, yes."

He slipped the ring on her finger.

She felt she would drown in the tenderness of his gaze. "Tonight too soon?"

"Are you serious? But there's so much to do. I could never be ready that soon."

"All you have to do is show up at the altar. Everything else has been arranged."

"I can't believe it. You have everything done?" She shot him a calculating grin.

A flash of mischievous humor touched his lips. "I have everything ready. I was just waiting for my bride to say yes."

She cocked her head to one side and raised a brow. "Pretty sure of yourself, weren't ya?"

"I love your accent."

Her smile widened. He teased her about her accent all of the time and she loved every minute of it. She loved every minute of everything he did. Then she remembered. "I just want to call Paige. I always dreamed she'd be my maid of honor. I have to call her."

"I'll see the minister while you make your call." He dropped a tender kiss on her lips.

She dialed Paige's cell phone number and let it ring and ring. No answer. Strange. Paige usually took the phone everywhere she went. She hung up and dialed again. Still no answer. She was probably out with Linc. But shouldn't she have her phone with her?

She hung up and waited for Jack to return. How would Paige react when she found out they were married? In fact, the only blemish on her ceremony was that Paige wouldn't be there.

Jack sauntered toward the table. "Everything's ready. Did you get hold of Paige?"

She shook her head. "Guess I'll have to do it without her. Mara glanced down at her white gauze dress. Good thing I wore this tonight."

Again, Jack's face reflected his love. "You could be naked and you would be perfect."

"Mmm. You say the sweetest things" Her eyes sparkled in anticipation.

"Come with me." He held out his hand.

She slipped hers into his and let him lead her to a carriage pulled by a matched pair of brightly decorated and finely groomed, chestnut-colored Belgian horses. The white carriage was covered with bridal lace and red bows; red bows that matched the ribbons braided through the horses' manes. In the back she noticed their luggage. She gave Jack a questioning glance.

His gaze followed hers. "You said yes."

"So I did." She settled against the leather seat waiting to be taken to wherever Jack had in mind.

The carriage lumbered down the cobblestone street toward the Grand Hotel. The night was cool but the bright moon washed the island in golden romance. As they drove by the beach the sound of gentle waves washing to shore echoed softly through the night. She sighed, "No one has ever had a more perfect night to get married." She tapped his chin, "Or a more perfect man to marry."

"And don't you ever forget it." Jack laughed lightly as he put his arm around her and pulled her close.

Mara thought of her best friend who was more like her sister. She was like Paige in that she hadn't planned on love until she retired. But hadn't she told Paige that you don't wait for love? If it comes before you expect it, a person should grab it and not let go? Yes, she had, and she certainly wasn't going to doubt her own words. She snuggled into Jack's chest.

"What are you thinking about?" Jack asked, his lips against her hair.

"You."

"Hmm, a very good subject."

She purred and snuggled closer. "We'll find out just how good in a little while."

He chuckled. "It seems to me this beautiful model I know said something about Jack being a dull boy."

"That was before she really got to know him. This Jack can work and play with the best of them."

The carriage stopped in front of the Grand Hotel. Jack helped Mara to the ground as a bellboy rushed down the steps to take their bags.

"I'd carry you up the steps, but I might make a spectacle of us both." He smiled down at her. "'Cuz I would not stop at the door. I would be on a dead run to our room with you in my arms."

"Don't you even think about it." She smiled up at him. They walked under the yellow awning along the walk and up the steps to the porch that looked a half block long. Several people rocked contentedly in white wicker furniture.

Jack held Mara's hand and led her inside the massive lobby. Tall columns rose to the high ceiling.

"Right this way." The bellboy led them to the reception desk.

Jack handed the receptionist his credit card and signed the register.

Mara smiled as he signed Mr. & Mrs. Jack Devlin.

"It looks so official." She peered through her lashes at Jack.

"It will be shortly." He kissed the tip of her nose.

They took the elevator to the fourth floor.

"The bridal suite, sir." The bellboy unlocked the oak-stained paneled door and handed Jack the ornate brass key.

Inside, a small entry led to a large sitting room. Jack escorted her through that room to the bedroom. A king size bed had a brass frame with garlands of fresh flowers twined around it. An old-fashioned woven carpet was centered on the highly polished hardwood floors. Soft, sheer drapes hung at the windows. The Victorian ambiance made her feel like a princess.

Jack tipped the boy and closed the door. He pulled Mara into his arms and found her lips with his own. "You don't know how happy you've made me."

Mara pushed against his chest. "Slow down, lover boy. Tonight you are my knight in shining armor. And the armor will stay on until you've made an honest woman of me."

A lusty laugh burst from Jack's throat. "You devil woman, you. Tease Sir Devlin, your Knight of the Round Table and then heartlessly turn him out."

She glanced at her left hand and lifted it, wiggling her ring finger. "I don't see a wedding ring there."

"You will, you will." His grin grew wider. "If I don't leave right now, I never will. Because when I take you in my arms, I will be your knight in shining armor and you will be an honest woman."

She smiled sweetly. "If you don't leave right now, I might not be able to let you go." She ushered him to the door where he hesitantly disappeared into the hall beyond.

A short while later a tap at the door drew her attention. She opened it to a small, elderly woman. "Mr. Devlin sent me to bring you to him."

"Wait just one minute." She dialed Paige's phone number again. It rang and rang just as before, but no answer.

Strange. Where was she? She felt so guilty for getting married and not having Paige with her.

With a frown of concern on her face, Mara grabbed her purse and followed the woman to the elevator. Where were they going? They crossed the porch and down the steps to the lawn. Jack waited for her in the white, Victorian gazebo.

She accepted his proffered hand and held his gaze. Misty green eyes melted into his smiling blue pools. They slowly turned toward the minister.

Beside Jack stood a tall, white-haired gentleman with a very distinguished appearance. Oddly enough she had a fleeting thought of Linc when she saw him. But her body and soul were fixed on the tall, handsome, dusky blond-haired man who would soon be her husband.

Cool breezes rushed from the Mackinac Straits and the sound of waves echoed through the night. The gazebo was lit only by candles and the tawny moon. Mara felt as if she had stepped back somewhere in time on this tiny jeweled island.

A minister with his Bible stood ready to make them man and wife. "Mara, repeat after me."

A band from the hotel played a soft ballad and filled the air with romance as she responded. "I Mara, take you Jack to be my wedded husband. To have and to hold from this day forward..."

The rest of the ceremony was only a blur until Jack reached for her hand. "With this ring I thee wed." He placed the narrow white-gold band with a single row of diamonds on her finger.

And then the minister said, "You may kiss the bride."

Jack gathered her in his arms, pulled back the veil and tenderly kissed her. A sob sounded behind them.

"Oh, Hester, you cry at every wedding," the minister said to the woman behind him as he closed his Bible.

Jack and Mara laughed as they turned and saw the older woman wiping her eyes on a hanky and blowing her nose.

"I know, Henry, but you know how sentimental I am."

Applause came from all around the gazebo as the minister announced, "Ladies and gentlemen, I would like to introduce Mr. and Mrs. Jack Devlin."

Mara glanced down and was surprised to see many of the hotel tourists standing and applauding them.

Jack shook the minister's hand. "Thank you." He turned to the man who had stood as his best man. "Mara, this is my uncle, Richard Devlin. Judge Devlin. Without him I couldn't have pulled this whole thing off."

Mara reached out her hand. "I'm pleased to meet you..." She paused, "Do I call you Judge Devlin or Uncle Richard?"

The man laughed and took her hand in his. "Uncle Rich will do, young lady." He leaned forward and placed a kiss on her cheek. "You two be happy."

They signed the license and stood gazing into each other's eyes. Jack motioned to the band leader who raised his hand to the band. After humming the first chord, Jack turned to Mara. "Could I have this dance?"

"Forever?" Mara said.

Jack smiled down at his new bride. "For as long as we live."

He gathered her in his arms and danced around the gazebo. Again the crowd applauded and joined the dance.

The phone at Linc's house rang. He glanced at his watch. Who in the hell would be calling him at 2:30 in the morning? He had been sitting on the deck thinking about Paige and all that had happened. He didn't appreciate the interruption, but then it might be a fire. The dry weather made the fields and forest prime for wildfires.

"Linc?" a harried voice asked when he answered it.

"Yes."

"This is Emma...from the inn? I'm sorry to bother you at this hour, but I didn't know who else to call."

"Calm down and tell me what's wrong," he said, his own voice growing agitated.

"It's Paige. She went out more than two hours ago and hasn't come back yet."

Linc knew Paige was upset. "She's probably just driving around."

"No. No, you don't understand. She walked. She didn't take her car. She hasn't come back and I'm worried about her."

The hairs at the back of Linc's neck stood on end. "She walked, you say?"

"Yes. She said she wouldn't be more than an hour. She was going to have a cup of hot chocolate with me when she returned. Only she hasn't."

"I'll be right there." He rushed through the house, grabbing his car keys from the dish on the gray marble counter.

Nuna came down the stairs. "Linc, where are you going at this hour?"

"Something's happened to Paige. I've got to find her."

He didn't remember driving to the inn but he simply burst through the back door. "Which way did she go?"

"Oh, Linc. I don't know. She just said she was gonna walk."

Linc raced out and cupped his hands on either side of his mouth. "P..a..i..g..e," he called. He listened. Nothing,

no sound, just the sound of night. "P..a..i..g..e," he frantically called again.

"I'm real worried." Emma pulled her sweater around
her round body as she stood next to him. "She's always
does exactly what she says she's going to do. She'd have
been here if she could. Something's happened, I can feel
it." Her voice cracked as she spoke.

"Go back inside. I'll find her."

He got into the truck and raced down the road to her
place. The lights from the vehicle flashed on the pile of
rubble. There was no movement, no sign of anyone.

He got out and called, "P..a..i..g..e." Again, nothing.

"Oh, God," he prayed aloud, "don't let her be hurt."
He'd never forgive himself if something happened to her.
He never should have left her alone in the state she was in.
He grabbed the flashlight from under his seat and flashed
the light around the yard. "P..a..i..g..e," he called again.

He rushed around the yard, flashing the light everywhere. She was nowhere. Where could she be? With her
car back at the Inn, she couldn't have gotten far on foot.
He retraced his steps.

What was that? He stopped and listened. Nothing. He
began to move, he had to find her, but where? There it was
again. What was it? Where was it coming from?

He stood deathly still, closed his eyes and listened, trying to fix the sound. There it was, a moan. It came from
the charred remains of her house. He moved toward the
pile of debris, flashing his light over it. As he approached
the blackened foundation of the house, he flashed his light
down into the cellar. "Oh, my God." He leaned over the
edge and saw Paige lying crumpled on the floor.

"Paige, hold on, I'm coming." He raced back to his
vehicle, grabbed the cellular phone and called 911. After
giving directions to the operator, he took a rope from the

back, tied it securely around a tree and let himself down into the hole.

She lay absolutely still. Linc checked for a pulse and let out a long breath as he felt the faint beating of her heart under his fingers. He removed his jacket and gently laid it over her. He couldn't risk moving her for fear he might injure her more.

After what seemed an eternity, he heard the screams of the ambulance and saw the flashing red lights reflect against the top of the foundation.

"Over here!" he yelled.

Linc stood back as the paramedics secured her neck with a foam collar and rolled her onto a backboard. Then they caught the stretcher that was lowered on ropes and expertly placed Paige on it. Slowly and carefully the two men guided the stretcher through the rubble, until it was clear and the rescue workers above could freely lift her and remove her to the waiting ambulance. Linc followed and climbed in. "I'm going with her."

The attendant nodded. "Okay, but what about your car?"

Linc ignored the question, looking at Paige. He took her cold hand in his. "It's going to be all right. You're going to be fine." He spoke gently. "You're not alone anymore."

On the fast trip to the hospital Linc simply held her hand and talked to her, telling her over and over, everything was going to be all right.

Linc jumped out as soon as the ambulance stopped. He watched helplessly as the attendants hustled Paige into the emergency room.

The nurse stopped him as Paige was wheeled through the swinging doors.

"I have to be with her."

"Are you her husband or a close relative?"

"No, but..."

The nurse shook her head. "Then, I'm afraid you can't come back here."

"I have to..."

The nurse stood in the doorway, blocking his entrance. "Please come to the desk and give me all the information you have about the accident."

Linc rammed his hands in his jean's pockets and watched as Paige disappeared into another room down that long hall.

"Her name?" The nurse asked.

Linc moved to the desk at the nurse's urging.

"Paige. Paige Turner."

"Address?"

"She lives in New York. She's here on vacation. Ah...she's staying at the Bayside Inn."

"Age?"

"I don't know. Twenty...five or six."

"Nearest relative?"

"She doesn't have any relatives...only a stepmother she doesn't get along with. And a roommate, but she's on Mackinac Island."

"Is there no way of getting in contact with this stepmother?"

"I don't..." He hesitated before finally saying, "No."

"Does she have insurance?"

Linc bounded to his feet. "I don't know and I don't care. She's in there and she's hurt. That's all I know. I found her like that and I damned well want to see her."

The nurse rose and stepped to the door. "I'll let the doctor know you're out here. You're not a relative?"

"No, her fiancé," he lied.

"Oh." The nurse nodded. "I'll see if I can get you in." She smiled sympathetically at him.

Linc paced the waiting room like a caged wolf. Damn, this was ridiculous. He stared at the doors that separated him from Paige. What right did they have to keep him from her. If anything happened to her, then...

"Hey, you can't go back there." The other nurse at the desk jumped from her chair.

"The woman I love is back there and no one is going to keep me out." He pushed through the doors and strode down the hall.

A sleepy-eyed doctor in a crumpled white coat was standing over Paige.

"How is she?" Linc stepped into the small examining room.

The doctor looked up. "Who are you?"

"I'm going to marry this woman." He stepped to Paige's side.

"She has a nasty bump on her head." Then he pointed to several dark bruises. She's going to be one sore lady. My examination hasn't revealed anything serious, but I think we should take x-rays, just to be sure." He flashed his little light into Paige's eyes.

She moaned and turned her head away.

"Is she going to be all right?"

"How did this happen?" the doctor asked, ignoring Linc's question.

"I don't know. The housekeeper at the inn where she's staying called me and said she didn't come back after a walk. I went to look for her and found her in the cellar of her burned-out house. I don't know how she got there or what she was doing there."

"Bear." Paige murmured.

"What did she say?" the doctor asked. "Bear?"

"It sounded like bear." Linc repeated.

"Linc..." she whispered. "A big black bear."

Linc took her hand in his. "I'm right here. You're going to be all right. The doctors are taking very good care of you."

The doctor peeled off his latex gloves and threw them into the wastebasket, lifted the chart and began writing. "I'm sending her for x-rays now and I'm going to keep her in the hospital for observation. So you might as well go back into the waiting room until she's in her room." He clicked his pen and slipped it in his pocket. "I'll send a nurse to take you to her as soon as she's ready."

Bear? She had said something about a bear. What had that meant? Surely she didn't think a bear attacked her. If she'd been attacked by a bear, everyone would know it. So, what had she meant?

Eight

Paige hovered between two worlds. She fought coming out of the safe cocoon of darkness, but the intense overhead light and distant voices disturbed her lethargy.

"Miss Turner? Can you hear me?" a voice from the light asked.

Her mouth was cotton-dry and her tongue felt stuck to the roof. She fluttered her eyes open and stared at the face above her. Where was she? Who was that strange woman in white?

She wanted to drift back into sleep, but the woman began taking her clothes off and washing her. The water, although warm, brought her fully awake. She shivered.

"We must get you cleaned up," the woman said gently. "You don't want to stay like this, do you?" she said as one might speak to a child.

"Where...am...I?" Paige asked. Realization suddenly hit her. The woman attending her was a nurse. What had happened? Why was she here?

"In the hospital. You took a nasty fall."

Of course. It all came rushing back. She'd been pushed into the cellar. Was she badly hurt? Had she broken any bones? There was pain everywhere.

"I want to...go home." She tried to fight the nurse, pulling back on the shirt the nurse was removing. But it was useless. The nurse was not only built like a marine sergeant but she had the strength of one.

"In a day or two." The nurse gently pushed her back and expertly stripped her of her clothing, sponged her with warm water and slipped the hospital gown around her. Then, apparently satisfied with her work, she pulled the sheet to Paige's chest, neatly folded it down and then pushed the button to lift the head of her bed.

"No, no...you don't understand. I have to go." Paige hadn't liked hospitals since her mother died. And when she lost her father too, she had declared she would never return.

"You've had quite a bump on your head. The doctor wants to keep an eye on you for a couple of days. Then you can go home." The nurse pushed aside the cart with the pan of water.

"Linc? Where's Linc?" She remembered hearing his voice through the haze. He had to be close by.

"Is that your friend outside? He's waiting to see you. He's very concerned."

"Please, may I see him?"

"I'll send him right in."

Linc bolted into the room and grasped Paige's hand in his. "What happened?" He leaned down and brushed a kiss over her forehead.

"I fell...I was pushed." She tried to pull together the events immediately preceding her fall.

Black eyes narrowed under blacker eyebrows. He looked like an approaching thunderstorm. "Pushed? Did you see who?"

"A bear." She knew it sounded ridiculous but that's what popped into her mind.

Linc's brows creased. "A bear? A bear attacked you?"

"I saw a bear." Linc's look made her wonder if she really did know what had happened. But, yes, she had seen a bear.

"Are you sure? If you were attacked by a bear, you would have more than bumps and bruises to show for it."

"I saw a bear. He was standing on his hind legs pawing the air. He opened his mouth to growl, only there was
no sound."

Linc's face flashed surprise. "No sound? Are you
sure?"

She nodded and grimaced as she put her hand on her
head. "Damn, that hurts." She cursed more at the inquisi-
tion than at her pain.

"Lie still and don't talk any more. You get some rest."

She placed her shaky hand on his arm. "Are you leaving?"

He gazed down at her. "I think I better."

"Please, don't leave." Two deep lines of concern
appeared between her eyes.

"I don't want to, but if I don't go, they'll throw me out.
But I'll be back first thing in the morning."

"Promise?"

A smile spread across his lips. "Try to keep me away."
He bent and kissed her tenderly. "Do you want to call
Mara?"

"Mara? Yes..." Mara always made things seem right.
Just to hear her voice would help. But it was late. The fer-
ries were no longer running. "No, no...I can't do that."

"No? Why not?" He looked surprised.

She glanced at the plain, round hospital clock on the
wall that showed it was well past three in the morning.
"It's too late. Why worry her tonight? She'll want to come
as soon as she hears I've been hurt, and she can't get off
the island tonight anyway. Let her at least get a good
night's rest."

"You two are really close, aren't you?"

Paige let her eyes drift closed. "Like sisters."

A tall, sandy-haired doctor came into the room reading
her chart. "Well, young lady, it seems you took quite a

fall." He scanned the pages before him and glanced up. "But your x-rays show no broken bones or fractures. That's a nasty bump on your head and I think we'll keep you for observation for a couple of days, since you don't have anyone to look after you."

Paige frowned. "I can look after myself."

The doctor shook his head. "I'm afraid not."

"But I hate hospitals. I'd get better faster if I was at home." She struggled to sit up in spite of the persisting pain.

The doctor threw Linc a glance that easily said, Can't you do something with her?

Linc took her hand again and tilted her chin. "You listen to the doctor and get better. Two days will fly by before you know it."

The doctor glanced at the couple. "By the way, we had to file a police report. You said you were shoved. There are some officers in the hall. They'd like a word with you."

Two officers came into the room, each holding his hat in his hands.

"Don't be long. She needs her rest," the doctor admonished the officers as he left the room. "And that applies to you too," he threw over his shoulder to Linc.

The first officer took a notebook from his pocket. "You told the doctor you were pushed. Did you see who did it?"

Paige shot Linc an uncertain glance. "I...uh...saw a bear."

"A bear?" the second officer asked disbelief.

"I was watching the bear and then I was shoved into the cellar."

The officers glanced at each other. "So the bear didn't shove you into the cellar?"

Again Paige glanced at Linc. "I...guess not. Someone pushed me. I remember thinking someone was there besides the bear."

"And you saw nothing but...this bear?" The speaking officer peered at the officer next to him. It was easy to read the doubt in his face.

"Yes."

"So you're saying someone came up behind you and shoved you into the cellar, is that right?"

"Yes."

The first officer cleared his throat. "Let me ask you another question. Aren't you the owner of the house that burned behind Nubs Nob? The old Turner place?"

"Yes. But what does that have to do with someone pushing me?"

The officer flipped his notepad shut and nodded to the other office. "I think we have all we need here." They both replaced their hats and headed for the door.

Linc rose from the bed. "So...what do you think?"

The officer turned. "We'll be in touch," he said, and put his hand to the brim of his hat.

Paige watched them leave and reached out to Linc. "They think I'm crazy."

Linc returned to his seat on the bed and gently brushed her hair away from her face. "No, I'm sure they don't think that."

"They think I burned my own house and now they think I'm crazy because I saw a bear. They probably think I jumped into the hole to divert attention from the arson." She closed her eyes as weariness settled over her. "I wish I'd never come back."

"It's going to be all right. Tomorrow things will look brighter. Remember my mother's saying about the sunshine?"

She nodded. She was sure his mother didn't mean that for her. But why hurt his feelings by saying so?

Again he bent and kissed her gently on the lips. Slipping something from around his neck, he handed it to her. "Here, keep this with you until I return."

She took the leather pouch attached to a leather necklace. "What is it?" She held it to her nose, smelling the sweet aroma of vanilla tobacco.

"It's a...well, it's a medicine bag. Kinda like a good luck charm. My grandfather gave it to me. And this little silver charm is a dream catcher."

She smiled and held the soft pouch in her hand. "Thank you. It seems I need all the luck I can get about now."

"Well, then you are in luck. You have me and I'm going to see to it that all of this mess gets straightened out."

A tingle raced along Paige's spine. His intense dark eyes suddenly became the focus of her whole existence. The conversation and the leather pouch were forgotten. Everything evaporated except for the overwhelming desire to drown in those beautiful eyes, to be kissed by that strong mouth.

She felt his warm gaze on her and as if in slow motion watched him lean toward her. Desire burned in his eyes. She saw his head tilt, his mouth relax, felt his hand very gently cradle the back of her head, felt his lips touch hers and she felt fire flare deep within her being. Her eyes fluttered closed as the gentle pressure of his mouth increased.

His kiss was miraculous, making all her troubles disappear. When he finally lifted his mouth, she felt weak. Her heart was pounding and her mind was fogged with passion.

A sensual smile crossed his mouth. "When you get home we will have to explore this area of our relationship further."

She squeezed the amulet to her chest. "Emm. I feel my luck changing already," she murmured, still mesmerized by his kiss and his fathomless, dark eyes.

"I do have to go." He gently ran his thumb over her kiss-swollen lips.

"I know," she whispered. She watched the strong muscles of his back flex under his shirt as he opened the door. She kept her eyes on the door until it closed. She drifted into sleep thinking of how lucky she was to have met him. Even if it was the fire of her beloved home that had brought them together.

Just as Linc had said, the two days passed swiftly and it was finally time for Paige to be released from the hospital. With nothing more than a few bumps and bruises, she could go home and take care of herself.

She felt for the leather pouch that hung around her neck. She had put it on when Linc had left that first night and had not taken it off since. In his absence, it was as if a part him was with her, as if his confidence and strength were there for her.

Before Linc arrived to take her home she once again reached for the phone and dialed Mara's phone number. For two days she hadn't been able to reach her. This time her friend answered.

"Mara? Where in the world have you been? I've been trying to call you for two days."

"Paige? How 'wah ya? Girlfriend, have I got a lot of things to tell you."

"How about telling me now? I was worried when I couldn't reach you."

"I tried to reach you a couple of nights ago and you didn't answer. I thought maybe you were with Linc or something. I tried two or three times."

"I had a little accident and—"

"Accident?" Mara's voice changed from casual to shrill, her New York accent very evident. "I knew it. I had a premonition. What kind of accident? Are you all right?"

Paige felt warm and comfortable. Mara had that effect on her. Everything would be all right now. "I fell into the cellar of my house a couple of nights ago. I'm lucky all I got was a nasty bump on my head and a few cuts and bruises." She gingerly touched her head. "I tried to get in touch but you never answered."

There was a gasp from Mara. "Oh, my gosh! We went to the casino in Sault Saint Marie. I left my cell phone in my bag locked inside the truck. I'm really sorry."

"I'm all right now. Linc will be here in a few minutes to take me back to the inn."

"Where are ya?"

"In the hospital?"

"Oh, Paige, I should have been there for you. I dreamt that I fell. I could feel the wind being knocked out of me. The dream was the night of the accident. I'm sorry. I should have tried harder to contact you and warn you." She paused for air. "We'll be there as soon as we can."

Paige found herself nodding. Her friend did have premonitions and rarely was wrong. If she had called, Paige would have heeded the warning. Suddenly she felt overwhelmed by all she had to think about, so she deliberately shoved the worries away. Mara would help her sort things out when she returned.

"I'll see you when you get here."

"See ya soon," Mara purred and the line went dead.

Paige eased her way into jeans and shirt, trying to avoid the tender bruises. She silently blessed Emma for bringing her clean clothes the night before. Other than the throbbing bump on her head, the rest of the pain was something she could deal with easily.

"Are you ready to go?" Linc entered the room with a bouquet of red roses.

"They're beautiful, thank you." She took the roses and breathed in their sweet perfume. "You can't imagine how ready I am. Who told you I loved roses?"

"A wise old owl."

Her eyes brightened with pleasure. "Right. Is the owl's name Mara? She tells a lot of my secrets," she said, remembering the quiche Emma had made especially for her.

He picked up the plastic bag with her soiled clothing from the accident and urged her to the door. Out in the hall an orderly waited with a wheelchair.

Paige frowned. "I don't need that."

"Hospital rules," the young man said as he firmly helped her into the chair.

This was all she needed. Wheelchairs were for people who really needed them. All she wanted to do was get out of here and begin living again.

Linc leaned down and whispered, "Don't make a scene. The sooner we get out of here the sooner we can be together." His husky voice carried a double meaning.

A smile grew in her eyes but she remained silent. She wanted to be with him as much as he wanted to be with her. Anyway, what good would it do to argue? The orderly was just following rules.

The elevator took them down to the lobby. Through the windows she glimpsed the sparkling water of Lake Michigan as it touched the distant horizon. It looked like a day that promised to be warm and sunny.

As the orderly pushed her through the doors to the out-side, a flurry of people rushed at them, seemingly from every direction, and cameras flashed.

"Miss Turner, is it true that you are spending your vaca-tion with your Indian lover?" a man shouted.

Another man pushed forward and thrust a microphone in her face. Behind him, trying to keep the camera bal-anced to catch everything, was a television crew. "How does it feel to have your vacation interrupted by an acci-dent? Was it an accident?"

A woman she recognized as a fashion reporter popped in front of her. "How long do you plan to stay in northern Michigan? Are you going to do a shoot here?"

Paige turned her head away, trying to shield herself from the insistent intruders. She was shocked. How did they find out she was here? Who had tipped them off? Her mind was whirling. She had to escape the bombardment.

Paige struggled to her feet, trying to get out of that damned confining wheelchair. Shock etched on his face, Linc tried to protect her. "Let the lady through," he shout-ed, making a path to his vehicle and yanking open the door for Paige.

A young man blocked her way, "Miss Turner, what are your plans for the future? Are you going to live in northern Michigan? Is your affair serious? What about your home? Did you burn it down? Did you need the insurance money that badly? Miss Turner, is your career waning?"

Linc roughly shoved the man aside. Paige ducked her head and climbed into Linc's truck, shuddering when Linc slammed the door. They were like a pack of vultures pick-ing every last morsel from her bones. Poor Linc. The one reporter had been so insulting. She was sure he was beyond anger. He had to be told. There was nothing else she could do.

Linc fought through the gathering to make his way to the other side of the vehicle. Questions about their relationship shot at him from every direction. He didn't answer. He swung into his truck and without looking at her, turned the ignition key and pulled out of the hospital drive.

A heavy silence hung for what seemed like an eternity. Then he asked, "Do you want to tell me what the hell that was all about? Who are you anyway?"

"You must understand why I kept it a secret."

"What secret? Are you Jack the Ripper? What is so bad that you would have to keep it from me? The press seem to know."

"It's not bad," she whispered. "It's just..."

"What?"

She laid a hand on his muscled arm and felt it tightly flex under her touch. Maybe this was going to be more difficult than she thought.

"I'm listening."

She didn't fail to catch the note of sarcasm in his voice.

"You told me something about being in the fashion industry. Just what is it you do?"

Her anger was growing to match his. She didn't owe him an explanation. After all they were only dating, not engaged or married.

"I'm a model." She kept her tone even but knew she was daring him to scoff.

"What kind of model?" His tone was accusatory.

"A fashion model. What kind do you think?" she retorted. He was acting like she was—she couldn't bring herself to even think it. She knew many prostitutes portrayed themselves as models, but to think he would imagine...

He maneuvered the vehicle through traffic and got to the other side of town, turning on the Harbor-Petoskey road. "It doesn't matter."

"Yes, it does."

His glance was bemused and opaque. "I was hoping...that you weren't a lady of the night, you know, like the Hollywood Madam."

Paige gasped, her gaze sharpened. He was like all of the rest. If a woman wasn't extremely thin or blond she couldn't possibly be a real model. "Linc, how could you think such a thing? Somehow I thought you were different. I guess you can't tell a book until you've read what's written on each page." She slumped back against the seat.

His glare pierced the distance between them. "On that point I would have to agree with you. You can't tell. In my defense, can you imagine how I felt and what I thought when we came out of the hospital and that barrage of paparazzi rushed at us like that?"

"I know what you thought and I'm sorry for how it made you feel." She thought of the racist comment slammed at him. Aching from the pain in her head and weary of the argument, she spoke her next words softly. "Reporters can be unfeeling people. I guess they have a job to do too." Even at the expense of others, she thought to herself.

He didn't respond and she didn't care. She was tired and in pain. He pulled up to the front door of the inn and walked her up the steps to where Emma was waiting to take over. Paige stared into his cold eyes. "Linc...thank you for everything."

Linc handed her hospital bag to Emma and mumbled, "No problem." He touched his fingers to his brow. *"Bama pii."* Sometimes English just did not say it right. This was farewell, he was not ready for goodbye. He left without looking back.

Bama pii echoed in his head. He did wish her well. But the deceit, did he really know who she was? Maybe everything about her was a lie. He shook his head to clear it. How could he have been so wrong? Or was he? He had no idea right now.

He drove aimlessly and finally pulled to the side of the road that led over the Mackinac Bridge. He was headed to the reservation. He was headed home. Linc knew he needed to talk to his grandfather but he had to calm down first. The bright blue-green waters of the straits calmed him. He felt a soft breeze and heard the laughing voices of children in a nearby park. How could everything seem so normal when his world was crumbling around him?

"Damn her," he swore aloud. "I was so sure she was the one in Grandfather's vision." His mother had been right, they weren't the right golden eyes. He thumped the heel of his hand on the steering wheel. He was such a chump. She had been leading him on, keeping secrets. If she wasn't ashamed of what she did and who she was, why all the secrecy?

The thought of his mother made him reach for his phone. Linc knew she wasn't home, but he could leave a message. He didn't want to talk to her, not right now.

He dropped the phone back into the cradle and returned his thoughts to Paige. He could still smell her soft, dark hair against his cheek. She was the woman he'd thought he wanted. But she didn't want him, not really. He was only someone to play with. What had she planned, a vacation with another diversion for the summer? Was that what he'd been, a summer diversion? God, what a fool he'd been. She was just another person who'd lied to him. The list was growing and he wanted nothing more than to tear up the list.

Linc crossed the bridge and continued along I-75 until he was on the reservation, at his grandfather's place. He was home. As usual the old man was nowhere in sight. When he was a child Linc had always tried to surprise him but somehow his grandfather always knew he was there. He heard the sounds of wood splitting from behind the small square house. He stepped around the building just as the old man stopped and wiped his brow. Linc stared at the back of the man he loved beyond his inherited love of the earth.

"*Ahneen*, Grey Wolf, it is good to have you home." His grandfather spoke his gentle greeting and then turned to face his grandson. Sweat dripped from his face and body.

Linc's heart swelled with love. "*Ahneen* Grandfather, how did you know I had come?"

The old man smiled. "The birds."

The answer was simple but Linc understood. His grandfather was completely in tune with the earth and her inhabitants. Reaching in his shirt pocket, he handed the Traditional Man a cigar. A gift of wrapped tobacco was offered for advice from the wise elders of the tribe. And his grandfather was the wisest of all. Linc knew outsiders called his grandfather "that Medicine Man," but to him and the rest of the Chippewa Tribe, he was a Traditional Man. "I need advice," he said with great respect.

His grandfather plunged the axe into the next log and stepped aside for a hopping crow. "Come, Grey Wolf." He pointed to the crow. "Our spiritual helper is here." They walked to the porch and sat facing each other. The old man reached for his pipe and filled it with kinikinik.

Linc waited until the Traditional Man tapped the red willow tobacco into his pipe and looked to him. "I've met the woman with the golden eyes but Mom thinks she may not be the right one. And now I wonder too."

The old man nodded. A ring of smoke hovered above his head. "I know." He stood and walked off the porch. "We will go to the sweat house and pray. There you can seek the answers to your questions."

Linc followed his grandfather down the wooded path. Before they entered they silently shucked their clothing down to briefs and dipped the towel ends in water. Pungent smoke and hot steam rolled out at them. The men held the wet ends of the towel to their faces to diminish the initial impact.

Linc dropped the towel from his face as his senses awakened to the smooth aroma of sweet grass. He walked around the fire and then stopped as his grandfather gave his spiritual name and threw his samah into the fire. Linc hadn't said his spiritual name in a couple of years but it was always there.

With his samah held in his left hand over the fire he called out, "Almighty One of the universe, it is Soaring Eagle, your child. I have come to ask for your guidance." The tobacco offering fell from his fingers into the fire. A soothing blue haze surrounded Soaring Eagle as he lowered himself to the earth next to his grandfather, joining the circle of his brothers. The prayers of many were mingled with his as he relieved his soul of its burden. Sweat rolled out of every pore, cleansing him of his pain. His eyes stung from the saltiness, but the cleansing purification was as welcoming as the pristine waters of Lake Superior.

The chanting voices quieted as the prayers were offered and reconciliation was made. The time of prayer left them quiet and introspective. Linc and his grandfather left and made their way up the path to the house. The old man spoke softly. "Now you must go to the mountain and seek your final truth."

Linc nodded and left without speaking. The clouds hung low over Thunder Mountain as he watched a soaring eagle float gracefully through the clouds and into the bright blue sky. He leaned against a jagged rock, wondering what significance his spirit guide's appearance held for him. He closed his eyes to see.

"A bear. Paige saw a bear," Linc shouted to the heavens. He knew it was a vision. A warning. His mind had cleared and allowed him to see the whole picture. Someone was trying to harm her, and it was up to him to protect her, to put aside the hurt and anger he felt for her lack of trust in him. His eyes followed his spirit guide.

The graceful bird soared around him, bringing him great inner peace, and then without reason crashed into the rock and fell at his feet. Linc scooped the bird into his arms and rushed to his grandfather's. He hoped he could save the life of the guide that had given him so much. The Traditional Man took the bird and quietly examined it, while Linc told him the story from the mountain. The old man glanced up. "He is dead. Your spirit guide has sacrificed himself for you."

Very gently the Traditional Man removed the pivotal feathers from either side of the sacrificed bird and handed them to his grandson. "You have been given a great honor. Somehow you will be given the ability to replace this marvelous creature. You must take the wing feathers. One is for you and the other for the woman with the golden eyes. This will bind you together and you will not be one without the other. You will always fly in the same direction. You will not keep a true path apart."

Linc accepted the sacrificial gift humbly, "I will not dishonor this gift. I know it is up to me to make right whatever is wrong."

The two men spent the rest of the day sharing. Linc gathered wood for the cooking range and together they prepared their meal. The evening drew nigh as they sat quietly conversing. When his grandfather rose to go to bed, Linc stood and waited until the old man was settled in.

He lowered himself into the crudely built rocking chair on the porch and stared into the sunset. The whole day unfolded in front of him. Although his heart was heavy as he grieved for the glorious bird which was now lifeless, he was thankful for the guidance he'd received. He knew he could accomplish the task he had been given, just as he knew he would always protect the eagle. He lifted his eyes to the sky. "There will always be eagles. I will see to it." He was at peace and one with the universe.

Nine

Paige leaned her head against the door of her closet, every nerve ending in her body quivering in shock and disbelief. What had happened today? Linc had been so angry over such a small thing. What did it matter how she earned a living, as long as it was legal and moral? Her face burned hot thinking of the conclusion he had jumped to. A prostitute! How could he?

His angry eyes burned in her memory. Maybe it wasn't her secret at all; maybe it was the racial insults the paparazzi had thrown at him. She could see him being a little upset that she hadn't told him, but to jump off the deep end like that? It didn't make any sense.

She closed her eyes and drew in a deep reinforcing breath. It really didn't concern him anyway. This was her life, her choice to keep her occupation to herself. What right did he have to expect her to tell him every little thing about herself right up front? It wasn't as if they had a commitment.

She jerked open the closet door and pulled her luggage from behind her clothing, tossing it on the bed. Her gaze was drawn to the phone. She grabbed the phone book beside her bed. There was only one thing left to do. Her long polished nails ran down the list of numbers.

She dialed and tapped the plastic of the mouthpiece as she impatiently waited for an answer.

"Hello," she said after about the seventh ring brought an airlines clerk, "can you tell me when the next flight for New York leaves?"

She nodded and waited again. "Ten-thirty in the morning. Good." She picked up a pen and jotted down the information.

"I'd like to make one way reservations for two to New York on that flight, please." She fought to keep her voice from shaking. This wasn't what she wanted to do; it was what she had to do. Slowly, she replaced the receiver.

She pulled open the drawers of the dresser and began packing her things. She blinked back tears that stung her eyes. She'd spent enough time crying; she wasn't going to cry again.

This is what she got for going against her own advice. This wasn't the right time for love or a relationship. She had her work and love should never have entered her life. Not yet. If she'd taken her own advice, this never would've happened.

Work, she thought. I'll call my agent and get another shoot. If I work hard and long I won't have time to think. She slung her lacy bras and silky panties carelessly into her bags.

As she zipped the last suitcase shut, she bridled at the sound of vehicles pulling in and reporters' voices hollering at the house. They had tracked her here from the hospital. When would they leave her alone? Why couldn't they just leave her alone?

She moved to the window and peered through the gauzy curtains. "Damn them!" she spat. A television crew was waiting alongside the road. She bristled, anger flowing along her veins.

Yes, work was what she needed. In work she would be too busy to think about her problems. The busy routine would soothe the deep despair of her loss. On the runway she would be hidden both inside and out. Then they could take all the damn pictures they wanted. And her agent would answer their miserable questions.

Paige stood with her back to the window. Would they follow her all the way to New York? "Forget them," she whispered angrily. Working with the press had always been easy before but this time they had insulted the man she cared deeply for. Even if they weren't going to be together, she didn't want him hurt. And she definitely didn't want to feel responsible for his pain. She carried enough emotional baggage of her own.

Her fingers twined around the leather charm Linc had given her. She couldn't bring herself to remove it because it was all she had left of him. God, you're pitiful, she thought. The guy dumps you on the doorstep, turns and walks away without looking back and still you feel something for him?

Satisfied with her decision to leave, she lined the bags by the door and lay on the bed. She stared unseeing at the ceiling. Her body ached from the fall but the most painful ache was in her heart. It ached from the pain of losing the two things she loved most. She knew losing Linc would mean many storm-filled days and lonely nights and losing her home was losing her past.

"Paige?" A knock sounded on her door. "Are you in there?"

Paige wiped her eyes. It took several moments to realize it was Mara. "Mara!" She was back.

She jumped from the bed, rushed to the door and threw back the bolt to let her in. "I'm so glad you're back." She threw her arms around her friend. "I need to talk to you."

"My God, have you seen the reporters down there?"

Paige leaned back and positioned herself to peer out the window. "I've seen them. They were outside the hospital when I was released and now they've followed me here."

"Damn sharks!" Mara hissed. "How did they find out you were here?"

Paige shook her head. "Who knows? They've got this stupid idea I burned my house to get insurance money. And they called Linc my Indian lover."

"Geeze." Mara frowned. "I'm sorry, I really am. I wish I had been here to help you through this. So, how are you feeling?" she asked, but her gaze moved to the luggage.

"I hurt a little, but the doctor says I'll be fine."

"Tell me what happened." Mara led her to the bed and sat down.

Paige sat beside her. "I was upset about the investigation of the house burning so I decided to take a walk to get my head on straight. I went to my place. Someone pushed me into the cellar."

Mara's expression was tight. "Pushed? You were pushed?"

"Yes, I was pushed."

"Who? Who would do a thing like that?"

Paige shook her head. "I don't know. I didn't see the person. I only felt their hands on my back, then I was falling into that awful, black hole, but not before I saw the bear."

"Bear?" Mara tilted her head. "Paige, are you sure you're all right? You aren't making any sense. A bear?"

"I saw a bear. A big black bear just before I was pushed."

Are you sure you didn't imagine that after being hurt?"

"No. I remember very clearly, there was a bear."

Mara reached out and brushed the stray tendrils of hair away from Paige's face. "Hon, if you'd been mauled by a bear, you'd have a lot more than a bump on your head and a few bruises."

"I know what I saw and I didn't say I was mauled. I just said I saw the bear before I was pushed into the cellar," Paige insisted.

Mara raised her hand in resignation. "Okay, okay. So you want to tell me why your luggage is by the door?"

Paige's faint smile was sad. "I've booked us on the ten-thirty flight to New York in the morning. I've had it with my so-called vacation. I'm sorry I ever came back. I'm sorry I dragged you away from New York. But we aren't going to stay here. We could have a better vacation lounging around our apartment."

Mara forced a demure smile. "What are you talking about?"

"We're going home . . . in the morning. I have to get back to work and . . ."

Mara shook her head and held up her left hand, "Now, wait just a darned minute here. What's really going on? Have you and Linc had a fight?"

Paige lowered her gaze. "Something like that."

Mara's laugh filled the room. "Well, patch it up, girl-friend. We aren't leavin' now."

"There isn't anything left to patch. We're leaving tomorrow and that's the end of it."

Mara flashed her left hand in front of Paige, causing the diamonds on her hand to catch the light.

Mara didn't have to say a word. It registered and the fact flashed in Paige's eyes. "Mara, you can't marry Jack. I think he's the one who. . ."

Mara placed a finger on Paige's lips to stop her from saying more. "We're already married. We were married on Mackinac Island. I love him and he loves me."

Paige's expression was one of mute wretchedness.

"Hey, come on. Be happy for me." Mara playfully pinched her friend.

Paige finally lifted her gaze to Mara's. "What about your career? What about . . .?"

"I can have both. Jack doesn't want me to quit modeling. I'll just do fewer shoots so I can be with him. Hopefully he'll go with me when I have to leave the country."

"But you don't know him, not really," Paige said, her voice weary with exasperation and shock. She began pacing and counting to herself. How could everything go so bad so fast?

Mara reached out and grabbed her hand as she passed, holding her still. "I know all I need to know. Remember I told you when true love comes around to grab it? Well, I did. He's Mr. Right. Please, be happy for me."

"Mara..." Right. Mr. Right. Mr. Arson is more like it. How could she be happy for her best friend who had just made the biggest mistake of her life? She glanced at Mara's glowing face. She would never be able to convince her of Jack's dark side. She plunked down on the bed and stared at her friend. Now she was completely alone. Linc had left. Mara was married to a criminal and her beloved home with all its memories was in ashes.

"Mara?" Jack's voice filtered from downstairs. "Can you come down here a minute?"

"Hey, everything's gonna be a-okay, really." She patted Paige's shoulder, then rose and left the room.

Paige was at a complete loss for words. Her whole world had just been blown apart. She'd never felt so alone.

She felt a sudden sting of tears. Damn, she never used to cry. Now she felt tears every time she turned around. She reached for the tissue box on the vanity.

Her gaze was drawn to the phone. She wanted to lift her hand, pick it up and call Linc, to smooth away the anger he had had when he had looked at her the last time. If she could just explain...

Of course it was too late for that. She knew it. It was too late for second chances, too late to search for the truth, too late for any kind of relationship with Linc. It was just too late.

She squeezed her eyes closed and tried to sink into a mindless void. Of course she couldn't shut out her emotions, her love, her friend and Linc. What had made her think she could?

Her gaze settled on the crystal where Emma had placed the bouquet of roses Linc had given her this morning. Why couldn't life be as beautiful as those flowers? With all this beauty around her, why did she have to have this agonizing throb deep inside that refused to go away?

She opened the window and let the warm breeze wash over her, willing it to cleanse her troubled soul. She lost track of time as she stared into nothing. It could have been a few minutes or an hour before she again became aware of the gathering outside the inn. Voices from below filtered through her brain. They were taking pictures. She slammed the window closed.

She had come in search of heaven and wound up in hell. Wasn't that just her luck? She glanced at her reflection in the mirror. She hadn't looked so ghastly since her father's death. If she stayed here, she wouldn't get any better. "You don't belong here. You never did," she whispered softly.

Her gaze fell to Linc's charm. She lightly touched it and this time removed it from her neck. She couldn't bear to pack it away, so she slipped it into a side pocket of her purse.

Paige stood quickly, with an air of determination. She couldn't let anyone talk her out her decision. She was leaving. No one could stop her, not Mara, not even Linc. As if he would, she thought.

Her gaze fell on the diamond earring. She whisked it off the dresser and made her way to the kitchen. Laughter gushed into the hallway, battering her. Paige stopped for a second to collect her thoughts and determination. Head held high, she marched into the room.

The laughter and talk died as everyone turned to her.

"Paige, you look tired. Would you like a cup of coffee? It's fresh," Emma offered as she hustled to grab a cup.

Paige shook her head. "No, thank you. I just came to tell you I am leaving for New York in the morning. I'd like to take care of my bill." She masked her inner turmoil with deceptive calmness.

Emma's brows creased, spreading worry lines. "But child, you've just gotten out of the hospital. You can't go traipsing halfway across the country like that. You need to rest for a few days. The doctor—"

"I'll be fine." She cut Emma short and turned to Mara, her best friend who now seemed like a stranger. Mara was one of them now. "I found your earring in my bedroom. You must have lost it when you were in such a damned big hurry to go away with him." She shot a sideways glance at Jack.

Mara held out her hand and accepted the diamond earring.

Jack stepped toward Paige. "Maybe you should reconsider your decision. After all, you are just recovering." He held his hand out as if to touch her arm.

She jerked her arm away and pulled it tightly to her side. All she needed was to hear his voice to have her nerves set on edge. She whirled to him directly. "What right do you have to say what I can or can't do? You don't think I know what you've done? You've ruined my life, my memories and all with the flick of a match and some gasoline. You set that fire, didn't you?"

Jack's eyes grew wide as he looked at Mara. His face pleaded with her to intervene. When she didn't, he shrugged his shoulders as if bewildered.

"Don't stand there and play the innocent with me." She glanced toward Mara and then back. 'That's why you married Mara. You thought it would help you in your ugly quest. How could you stoop that low just to get your grubby hands on my property?"

"Now see here," Jack's voice hardened.

"No." Paige pointed her finger at him. "You see here. Have you told her that you want my land to increase the size of this resort? Have you told her you would do anything to get it? That's what you told Emma the other night. Isn't it?" Her voice had reached a fever pitch, surprising even her.

His face paled. "You misunderstood what I said."

"Oh, did I really? Didn't you say you'd do anything to get it?" She gasped for air. "Well, let me tell you something. Hell will freeze over before you even come close, Mister Arson. And then I'd fight you to the death, to see you didn't get your guilty hands on that land! I don't care if it sits there a hundred years, you'll never get it, never!"

Mara's surprise at her friend's outburst was etched in her face. She glanced from Paige to Jack. "Paige, I can't imagine what's gotten into you." She spoke quietly in a calming voice. Stepping toward her, she added, "You need rest. You're not yourself."

"Right," Paige shot back. Now even Mara was treating her as if she had gone crazy. Well, it wasn't she who had a screw loose. She glared at Mara. "Like I'm the one who ran off and married a man I didn't know! A man with questionable motives and character. I don't think it's me who's not herself. Take a good look at yourself, girlfriend." She spat the words sarcastically. Whirling on her heel, she rushed from the room, ignoring the whispered shock that followed her.

She had a temper, she'd give herself that. Not that she was proud of it. She tried to control it most of the time, tried to see the other person's point of view, but this had gone way past that. Jack was a snake and he manipulated people. He had Mara under his spell. Damn, why did she give him the satisfaction of blowing up like that?

She stood by the window in her room watching the reporters scatter for shelter as a spring thunderstorm shot lightning at them and doused them with torrents of rain. At least the weather had changed to fit her mood. Something was going right.

The sharp ring of the phone startled her. Now who could that be. Linc? He was the only one who might be calling. But she doubted it.

Hesitantly she reached for the ringing intruder. Had he decided to apologize? Hope and fear wrapped around her. She wanted—no, needed—his love and support now more than ever. Yet loving him was causing her nothing but pain. She pictured his long deeply bronzed fingers gripping the phone; his mouth with that silly quirk she loved so much and his deep coal black eyes that pierced through to her soul. Tingling chills ran through her as she hoped it was and wasn't him. Tentatively she picked up the phone.

"Hello." Her heart pounded in her chest.

"Oh, Paige dear, I'm so glad I found you in," the familiar, unwelcome voice from the past greeted her.

Paige felt her face fall and her shoulders drop. Her hopes and fears were dashed. "Ada?" she questioned, but she would never forget her stepmother's voice.

"Of course it's me, dear. I just read all of those miserable lies printed in the newspapers. Oh, my darling girl!

How could this have happened to you? I had to come and be with you."

Paige closed her eyes and shook her head. This was all she needed right now. What timing! Her stepmother was the last person she wanted help from. And what was this "darling girl" thing? She sighed heavily. "I'm fine, Ada. Really."

"Don't try to fool me. I can tell by your voice you're distraught. I knew you'd need family at a time like this."

"Ada, we're not family. We've never been family." Paige's voice sounded more frigid than the waters of Lake Superior.

There was a long silence on the line. Then Ada said, "I know we've had our differences, dear, and some of them were my fault. I was never the mother you needed."

Paige broke in. "I had a mother. She might be gone, but she's still my mother."

"Of course she is, dear. I wouldn't have it otherwise. But I want to make up for all the bad years between us. I can't stand by and watch you go through this alone."

"I'll be fine, really. You don't have to come." The woman sounded sincere but it was too late for her too.

"I'm already here. I'm at the Pellston airport."

Paige touched the lump on her head. It was beginning to throb. This was just great! All the trouble over the house and Linc and now her stepmother. Could things get any worse? She slumped to the bed.

"Did you hear me, dear? Hello, are you still there?"

"I heard you."

"Well, do you have a car? I mean, I hate to hire a cab to bring me all the way to Harbor Springs."

"You want me to come get you?"

"Oh, would you, dear?" Her voice dripped of honey. "I'll be waiting."

Paige sat for what seemed an eternity, glaring at the phone in her hand. She was stuck. She had to go get Ada; she couldn't leave her sitting in that airport, although that's what she felt like doing. God, what a mess this whole thing had turned out to be.

Paige dragged herself from the bed, swallowed her pride and went to Emma. "I have to pick up my step-mother from the airport. Is there a way to get out of here without them?" She pointed at the press huddled out of the storm in front of the house.

Emma's face darkened in concern. "Do you think you ought to be driving? Let me call Mara and—"

"No!" Paige exclaimed. "I can do this."

Emma gave her directions and the keys to her car. "You shouldn't be going out by yourself, but if you must, take my car. They won't know it. Please be careful, Paige. And about the other problems, I know they will all work out for the best."

Paige smiled at the eternal optimist. "Thank you, Emma. But I can't see how." She left quickly to avoid any further conversation on the subject.

Heavy rain made driving the back roads to the airport more difficult. Potholes were everywhere. Paige felt as if she were driving an obstacle course. Much like her life. She'd hit more of the holes than she missed. The lightning seemed to aim its arrows right at her. "Why not?" she said loudly. "Everybody else does."

The lights of the airport loomed through the heavy downpour. Her stomach knotted and she couldn't shake the feeling of impending doom. Not like it wasn't already bad, but somehow she knew it was going to get worse. Ada never made anything better. The last person on earth she wanted to see was that old witch. What did she really want? She knew from firsthand experience that Ada wasn't to be trusted. She glanced toward the darkened sky. "Only because she was once your wife, Daddy, I'll pick her up but I don't have to stay with her." It's really bad you only have nature, deceased relatives and yourself to talk to, she thought, scoffing at herself.

She glanced around the terminal and didn't see Ada but heard the voice that she dreaded. "Over here." A woman in her fifties with bottle-red hair waved to her.

"Hello, Ada." Paige smiled tightly. Ada was still Ada. Still trying to pass for white and acting and dressing as if she were still in her twenties.

Ada threw her arms around Paige and hugged her. "It's so good to see you." She glanced around. "But let me tell you this, nothing but you having all this trouble would have gotten me to set foot in northern Michigan again, I can tell you that. God, I hate this place." She pulled her sweater jacket around her. "It's windy, cold and damp."

Right, Paige thought. "My car is parked just out the front door. Let's get your luggage."

As they drove back to the inn, Ada chatted all the way as if they were lifelong friends. Paige retraced her trek with about the same luck as before with the potholes, and arrived at the back entrance without the press suspecting a thing. At least she had done something right.

"This is a lovely place—for northern Michigan, that is. They turned that rambling old mausoleum into an inn. What a novel idea." Ada held her umbrella out of the car, popped it open as she pulled herself under it.

Paige ran around to join her and led her to the back door of the inn. They hung the umbrella and their wet jackets in the mud room and then stepped into the bright kitchen. Paige was anxious to get the woman settled and get away from her. "You can get a room here for the night, but I'm leaving in the morning."

"Leaving?" Ada stared up at her. "You can't leave now, dear. There's an investigation going on. If you leave now, you could be in real trouble."

"Trouble?" Paige hadn't thought about that. "I can't leave? Are you sure?"

Ada shook her head. "I don't think so, at least not until the police and insurance investigations are finished. It would make you look guilty."

Paige squinted her eyes suspiciously. "How do you know so much about what's been happening to me?"

"My dear child, you are headline news." She drew out a tabloid. "See," she said. "Washed-up fashion model, Paige Turner, burns childhood home and moves in with Indian lover."

Paige felt screams of frustration at the back of her throat. "Oh, my God." There was a picture of her and Linc in front of a teepee. She grabbed the trashy paper. "Even the picture is a lie. They've altered it to insult Linc and his people." It's a wonder they didn't have a picture of me in front of an African hut instead of my Victorian."

"I know, dear, but you must be very careful of what you do and who you are seen with from now on. People will be watching your every move, especially the authorities. You must think of your career."

Paige's stomach clenched tightly. "I don't want to stay here. The reporters are heating up something that is already a living hell. I have to get away." She tried to maintain her fragile control.

"Where do you want to go?" Ada asked.

"I don't know. But I want to get away from here for a while."

Ada put her arm around her. "Why don't we go away, just you and me?"

Paige glanced at Ada. Maybe she really had come to help. People change. She'd seen evidence of that in the past few weeks. "Where?"

Ada shrugged. "Would you like to go up to Sault Saint Marie for a couple of days? We could visit the Sault locks and do some gambling at the casino and take in a dinner show. Bill Cosby will be there for a couple of shows." She glanced at the younger woman. "Maybe we could do some shopping. I hear it has many lovely shops." A beguiling smile spread over her thick red lips.

"I don't know...you said I couldn't leave."

"You're not leaving the state," the older woman said thoughtfully. "But we'll call the fire marshal and tell him where you're going. Come on. It will do you good. We could leave first thing in the morning."

Part of her wanted to believe Ada had changed, but a part in the back of her mind nagged a warning. But who else was there to help? She nodded. She was weary and needed a change. "All right, we'll go for a few days."

"Good. This will give me the chance to make up for a lot of the wrong I've done you. We'll leave first thing in the morning."

Paige noticed Emma sitting in her little office off the kitchen. She was sure she had overheard everything, but she didn't care. She asked Emma to give Ada a room next to hers. Ada was tired and exhausted from her trip and wanted to rest.

She returned to her room sorry she had agreed to go with her stepmother. She should just return to New York and let the police find her when they wanted her. She opened her door to find Mara sitting in the Queen Ann chair by the rounded bay windows.

"May I come in?" she shot sarcastically. "Are you adding breaking and entering to your list with friend betrayal or have you taken the housekeeping job here?"

Mara shook her head. "Whether you believe it or not I am your friend, I love you. That's why I am here. I spoke with Emma." She paused. "What are you doing?"

Paige shrugged her shoulders. That didn't take Emma long, she thought. "What do you mean?"

"Your stepmother. You and she have never gotten along. How can you trust her now?"

Paige laughed sarcastically. "You should ask that! Who can I trust anymore? I ask you that?" In her heart she knew Mara had spoken the truth about Ada but she wasn't ready to listen.

"Paige, that's not fair. I've never done anything to hurt you. We've been together for years and I've never hurt you."

"Until Jack."

"You don't know Jack."

Paige crossed to the window, stopping to watch the rain wash the glass panes. "I think I do. Well, I know his kind anyway." She turned to face Mara. "I suppose Jack trying to get my land any way he can, is okay with you. He'll use anything, including you, to get what he wants."

"You're wrong about Jack."

"If you say so." Paige turned away. And the sun doesn't rise in the east either, she thought. But there was no convincing Mara of that. She'd have to find out for herself what kind of a rat her husband really was.

"I didn't come here to argue with you," Mara continued. "I wanted to return this earring. It isn't mine."

Paige stared at the diamond in her friend's hand. "It's not yours?"

"No. Mine **are** in my ears." She pulled back her long blond hair to show Paige.

"Then whose is it? Emma?"

Mara shook her head. "I asked Emma and she laughed. She said she couldn't afford diamonds, and wouldn't wear them if she could. So I don't know who it belongs to."

Paige took the earring and turned it over and over in her hand. "Strange."

Mara took a step forward. "I can't leave our relationship like this. We've been like sisters. I don't want a rift between us."

Paige tilted her head and clicked her tongue. "I'm afraid there is and his name is Jack."

"I'll pretend I didn't hear that."

"I'm sorry, that's the way I feel. It seems you're pretending not to hear a lot of things involving Jack. He's the cause of all my troubles and I'm going to prove it."

Mara's face paled under pink cheeks. "You can't really believe I'd marry a man who was trying to hurt my best friend. What do you mean you're going to prove it?"

"I'm not sure, but believe me, I will leave no stone unturned. And I don't give a damn how much it costs. I'm going to get to the bottom of this no matter who it hurts."

"You've changed."

Paige's eyes were stony with hurt and anger. "You have all the things done to you that have been done to me, and you'd change too. I've had my house destroyed, my name scandalized, and had someone try to kill me. And your husband will stop at nothing to get my land. Now if that isn't enough to change a person, I don't know what is."

"I know it's been rough, but it's not Jack's fault."

Paige threw up her hands and released a long breath. "I'm not going to argue with you. Someone is out to get me and who else has a motive?"

"Jack wouldn't do that. He may want your land but he wouldn't harm you. Besides, he was with me on the island when you were pushed."

"That's convenient, now isn't it?"

"God, Paige, just listen to yourself. You suspect everyone. You sound paranoid. Next you'll be telling me Linc is a suspect."

Paige laughed harshly, her mind still gloomily colored with the memory of Winona's words. "Well, the Chippewa tribe wants the land for another casino, so he's probably in the running."

"Linc really loves you."

"Right. That's why he hates me for not telling him I am a model."

"Is that what you and Linc had a fight about, your being a model?"

"Among other things."

"You had a fight about not telling him? He hates you because of that?" Mara shook her head. "You're wrong, dead wrong. Linc doesn't hate you. I've seen the way the guy looks at you. He's in love with you." Pain flickered in Mara's eyes.

Paige turned away. "He has an odd way of showing it."

Mara heaved a sigh. "I don't know what more I can say, except I still love you and I'm trying to understand your hurt. This whole thing has been rough on you, but to turn to the woman who made your life miserable is crazy. You know you can't trust her, you never could."

Paige kept her back to Mara. "There are a lot of people I can't trust anymore."

Paige couldn't see Mara's face but she knew if she turned around, hurt would have masked her usually warm, smiling features. Why did everything have to turn upside down? But what could she do now? Mara was married to a man with a questionable character. Questionable! That was an understatement.

She heard soft footsteps move toward the door. "Paige, I know you don't believe me, but I'm here for you if you need me. I'll never turn my back on you, I promise. And neither will Jack."

The door closed quietly. She heard Mara's steps descend the stairs. Her life had become a bitter battle and her sense of loss was beyond tears.

A heaviness centered in Paige's chest. What had happened? Her friend had left and she'd let her go. Oh, Mara, how can we ever get things back to where they were? Even as she thought those words, she knew it was impossible. Time stands still for no one and there was no going back. Thunder roared through the sky and rumbled in her heart while lightning shot its hissing prongs in her direction. She could only plunge forward into the dark unknown. She sat in lonely silence trying to swallow the lump that lingered in her throat.

Ten

The bright, early sun of the next morning found Linc restless. Quietly he slid off the cot in his grandfather's small house. He needed to escape to the serenity of the trails and forest on the reservation.

Visiting with his grandfather had cleared his muddled thoughts and put him more in tune with nature than he had been for a long time. He no longer had doubts about Paige and where she belonged in his life.

The sun warmed his face and a warm, moist zephyr swept past him, refreshing and strengthening him. He drew in a deep satisfied breath. He knew what he must do.

He'd had time to think about why Paige felt the need to keep some things private. She'd been protecting her innerself. She must have experienced a great deal of heartache. He understood that need for privacy because he too held his life close to his chest. Now he knew that she was the woman who would make his life whole. But God, he felt like a heel. He must let her know what he had discovered about her and himself.

Without giving her a chance, he had foolishly misjudged her. He felt sick when he remembered the look of anger and hurt etched in her beautiful face. He cringed at the thought of her darkened, golden eyes, eyes that had held a vacant look when he questioned her. He couldn't believe the pain he had delivered to the woman he loved.

All his life he had set such high standards for himself and others. Standards that were self-imposed and should not be applied to others. How could he judge others by his life? He was a fool to let his life's experience come between him and Paige.

"Linc!" A juvenile voice filtered through his thoughts. "Linc!"

He turned as a young boy with fly-away black hair came running toward him.

"Hey, slow down, fella. You're going to run those legs off." He reached out and ruffled the boy's hair.

"You got a phone call," the boy said, all out of breath.

Linc's gaze darkened. Only his mother knew he had come to the reservation and she wouldn't disturb him unless it was an emergency. His mind raced. "What now?" he spoke to the eagle making a low swoop over him. His trot turned into a dead run back to his grandfather's house.

The small boy did his best to keep up with Linc's long strides.

"You gotta call back," the boy's voice called after him.

Linc's grandfather was at the back of the house stacking the wood he had chopped the day before. The sun was still only a bright red glow in the eastern sky. His grandfather always got up early. It was his way.

"Someone called?"

His grandfather nodded, his silver-grey hair falling over his weather-worn forehead. "The number is by the phone," his grandfather said without breaking pace in his movements.

Linc rushed into the small, austere house and picked up the paper beside the phone. It wasn't his mother's number. It was the number of the inn. Paige! His fingers quickly dialed and waited for someone to answer the phone. "Come on, come on," he ordered someone to answer the phone.

"Hello?"

"This is Lincoln Cross returning your call."

He could hear Emma's smile over the phone. "Oh, Linc...it's good to hear your voice. Mara wants to speak with you. Just a minute."

He heard her place the receiver on the kitchen counter with a clunk, and listened while hurried footsteps stopped and then the receiver crackled to life with Mara's voice.

"Linc. Thank God I finally got hold of you."

"How did you know where to find me?" He crumpled the notepaper and tossed it in the hand-woven trash basket beside the back door, mentally giving himself two points.

"When she left I called your house. Your mother told me where you were. You gotta find her."

"Calm down and tell me what's wrong. Her? Who? Paige?" He knew without being told. Damn. He never should have left.

"Linc, she's gone."

Prickles of tension ran down his spine. "Gone? Gone where?"

"Her stepmother arrived yesterday. Something's not right here. She and Paige never got along and suddenly she comes in out of the blue and plays the attentive mother. Linc, you've got to do something."

"Where is she?"

"I don't know for sure. Paige was planning to return to New York this morning. But Emma overheard them making plans to go to the U.P. I thought I caught something about Sault Saint Marie, you know, the Soo."

What was going on there? Why would Paige come to the Upper Peninsula? "Mara, what's happened? Paige and you are so close."

There was a long silence and then Mara heaved a sigh. "Jack and I got married. Paige took this as a sign of not just rejection, but as if I became the enemy. She hates Jack and thinks he burned her house and was responsible for shoving her into the cellar." Her voice cracked.

"Damn." He had considered Jack a suspect too until he remembered all of Jack's connections. He didn't need to go that far. Or did he? "You married Jack?" he asked as if he had just heard her.

"Linc, it's a long story. We can discuss it later. Right now you have to find her. I don't trust her stepmother. Why has she come back after all this time? She's never given a rip for Paige and now she's as sweet as honey."

"Are you sure the woman hasn't turned over a new leaf? People change you know," he said, hoping against hope that the dark foreboding around him was unreasonable fear. He shook his head. Mara was right; he could feel something was wrong. He had to reach Paige, make her put aside her anger and listen to him explain that he was a big fool with too damned much pride.

"That woman hasn't ever been nice or kind without a motive." Mara spoke hurriedly, trying to convince him. "And Linc?"

"Yes."

"The reporters have been swarming all over the place. They're still out there, like a bunch of vultures. They haven't caught on to the fact she isn't here any more."

"How did she get away without being seen?"

Mara laughed. "Emma showed her the back road through the woods to the highway. The reporters never saw them go. But I'm worried about that stepmother of hers. Paige is very vulnerable right now. I'm really worried."

"I'll find her, I promise." His guilt for pushing Paige away from the safety of his arms stabbed at his conscience. And his feeling of uneasiness grew as he thought about her unscrupulous stepmother. He hung up the phone.

Damn, this was his fault. If he hadn't gotten angry, none of this would ever have happened. He pushed his fingers through his hair. Now, to find her. If she was here in the Soo, he would use his good ol' boy network to find her.

He walked out to where his grandfather was still working. "I have to go out for a while."

"I know." the old man nodded. His grandfather's words were short and to the point.

"I will pick you up after I find Paige. I want you to see her house or what's left of it."

"I'll be ready."

Linc turned on his heel and quickly strode toward his truck. He had to find her. The U.P. was a big place, but her stepmother was a city person. She wouldn't feel comfortable in the wilderness. The casino was the only reasonable place to begin his search. That was where his good ol' boy network was.

"Everything is going to be just fine, you wait and see." Ada patted Paige's arm.

"Maybe." Paige pulled her hooded jacket closed and zipped it up under her chin. The breeze off St. Mary's River was stiff and a bit cool. If only she could believe everything was going to be all right. If only she could get Linc out of her head...out of her heart.

Ada slipped her arm around Paige's shoulder. "Time heals everything," she assured. "After this whole thing is behind you, you'll look back and wonder why you were ever so upset."

Paige doubted that. There would never be another man in her life like Linc. Even though she was angry with him, she knew he would always be in that special place in her heart.

She closed her eyes and felt his presence, as if he were standing next to her, protecting her. Of course that was silly, he was still in the Lower Peninsula. And he was still very angry and wanted nothing to do with her. But it was warm and comforting to close her eyes and see him in her mind's eye. It was so real . . .

"Would you like to take a tour of the locks?"

Paige shrugged. It didn't matter what they did. Nothing mattered any more. Her life was empty and dark. "I don't care, if you'd like."

"Hey." Ada playfully shook her. "This little trip is for you. I have to bring you out of the doldrums." She thought for a moment. "I know." Her face brightened excitedly. "Would you like to go over into Canada and do a little shopping? Shopping always helps when I feel bad."

Paige turned toward the swiftly flowing river. Why had she let Ada talk her into this stupid trip anyway? What in the world was she doing here? She didn't want to go to the locks, she didn't want to go shopping and she certainly didn't want to stand on the shore talking about it.

"I don't care. I guess." There was no sense in hurting Ada's feelings. She'd come a long way just to be with her.

The older woman's face enlivened. "Great. Let's go shopping and then tonight we can have dinner in the Dream Catcher's Lounge at Kewadin Casino and do a little gambling after."

They spent the morning shopping at Station Mall. Paige always marveled at how two cities named the same and separated by a river and the border of two countries could be so different. No more than a couple of miles separated Sault Saint Marie, Michigan, and Sault Saint Marie, Ontario. Yet it might as well be hundreds. Just like her and Linc. Alike in so may ways but miles apart in too many.

Ada bought lunch and brought it to the table. "You must keep up your strength."

Paige shook her head. "I'm not hungry."

Ada pushed a cup to her. "At least drink your tea. You'll feel better." The older woman's narrow face smiled warmly at her stepdaughter.

Paige obliged, grimacing as the unusually bitter tea met her taste buds. "Thank you." She smiled at Ada, adding some sugar to the strong tea.

When she finished her tea, Ada gathered their dishes and took them to the counter and whisked Paige off to shop. Ada seemed to buy the store out. Paige bought nothing. There was nothing she needed except to escape her troubles. If only she could make it right with Linc. If only she hadn't come home. If only she hadn't called Mara. If only.

After returning to the Kewadin Inn, Paige was totally exhausted. "I need some rest." Paige stood in the hall leaning on the staircase leading to her room. "I don't know what's the matter with me, but I feel like I could sleep forever." Her head felt big and her limbs were weak, her legs heavy as if they would no longer hold her up.

Ada patted her shoulder. "Darling, you've just been released from the hospital, of course you're weak. You take a nice nap. Don't worry about me. I can entertain myself." She escorted her stepdaughter into her room. "I'll wake you about an hour before dinner if you're not awake by then."

Paige lay down and slept for most of the afternoon. Her dreams were filled with the flames of hot fires engulfing her. In the flames she saw the bear on his hind legs with his mouth open in a silent roar and Linc running toward her. His arms were waving for her to come to him. But she couldn't leave the fire. Frantically he motioned for her to run. But from what, to what? What was he trying to tell her? She struggled to move through the mist but couldn't reach him. He was always just out of reach, his face was filled with dark concern and urgency. As she finally freed herself of the hot flames, she stumbled into quicksand. Horror surrounded her as she felt the smothering slime locking itself around her, squeezing the living breath from her body.

She screamed and screamed, but Linc couldn't reach her. He held out his hand but she couldn't touch him. She felt herself sinking lower and lower into the muck. Oh, God, she was going to die.

With a jerk she awoke and bolted upright in the bed. Her head ached. Her arms felt as if they had lead weights attached, and when she moved her legs to get up, they also felt too heavy to move. Then she remembered her dream. Perspiration beaded on her forehead and upper lip. She quivered all over as every nerve ending in her body rebelled against her nightmare.

She shook her head to clear it. Paige knew if she lay down she would go back to sleep. And she wanted to. But the clock said quarter of six. Not wanting to disappoint Ada, Paige knew she had to get ready for dinner and a little gambling. She groaned. It was the last thing she wanted to do.

She slipped from the bed and laboriously moved to the bathroom counting on a nice hot shower to revive her.

As the hot water caressed her naked body, her mind strayed to Linc's hands roaming over her as they danced. As much as she tried to think of something else, he stayed in her thoughts.

He was a brilliant man who lived very well in the modern world. Yet there was a deeper side, a spiritual, simplistic side that made him at one with nature. She would never forget him. No man could ever measure up to him...no man ever would.

She envied him. He had a culture he clung fiercely to, in fact, two cultures. She had never taken time to look into her roots, to find out where she came from, where her ancestors came from. She was just another African-American who never bothered with the culture of her people. Were they brought here as slaves? Did she have relatives in Africa, distant relatives that had a proud heritage, that knew the family history she didn't and probably never would?

Tears welled in her eyes. She'd lost Linc and to make matters worse, she didn't even know who she was.

He was a paradox. It would take her a lifetime to learn the depth of him. These thoughts were stupid. What did it matter? She would never see him again after this investigation was over. His last words had been a definite farewell. She didn't have to be told the meaning of the words he'd used when he'd left. She'd felt it when the words dropped from his lips. It had been a final goodbye.

She thought about her job and wondered where she would go on her next shoot? Wouldn't it be ironic if she were sent to Africa?

But Linc's image haunted her, flashed before her eyes, especially the last time they were together. He hadn't believed she could be a model. But he had said she could have been a prostitute. That hurt, really hurt.

Yet, she found herself wanting to explain why she had kept secrets from him. Of course that was out of the question. She'd already realized there would be no second chance.

Enough of this feeling sorry for herself. Wallowing in self-pity wasn't doing anybody any good. She closed her eyes and let the water cascade over her, willing her thoughts to empty. But through the steamy mist, Linc appeared. His dark, phantom-like effigy emerged before her, taunting her, daring her to forget him.

She wanted to reach out and touch him, to run her fingers through the ebony hair that fell in wet waves over his forehead. His bronze chest rippled with taut muscles that gave him the craggy look of an unfinished sculpture.

Her gaze moved down to his smooth, tight stomach and stopped. She wanted him to reach out and touch her, to use his healing power to soothe away her bruises and pain. Her gaze fixed on his mouth and she yearned to feel his lips on hers.

This is a dream, it can't be real. Cautiously she let her long fingers touch the inviting lips. His arms wrapped around her and she was led willing into a fevered grasp. He had forgiven her. He was here. His hands moved down her body as they had when they danced, only now her body was naked and slick with soap.

He caressed her breast, her hips and embraced her lips with his. He held her captive, his own hardness pressing against her. His fingers sought out her soft, fleshy mound and caressed her tenderly. Waves of passion roared through her body.

An animal moan escaped her lips as she pressed against him, willing him to enter her right there in the shower, to make them finally one.

The passion-drugged haze enveloped her. "Linc? How...? Is that really you?" she whispered on his lips and then leaned back to look at him. A sensual grin lifted his mouth. She reached out to pull him back into her grasp, but she could no longer feel him. Her eyes flew open.

"Linc?" Like a movie in slow motion, he disappeared into the mist. "No," she cried, reaching to grab him. "Don't go." Her arms fell to her side, empty. It had been a dream. But it had seemed so real.

Paige grew cold inside. Now she was hallucinating. Maybe the bump on her head was worse than she'd thought. A shudder ran through her. She was alone in the steamy shower with only a memory. She leaned back and rested her head on the glass door. Whatever had just happened she didn't want to go there again, at least not alone.

She had to get out of the shower, away from those heated thoughts. Paige dressed quickly, pulling her low riding jeans to her navel and snapping them with determination. Tucking her tee-shirt into the pants, she tossed on the matching denim jacket. She had just finished her makeup and put a small silver clasp at the bottom of her long heavy braid when a tap sounded at the door. She didn't feel like fussing with her hair tonight. This would have to do.

"Come in, Ada." She stepped back to allow her stepmother entry.

Ada's eyes swept over her jeans and jacket. "I like that red tee shirt with that. You've certainly learned a great deal about fashion." She leaned into the mirror and ran her little finger over her ultra-thin brow. "I hear Kenny Rogers is going to entertain at the dinner club this evening."

"Oh?" That was as close to a compliment as Paige had ever heard fall from those red lips. Maybe part of her hatred of Ada was her fault. She just hadn't wanted anyone to take her mother's place.

"Yes." Ada straightened her too-tight skirt and tightened the braided belt around her waist. "And there's no one I like to listen to more than Kenny," she said, as if she knew him personally. "I guess Cosby isn't going to be here until next weekend. Well, are you ready?"

Paige nodded. "As ready as I'll ever be, I guess."

The dinner was much like lunch. Paige pushed her food around her plate, her appetite abandoning her.

"Come on, you gotta eat. You'll make yourself sick." Ada was obviously enjoying her food. "You act more like a lovesick puppy than someone who has just had a nasty fall. Besides, you don't know what you're missing. This whitefish is delicious."

Paige stiffened. Was it that obvious? Was she really acting like that? She couldn't seem to clear the clouds that had gathered in her mind.

Ada stared at her. "That's it, isn't it? You're in love."

"No." Paige turned her gaze away and watched the singer performing. Only it wasn't Kenny Rogers, it was someone she'd never heard of.

Ada eyed her carefully. "Whatever, dear. I do understand loving someone you can't have." Her eyes met Paige's. "I suffered a great loss when your father passed." Ada reached across the table and placed her hand on Paige's arm. "Who is he? Is it that Indian the tabloids are plastering all over the front page?"

Was that anxiety on Ada's face or concern? Paige shook her head. "He's a Native American." Then she shrugged her shoulders. "It doesn't matter. It's over." She noticed Ada relax.

"Are you sure of that? I mean, you've been moping around like a sick puppy."

"It's over," Paige said curtly.

Ada raised her eyebrows and held up her hand. "All right dear. I was just asking. I didn't mean to intrude where I shouldn't."

"It's forgotten," Paige murmured.

Ada rattled on and on but Paige's mind was elsewhere. She tried not to think about Linc, but he was always there, just a thought away. Why couldn't she forget him at least for a few minutes?

"Are you all right?"

Paige felt Ada shaking her arm.

"I said, are you all right?"

Paige blinked and unwillingly dragged her thoughts back to her stepmother. "What?"

"Where were you? You seemed a million miles away."

Paige felt color rise in her cheeks, warming them. "I was thinking."

"About this man?"

"What man?"

Ada made a face and heaved a sigh. "Come on, tell me about it. It might help to get it off your chest."

Paige hesitated. She didn't want to talk about Linc. It was too personal, too hurtful.

Ada watched her. "All right, then let me ask you this. Does he live in Harbor Springs?"

Paige nodded.

"Then you met him when you came back?"

Again, Paige nodded.

"Do I know him."

"No."

"It's not that Jack that your friend married, is it? You aren't in love with . . ."

Paige couldn't help smiling at that. "No . . . I'm not in love with Jack. I don't even like him and I certainly don't trust him. I think he's the one who burned my house."

Ada jerked her brow questioningly, as if somehow she liked the idea. "Really? What makes you think that?"

"He wants the property to increase his resort. I guess he wants to add a golf course or some such thing." She grimaced. "But the house burned on my first night back. He never even asked to see if I wanted to sell."

"Strange," Ada mused.

"Of course, I had no intention of selling. I wanted to make it my home after I retire from my career."

Ada was thoughtful for a few moments. "And you think he pushed you too?"

A hesitant smile trembled over her lips. "Oh, he has the perfect alibi. He was on Mackinac Island getting married to Mara when I was pushed. But he could have arranged it."

"And your friend married this man? I'm so sorry." She clicked her tongue and shook her head.

Paige nodded. "I know. I've never felt so alone."

Ada reached across the table again. "You're not alone, dear. You have me now. And I will never leave you."

Out of the corner of her eye Paige caught a glimpse of a tall, dark-haired man moving in the opposite direction. Prickles of gooseflesh rose on her skin. Linc. She turned her head just in time to see him disappear through the crowd.

"I'll be right back." She hurriedly rose, scraping back her chair.

Ada's eyes grew wide in surprise and her mouth formed a question.

Paige didn't let her ask it. She offered, "I won't be long." Without another look at her stepmother, she hurried in the direction she had seen Linc or the man who she thought was Linc. What would he be doing up here? Had he followed her? No, he had no idea she would be at the casino.

She threaded her way through the crowd and out into the lounge. Disappointment inundated her. Whoever it was, was gone. She moved into the room and gazed around, looking for that tall, broad-shouldered man in a white shirt. But there was no one who fit that description in sight.

She felt as if she were being stalked by a memory. Why couldn't she put all this behind her? It was love. It had to be. Yes, she must admit she loved him. No matter how angry he'd made her, she loved him. Would every tall, dark-haired man remind her of Linc?

Slowly, her heart heavy, she returned to the table where Ada waited.

"What was that all about?"

"I thought I saw someone."

"This man of yours, no doubt?"

Paige took a sip of ice water. "He's not mine. It doesn't matter anyway," she denied too vehemently.

"Well, if you don't want to talk about it . . ."

"I don't," Paige said bluntly.

Ada picked up the bill and carefully read it.

"Come. I'd like to win a little money while I'm here."

Paige followed Ada as she paid the bill. "Let me pay my share." Paige reached into her purse.

Ada stopped her hand. "Nonsense. This is my treat." She handed the hostess the check.

The sounds of the casino became louder and louder, crashing in around her. Bells rang and gongs went off as people won and lost at the slot machines. The room sounded like a thousand different video games playing at the same time. The noise made her head throb. Smoke from pipes, cigars and cigarettes filled the air, irritating her throat and burning her eyes.

Ada sat at an empty dollar slot and began depositing the dollar tokens. Paige glanced around at the throngs of people who were obviously enjoying this expensive pastime.

She might enjoy this at another time too, but tonight her head throbbed and her heart ached.

She placed her hand on Ada's shoulder. "I'm going outside for a little fresh air." Ada nodded without turning to look, her eyes fixed on the flashing lights.

Paige walked toward the door, toward the peace and quiet of the outside evening.

The sun had set, leaving only a slight glow in the west, and a cool Canadian breeze swept over the large porch-like entrance. Paige moved around the parking lot, glad to be away from the smoky and noise-filled casino. How long would Ada be? All she wanted to do was return to the inn and sleep.

She remembered seeing an art gallery as she and Ada walked from the Dream Catcher restaurant to the casino. She retraced her steps until she came to the Bawating Art Gallery. She made her way through the glass doors and was greeted with a quiet, reverential sounding music that had the power to relax her soul.

This was the one room where there was a non-smoking policy. Paige drew in a deep breath and gazed at the paintings hanging on the wall. Her gaze was drawn to the painting of a young woman holding her child toward the heavens, giving the child a spiritual name. Did Linc have a spiritual name?

"It is good you've come." A soft, gentle voice filtered through her thoughts.

"What?" Paige turned to a kind-looking woman with a fawn complexion, raven colored hair and midnight eyes.

"There are things you must resolve. Beware of the one closest to you."

Paige could only stare at the stranger. What did she mean? Who? Mara? Linc? Ada? The woman's gaze moved back and forth as if she were reading her mind, her heart, her very soul. Don't be silly, she chided herself. That's not possible.

"I'm sorry, I don't understand," Paige whispered.

"With your spiritual guide, you will have your answers. Listen to your guide and don't be afraid to follow your heart."

"I don't understand." Paige whispered.

"You will. You are from a strong and proud people too. You have ancestors that will help you. Never turn your back on the past."

Paige was at a loss for words. She glanced at the painting and then back to the woman. She was gone, like a ghost evaporating into the night.

She whirled around, searching the art gallery for the woman, but she was nowhere to be seen. She felt a chill building at the base of her spine and rapidly travel to her neck. She shuddered. What was that all about? Her eyes searched the room again.

Before she had time to contemplate the woman's words, Linc's voice streamed toward her. She bristled and then flushed as his nearness drifted over her. She'd know that voice anywhere. She kept her back to the voice, afraid to turn around.

"Sure, the house is gone. Everything was destroyed in the fire, but she is determined to rebuild."

"And you drew up plans for a new one?"

"Of course. She asked me to," Linc answered.

"You realize how valuable that property is to our tribe? A casino at that spot would be prime. With all the tourism and money in Emmet County, it's worth a fortune. It would be the most productive casino our nation owned."

"I'm sure it would. But she is stubborn." Linc laughed. "You are determined to spread the Red Man's revenge, aren't you?"

His companion laughed in return. "It isn't revenge. It's our way out of poverty. Don't you think it's about time, my brother?"

Paige shivered and her shoulders dropped. Linc did want the property. She perked her ears. She might as well hear the rest of the story. Their voices lowered as they passed close by her. Winona had been right. The Chippewa tribe did want the land. And Linc had known all along. Damn. Talk about secrets! It looked as if he had some of his own.

She couldn't hear what they said next, only the jumble of muted voices. Paige turned to get a better look at the two men as they stood by the door. The man facing her had his gaze on Linc.

"You know Linc, you're a damned apple." He lightly punched him in the shoulder.

She watched as both men left the art gallery, feeling as if her life would drain from her body. Linc was behind the Nation wanting her property for another casino. Talk about betrayal and deceit. And he'd judged her so harshly for keeping her little secret. God, what a hypocrite!

She squared her shoulders and marched out through the doors. The cool evening breeze touched her face but did not calm her burning pain. She spotted Linc as he stood alone under the entrance lights and she strode toward him.

"Linc," she called.

He turned toward her voice. "Paige! Thank God. I've been looking all over for you."

"I'll just bet you have." She shivered in anger. So much anger flowed along her veins, she had no idea where to begin to tell him what she thought of him.

"Mara sent me to look for you. She's worried."

"Strange. She didn't give me a second thought when she married one of my enemies."

His face was splashed in moonlight which accentuated his dark handsome features. "I don't think you're being fair to her. She loves you like a sister."

"Mara has a funny way of showing it." She glared directly into his eyes. "So much for love, huh?"

His frown deepened. "What are you talking about? Mara loves you and so do I."

"You don't love me, you want my property just as much as Jack. You both want it for money." She inhaled deeply. "Well, let me tell you the same thing I told him. Hell will freeze over before you get as much as one grain of sand from that land!"

"Paige . . ." He stepped toward her. "What's wrong? I know we had a silly argument, but I realize now..."

She backed away. He wasn't going to touch her, never again. "You know very well. You want the land for a casino, you and your precious Nation! No one is going to get my property. It's mine. Do you hear me? Mine!" She spat out the words contemptuously. She cringed inside listening to her own voice. She sounded like she was crazy. But the land was all she had left of her parents. He knew that. He had brought her the album.

Several couples walked past them, watching in amusement as Paige ripped into Linc. She didn't care. He had been more deceitful than she ever could imagine and she wanted him to know beyond a doubt she had caught on to his game.

Her head began to swim. The pounding became more intense and she felt the blood drain from her face. No, she couldn't become ill now, not here. But she did.

"Paige." Linc reached out to steady her. "Let me help you."

"No!" She pushed away, but faltered.

His iron grasp kept her knees from buckling. He placed his arm around her and held her steady. "If I move away you'll fall on your face. I think you've had enough falls for a while. Where's your car?"

"We walked," she murmured softly. "Ada is still gambling."

Linc guided her toward the parking lot. "Where are you staying?"

"The Kewadin Inn."

"I'm going to take you there." He held her fast. "This was a stupid, crazy stunt you pulled. You just got out of the hospital. You had no right to go off like this, making everyone worry about you." His voice hardened in worry and concern.

Her throbbing head worsened. She felt faint and sick to her stomach. She was ill. Too sick to fight him. And the thought of getting back to the inn and sleeping sounded better by the minute.

"Ada," she murmured as Linc helped her into the truck.

He reclined the seat and placed a small pillow beneath her head. "You just lean back and rest. I'll have you there shortly. And then I'll tell your stepmother.

Relief ran through her as she closed her eyes and instantly drifted into a deep sleep.

She felt the truck roll to a stop but didn't lift her head until she heard the door slam. Where was she? She struggled to sit up, her eyes barely focusing. "Where . . ."

"Back in Harbor Springs."

"Harbor...?" She gazed at the inn as Linc got out to help her inside. "Linc? What are you doing here?" Her mind was fraught with confusion. "How? Why?" she stammered.

"Because you needed to be where you can rest and get your health back. You can't be gallivanting all over the countryside after the accident you had."

"I was pushed," she said belligerently.

He nodded. "Yes. Pushed. In any case, you need bed rest."

She felt too drained to fight him. She did need rest; she was exhausted and spent. Linc reached in to scoop her into his arms. "No." In her hazy mind she still thought of her weight. She couldn't let him pick her up and discover how heavy she was. She leaned on him as he helped her out of the truck and into the inn.

"Paige! Thank God." Mara rushed forward. "I've been so worried. Ada has been calling. She sounded frantic."

"I'm sorry. Would you make sure you let Ada know where I am so she won't worry?" Paige responded in a weak voice.

Mara rushed to take over. "Sure we will." She glanced at Linc, "I'll take her to her room and help her into bed."

"And I'll make a cup of my herbal tea. It's a blend my mother always used when a person needed to strengthen their system." Emma hustled from the room.

Paige began to slide down. This time Linc whisked her into his arms and carried her up the stairs to her room. Mara followed behind, giving Linc instructions. Over her shoulder she hollered at Jack, "Tell Ada that we have Paige and she is going to stay here until she is well."

Linc laid her on the bed as Mara had said. Then he sat beside her. Smoothing her hair away from her face, he spoke softly. "I do love you and I will prove it. But first you have to rest and recover." He lightly brushed his lips over her forehead. "I'm sorry for being such an ass. It won't happen again."

Paige opened her eyes and gazed into his, but didn't speak.

Mara brought a damp washcloth and wiped Paige's face. She turned to Linc. "Why don't you go downstairs. I'll get her ready for bed."

Linc nodded. "Call me if you need anything."

"You'd be the first person that I called."

Paige was beyond the point of caring. When she was well she would deal with all of them. Right now all she wanted to do was sleep. Tomorrow was another day. She'd face her problems then.

Eleven

Linc hesitated at the bottom of the stairs as Emma hustled by him with the herbal tea. He hated leaving Paige, even if only for a few minutes. Now that he had her, at least physically, he didn't want to be separated.

Emma glanced at him. "Don't worry yourself none. In a few days she'll be as right as rain." She took a couple more steps and called over her shoulder, "There's fresh coffee in the kitchen. Help yourself."

"Thank you. You're a good woman, Emma. We wouldn't know what to do without you."

Emma clucked her tongue, warmth staining her face. "I know you're only saying that 'cause it's true." She gave a nervous giggle. Her voice was filled with the embarrassment of someone who didn't receive many compliments.

Linc wondered how this kind woman could put up with a boss like Jack. There must be something good about him, but he failed to see what. He wanted to stay close to Paige but the last thing he wanted was to spend time talking to Jack. That guy just rubbed him the wrong way. Yet he couldn't bring himself to leave.

He needed to talk to Mara to see how Paige was doing. More importantly, he wanted to be there to make things right with the woman he loved. He had to apologize for being an idiot about her secrecy. She had been right. It hadn't been any of his business. He would work to gain her trust.

He stepped past Jack who was on the phone at the breakfast bar and listened as his childhood nemesis explained the situation to Ada. He grabbed a coffee mug and filled it. Straddling a stool, he leaned on the bar and studied the steam rolling from the cup.

Linc knew he had to find a way to get things on track. He and Paige belonged together. That wouldn't happen until the fire investigation was cleared up and Paige was well again. She looked worse tonight than when she left the hospital. Somehow he would clear her name and free her from her problems. Something, no, someone was trying to harm her. She had said she was pushed, and he believed her. But why would someone want her hurt or dead? He shuddered at the last thought.

Linc looked up when Jack dropped the phone heavily in its cradle. "Mara's been worried out of her mind." Jack said, pouring himself a cup of coffee and then offering to refill Linc's cup.

Linc nodded. He was tired and exhausted. The last thing he needed right now was a confrontation with Jack. But he needed to know if Jack was the arsonist. And worse yet, if Jack had arranged to have Paige pushed into the burned cellar. He glared at the man who had tormented him when they were children. He didn't like him. Maybe that was why he was willing to believe the worst. Whatever it was, he wanted to lay all of the cards on the table at once. He noticed Jack shifting under his glare. "Do you mind telling me how the hell you pulled it off?"

"What?" Jack's eyebrows shot up and then crowded together over the bridge of his nose.

Linc slid off the stool and paced the kitchen floor. He was agitated and knew he shouldn't be talking to Jack. Not when he felt like this, but he marched on. "Paige. Why did you do it? She never did anything to harm you. You never even asked about her property. You just burned the house without finding out if she would sell."

Jack jerked from his seat and planted himself in Linc's path. "Now wait just a damned minute! Are you accusing me of burning her house?"

Linc's eyes darkened, snapping with fury. "Well, it looks like little Jackie Devlin understands English." Jack opened his mouth to respond but Linc cut him off. "I want to know how you managed to be on Mackinac Island and shove her in the cellar. Who did you hire to do your dirty work?"

Jack's face paled and his eyes grew stormy blue. "I think you should leave and cool off before one of us does something we'll regret." It was obvious by the set of his jaw and the flaring of his nostrils he was trying to control his anger.

Linc sneered. "Believe me, I wouldn't regret working over the guy who seems hell-bent on destroying the woman I love." His fist clenched and unclenched at his side. The men were standing within reaching distance of each other. "If you didn't have so damned many connections I'd wipe up the floor with you, just as I did when we were kids." He raked his fingers through his hair. Getting himself locked up for assault and battery wouldn't do Paige any good but it would make him feel better to let Jack have it. He sucked in a deep breath. "God, how could you do it? Do you love money that much?" He slumped back on the stool.

Jack took a step in his direction. "In case you haven't noticed, we are about the same size now. Go for it."

Linc glared at him. It was true, both men were well over six feet and built much the same. He probably couldn't stomp his ass any more but he'd have a good time trying. "You'd like that wouldn't you? You'd love to call your Uncle Richard and have my ass thrown in jail for assault. You've wanted to do something like that for a long time."

"What the hell are you trying to prove? That you're a complete buffoon? Well, you've proved it. I did nothing.

Not a damned thing! And I'd rather have the chance to kick your ass than to have you put in jail," Jack challenged.

Linc watched Jack as he leaned against the counter and folded his arms over his chest, proudly standing his ground. There was no backing down. No hesitation. If he was acting he was damned good. But who else could it be? "Then who did?" he asked. "You, my friend, are the only one who would profit. You want her property."

Jack stared at him openly. "I wanted her property, yes. I still do, but not like that. I didn't set her house on fire. And to set matters straight, I didn't marry Mara to get to Paige. I love Mara. She's the best thing that ever happened to me."

Linc's heart tightened. There was a truthfulness to Jack's words. He'd known him for a long time and this wasn't the way he acted when he was guilty. This guy that he had spent a lifetime hating—no, envying—was in love and probably didn't burn the house. As long as he was being honest with himself, he would have to admit that he had hoped it was Jack. Childhood anger carried one helluva lasting punch. He shook his head.

Before he could respond, Mara entered the kitchen and looked from one to the other, questions flashing in her eyes.

"I could hear the two of you all the way upstairs. What's going on?"

Jack pulled her close. "Linc here thinks I'm the arsonist."

Mara released an exasperated breath. "He didn't do it. I know he didn't. Paige told me what she overheard between Jack and Emma, but that's just Jack." She smiled at him lovingly and placed a quick kiss on his cheek. "He talks a bigger game than he plays."

Jack pulled her tightly against him. "My wife knows me better than I know myself."

Linc ran his fingers through his dark hair and then shoved his hands deep in his pockets. "Then who did? Who but Jack would profit from Paige's loss?"

Jack frowned. "I'm telling you the truth. I didn't have anything to do with any of this. I don't know who is behind it, but I'm not."

Linc glared at him. "You've always been a liar. Why should I believe you now?"

"Liar?" Jack asked. "When have I lied to you?"

"You have a short memory, don't you? You were always lying to your father about me. You were always trying to turn him against me. Did you think I'd forgotten?"

Surprise and shock crossed Jack's face. "God, Linc, we were just kids. Did you think I wanted to share my father with you? And then to learn that you were my brother almost killed me."

A pregnant silence stretched between them. Linc felt as if the earth had been knocked from beneath his feet. What in the hell was Jack talking about? Devlin . . . his father? He and Jack were brothers? No, it wasn't possible. Linc stared at Jack, studying his features. "What do you mean 'my brother'?"

Jack's eyes grew wide and his lips thinned. "Oh, come on. You must know. My dad spent every spare minute he could with your mother. Surely you saw that. And there was all that gossip about me and my bastard half-breed brother."

"What kind of malicious game are you playing?" But was he playing games? Linc remembered the nights Devlin came to the house when he was just a youngster. He always said he had paper work for his mother. But was that true or was that just another lie in a long line of lies? And there was that one time he got up in the wee hours of the morning and found Devlin still at the house. Had he stayed all night?

"No game, brother. My father is your father," Jack said, a touch of impatience in his tone. Then his voice softened. "With both of my parents dead, I guess it's a little ironic that you are all of the blood family I have left, except for Uncle Rich, of course.

Mara jerked a look at Jack and grabbed his arm. "Oh hon, I'm so sorry for both of you," she whispered. She looked from one to the other. "Now that this is finally out in the open, I think you should put aside your differences and try to be, at the least, friends."

"You're lying!" Linc said in a harsh, bitter tone, ignoring Mara's entreaty. Not Mr. Devlin. No, it wasn't possible. His mother and . . . "This is just another one of your lies to cover up what you've done." The words rushed angrily from Linc's lips, God, was it possible that Jack's father and his mother had been lovers?

Jack shrugged his shoulders. "Believe what you want. It obviously won't do any good to talk to you."

"How do I know you're telling the truth?" Linc demanded. "How do you know?"

"I heard my parents arguing one night when I was about thirteen. It seems my mother had been flaunting a recent affair in Dad's face. When he became angry, she threw the past in his face and you were part of it. Our father told her to leave his sons out of the argument...you and me."

Linc felt as if someone had punched him in the stomach. All this time his mother and Devlin! He glanced at the other man—his brother. They both bore the burden of their parents' indiscretions. He drew in a deep reinforcing breath, and called on the spirits to help him through this turmoil.

"I have to leave." Linc made his way to the back door. "I have to think." He had to think all right. This had been a night for revelations.

Jack's voice stopped him. "You would have known in a year anyway."

Linc turned. "Why...what do you mean?"

"You're in the will, you know. We equally share everything when we both turn thirty-five. I guess Dad wanted us to be settled down before we got our hands on that kind of money."

Linc felt sick. "I don't want his money. I never wanted anything but a father and you're the one who had that."

"Did I? Did I really?" Jack's hands curled into tight fists of anger.

The two men stood glaring at each other. For the first time Linc saw Jack through different eyes. If this was indeed his brother, his blood . . .

Linc nodded. "Yes, you had a father. I was the one who didn't."

Jack's features hardened. "Didn't you? He may have lived in our house, but his love was in yours. I envied you that and hated you for it." Jack grabbed the back of his neck and rubbed as if he had a lot of tension and pain. "Oh, he lived here with my mother and me, but when he bragged, he bragged about you...about your scores at basketball, your homeruns and your touchdowns. And when you went to college, he bragged about your grades and the kind of young man you had grown into. Is it any wonder I hated you?"

Linc was confused. Was it possible? He thought about Jack and how they had fought when they had been kids. Had Jack only been protecting his family the only way he knew how? He was uncomfortable with the fact that Jack might be telling the truth. He had to get away.

"Ask your mother, if you don't believe me." Jack's voice followed Linc out the door.

He felt a ripple of unease travel down his spine. He had asked his mother. She had told him that the man's wife had been pregnant at the same time as she. And Jack was his age within a couple of months. They had been in the same grade at school. Were they really brothers? How had he managed to go through life never picking up on something like this? Jack said there had been gossip. Why hadn't he heard it?

Linc walked right past his truck. He was too keyed up to go home right now. He moved through the field and into the woods where night animals had come out to play. The trees looked gnarled and twisted by the light of the moon.

His footsteps slowed as his gaze darted first left then right. A hair-raising sensation inched along his back. He could feel someone watching him.

His eyes narrowed and he turned completely around, searching the shadows and crevices of the woods. There was nothing there. He released the breath he had been holding and then pressed his hands to either side of his head, which felt as if it were going to explode.

Linc stretched his arms to the sky. He wanted to cry out to the spirits, What have you done? But he couldn't. He walked, faster and faster until he broke into a dead run. His heart raged in his chest as his breathing became more rapid. Once again in a short period of time he was trying to run from his feelings.

He ran to become one with the night spirits. The spirit of the wind whispered dryly through the branches and rustled through tall grass, opening a path. The spirit moon peeked from behind a dark cloud, sending out fingers of ethereal light. The spirit of the wind sighed once more, bringing a keen awareness of his surroundings.

He stopped short as he saw movement out of the corner of his eye. He peered into the darkness. There in front of him was a black bear standing on its hind feet, pawing at the darkened sky. Its mouth was open in silent roar. This was what Paige had seen. It was a sign. All of the spirits were there to help him; the bear, the moon and even the wind were all speaking to him. Linc at once felt an inner peace. He knew that somehow everything would work out.

Linc returned to his truck. Before he slid beneath the steering wheel, he glanced up at Paige's window and saw soft light glowing from within. He knew she slept. He could feel it. He also knew their destinies were twined together as one. Convincing her of that might be another story, though.

He lowered his gaze to the first floor of the house. Inside was the man claiming to be his brother. Had he found the answer to this part of his quest so easily? Had the spirits affirmed the truth of Jack's allegations? There was only one way to find out. He would have to confront his mother, but this time he would demand answers. Judging her deeds wasn't for him to do. She was his mother and he loved her no matter what she had done. He quietly closed the door and drove toward home.

Linc went straight into the house. He found his mother in the living room asleep under her blanket. Her feet were perched on the small pine stool, her head tilted to one side. A book on the floor had obviously slipped from her hand. The fire had gone low. Linc quietly picked up a birch log and settled it on the hot embers in the grate.

He stared at the woman who had given him life. The worn look had softened in sleep. Strands of fine gray hair had escaped her braid and framed her face. She was a beautiful and strong-willed woman. Her life hadn't been a bed of roses. Nothing but love could have sent her down the path she chose...or that was chosen for her.

Nuna flinched. Her eyes flew open and fixed on her son. "You're back."

He nodded and brushed the sawdust from his hands. Their eyes met in quiet study.

"You know," she said quietly.

He nodded again. "I know."

"Jack told you," she said softly, her voice almost a whisper.

"Yes." Linc kept his eyes riveted on his mother's face. There would be no more lies, no secrets; they would have an easier path now.

"His father was afraid he had found out."

"It's true, then?"

Nuna nodded. Years of melancholy washed from her face. "Yes, it's true."

Jack had been telling the truth. Not only were they brothers but Devlin had been his father. He sat on the sofa and closed his eyes. He had thought he'd be angry and struggle with feelings of betrayal when and if he found out. But it was not so. He suddenly felt at peace.

"You're not angry?"

"No. I'm actually relieved."

She sighed and shifted in her chair. "No more secrets."

Linc nodded. "No more secrets."

"Does that include Paige Turner?"

He reached out and took his mother's hand. "Yes, especially Paige. Grandfather helped me to understand that Paige and I are destined to be together. At the sweat house it was made clear and on Thunder Mountain my spirit guide, the eagle, gave its life for us."

Nuna's dark eyes softened as she pondered her son's words. "Then she is the woman with the golden eyes...the right woman."

A grin spread across Linc's face. "She is. As soon as I convince her of that, the better. And I hope you will be happy for me. For us."

She squeezed his hand. "All I want is your happiness." She smiled warmly.

For a moment she was somewhere else. Linc studied her as she made a trip deep within her soul.

She finally dropped her gaze on her son as she said in a tone of great peace, "If Paige makes you happy, then I'm happy."

Nuna held her hand out to her son, "Come sit beside me." Linc grasped her hand and held it tightly. He lowered his long body to the pine stool and gazed into his mother's eyes. "If you want to tell me, I'm ready to listen."

Her eyelids fluttered as she gathered her thoughts. "Your father was a good man." Her face glowed in remembrance. "He and Jack's mother, Evelyn, were more or less forced into marriage by their families. It was the money-wise thing for the two families. They tried to make the marriage work, but it just wasn't meant to be. Jack's parents went their separate ways. For them this was the only solution, but neither of them counted on the other falling in love with someone else."

Linc pulled in a long breath and looked away. He wanted to ask why both women became pregnant at the same time if his father wasn't in love with Jack's mother, but was willing to just accept the parts of the story she wanted to share. He waited, knowing she wasn't finished.

She squeezed his hand, drawing his gaze back to hers. "When I told John you were coming, he was thrilled. When he left that night he was on his way to tell Evelyn he wanted a divorce. He stopped at the tavern to celebrate and gain courage." She patted Linc's hand. "You must understand he was very young and would be going against his family's wishes." She brushed a wisp of hair from her forehead. "Anyway, when he got to Evelyn he was very drunk. When he asked for the divorce, of course she was hurt and angry. She told him she would never give him his freedom." She drew in a deep breath. "Your father was hurt and angry. He told her it was time for her to be his wife in every way...thus Jack your brother was conceived. He was born six weeks after you."

Linc didn't say anything, but the bitterness he had felt was evaporating. Years of envy and hate were sliding into understanding. Jack had suffered as he had. The sins of the fathers, he thought.

He started to stand but his mother held him tightly, her eyes bright with memory. "There's more. John and I were going to marry but the two families fought it. They finally told your father that if he married me, he would be without a job and neither of his sons would be recognized in the families' wills. We knew we could make it without their money but we didn't know what would happen to Jack and to Evelyn. So for the sake of his children he stayed, in name only, with her." She paused and began again.

"When your father died, Evelyn came to me. She thanked me for the sacrifice and I thanked her for hers. After all, if she hadn't been tied to your father she might have found happiness. She told me she was dying and asked me to watch after her son." She smiled wanly. "I've tried, but that Jack has been a rebel. Your Uncle Richard and I have spent many hours trying to keep that young man out of trouble."

"Why didn't you tell me this long ago?"

I was waiting for the right time. I kept my promise. When you found out, it would be because it was meant to be."

Linc pulled his mother into his arms. "You are a good woman, Nuna Cross. Thank you for being my mother."

Ada placed a hand on Emma's shoulder. "Don't you worry about a thing. You run your errands and I'll watch after my stepdaughter."

Emma smiled at the other woman. "She hasn't been awake since we put her to bed last night. I'd like to make sure she's all right. Besides, when Jack and Mara went to his apartment they told me not to leave her for a minute."

"Well, that was before I came back. Now I am here and I'll take over. You run along."

Emma nodded hesitantly. "Well, I do have some shopping I need to get done. We have guests coming in a few days."

Ada picked up a duffel bag and smiled to herself as she slipped into Paige's room. She unpacked a few items from the bag and then sat in the chair across from her stepdaughter.

Sensing movement, Paige slowly opened her eyes. She could see she was in her bed at the Bayside Inn but she wasn't quite sure how she got there. The last thing she remembered was Linc loading her into his truck at the casino. "Linc?" She glanced around the room.

"You're awake." Ada hustled from the Queen Anne chair by the window. "How are you feeling?"

Paige lifted her head and propped herself on her elbows to get a better look. "How did you get here?" The last time she'd seen her she was enjoying her slot machine.

"When I heard Linc had brought you back, I came as soon as I could. You should have told me you were ill. I'd have brought you back." Ada reached behind Paige and fluffed the pillows.

"I'm fine, really. It's just that so much has gone on and I was exhausted . . . mentally exhausted."

Ada poured a steaming liquid from a small thermos on the dressing table and held it out to her. "Emma made this broth especially for you."

"I'm not hungry." Paige gently shoved it away.

Ada sat on the side of the bed and held out the cup. "Maybe not, but I'm not about to let you get sicker. Now you drink this broth, young lady," she said in a voice used for wayward children.

Paige brought herself upright and accepted the cup. Wrapping her fingers around its warmth she inhaled deeply. It smelled delicious. She was surprised to realize she was ravished, and after a few sips drank the whole cup.

Ada's eyes sparkled as a smile lit her face. She took the empty cup and sat it on the table. "That's much better. Now you just rest and get your strength back." She fussed with the blanket that covered Paige. "You don't know how worried I've been. You slept half the day away."

"I feel fine, really. What time is it?" She reached for the bedside clock and turned it toward her. "Oh, my gosh! It's almost four o'clock."

"Yes. You slept the better part of the day."

Paige threw back the sheet and light blanket that covered her. "I can't lie in bed all day." She sat up and stretched.

"You can," Ada insisted. "You must rest and get your strength back. I promised everyone I'd watch you."

Paige laughed. "You can watch me but I'm going to shower and get dressed."

But before she could rise from the bed, the phone rang.

"Hello?" Paige answered.

"Paige, this is Jack."

What did he want? "I don't think..."

"Paige, please listen to me. I think I know who is behind all these attacks on you. I have to go away for a few days to get the proof I need. But I want you to do me a favor."

"A favor? What kind of favor?"

"Take care of Mara for me. She loves you like a sister and I know in spite of what you think at the moment, you love her too. I know you think I married her just to gain your trust and property, but I swear to you, Paige, I didn't. I love Mara more than life itself. I would do anything for her and that includes forgetting about your land. I love her, Paige. I want you to know that."

What in the world? Was he serious? Could he be serious?

"Paige, are you still there?"

"Yes."

"Will you do this for me?"

"But what are you talking about? Why are you going away?"

"I'll explain everything when I get back. Trust me. When I return, everything will make perfect sense. Will you do this one thing for me?"

Could she have been wrong about Jack all along? Was he really a good guy after all?

"Paige?" Jack's voice pulled her from her thoughts.

"Yes."

"Will you...trust me and take care of Mara for me?"

"Yes, I will. Just this once."

"Thank you. I'll see you when I get back. You won't be sorry, Paige. I promise."

"Good-bye." She placed the phone back on the stand. "Who was that?"

"Just a personal call," Paige lied. For some reason, she couldn't confide in Ada.

The hot shower and fresh clothing made Paige feel like a new woman. She emerged from the bathroom fussing with her hair, pulling it back and clasping it at her nape. "Where is everyone?"

"Emma went to the store. Mara and Jack went to his apartment to get a few things he needed. They're going to stay here for a while. Until things settle down."

"Oh." Paige felt disappointment that Mara and Emma weren't there.

Ada began straightening the room and fussing over the mess it was. She finished by making the bed, pulling and tucking the sheets and each blanket until they were perfect. "Would you like a cup of coffee or something?"

"No, I'm fine."

"Then I think I'll have something." Ada reached for the door and stumbled. "Oh..."

"What's wrong?" Paige rushed across the room just in time to stop her from falling.

"My medicine...my purse."

Paige led her to the bed and helped her lie down. She rushed into Ada's room to get her purse.

"Small...bottle." Ada said weakly as Paige searched the purse.

She found the bottle, only it was empty. "Do you have more?"

Ada shook her head. "No. Prescription."

Paige shuffled through the purse until she found the doctor's prescription tucked inside the small inside pocket. "I'll go get this filled. But I can't leave you alone. I'll call 911 for help."

Ada shook her head. "No, just go. Get the medicine, quickly. It's my heart."

"I'm going to call 911." She reached for the phone.

"No! I just...need...my medicine. Please...hurry."

Paige placed the phone on the bed beside the ill woman. "If it gets worse, call 911."

"All right. Please...hurry." Her voice grew raspy.

Paige rushed out of the house and into her car. She didn't even realize she was driving until the tires squealed as she pulled hurriedly out of the drive. She'd remembered seeing a pharmacy nearby when she had gone shopping with Linc. Linc, she thought, that all seemed so long ago. She shook her head to clear it. She'd think about that later. Right now she had to get the prescription filled. Ada had been so good to her and now it was her chance to return the favor.

Her vision suddenly blurred and her hand flew to her eyes. She tried to wipe them with a tissue but nothing helped. She didn't feel well. A wave of nausea rolled through her. Frantically she tried to steer the car to the side of the road. She narrowed her eyes trying to see the cars coming toward her, but they were in a distant haze.

The side of the road. Where was it? Her stomach twisted with a burning pain, then cramped until she wanted to double up. Another wave of nausea and cramps hit her as she reached her foot for the brake. She couldn't find it, couldn't feel it.

Another pain seized her, again almost doubling her over. She felt the car weave and heard the sound of someone blasting their horn. She felt herself sinking into oblivion but rebelled against it, fought to keep awake.

She heard the screech of tires and opened her mouth to cry out. The crashing sound of metal ripped through her ears and vibrated in her head. Then it was over as she drowned in blackness.

Paige was barely conscious of being strapped to a stretcher and hoisted into an ambulance. She shuddered as another wave of pain gripped her. Someone moaned. Had that been her?

"It's going to be all right." A voice from the haze spoke reassuringly to her.

After endless time she was moved again and she opened her eyes to lights flashing by. Where was she?

Another wave of nausea swept over her, burning spasms twisted her stomach. The whirling sensation overtook her and she fell into darkness again.

Through the fog she heard someone calling her name. "Paige? Paige, can you hear me?"

She groaned. Who was it?

"Come on, Paige, fight it," he commanded. "Come back to me."

A face swam before her. "Come on, I know you can hear me." A hand gripped her chin.

"Linc?"

"Come on, babe, fight it!"

"Linc?" she murmured again.

"I think perhaps you'd better leave now." Another voice invaded Paige's hazy domain.

"Not until I know she's all right." He bent close to her face. "Come on, Paige, come back to me. I love you. Don't leave me now."

"I'm going to get the doctor if you don't leave right now," the voice threatened.

"I don't give a damn what you do," the first voice said. "Paige, do you hear me? I love you. I'm going to marry you as soon as possible."

"Marry?" she murmured, the word hurting her raw throat.

He laughed and squeezed her hand. He wanted to hug her but feared to. "Yes, marry you. You aren't going to get away from me this easily."

"What's going on here?" A doctor carrying a chart entered the room.

"She's going to be all right," Linc said, still holding her.

"Who are you?"

"I'm her fiancé. One of the nurses called me after finding my number in her purse."

Linc stepped aside as the doctor listened to her heart, felt her pulse and shined a light into her eyes. "You had a nasty accident, young lady. You're lucky you were wearing your seatbelt." He wrote something on the chart. "Are you prone to seizures?"

"No."

"You've never had a seizure of any kind?"

"No."

"I'll need to run some further tests. We did check for blood alcohol. It was negative." He seemed to be talking to himself more than the two people in the room with him.

"What kind of tests?" Paige whimpered.

"We have to find out why you were driving so erratically and why you blacked out at the wheel." He shoved the pen in his pocket. "If you aren't on any prescription drugs and aren't taking illegal drugs, something has to be causing the problem. I think we'll get a CAT scan of your head."

"I'm sure I'll be okay, it's probably from the bump on my head." Paige insisted.

The doctor flipped the pages of the chart over the clipboard. "Yes, I see we just released you a couple of days ago. And that was an accident too?"

Paige nodded, feeling defeated by the suspicious look on the doctor's face.

"I need to ask you again. Have you been taking anything?

All of the signs say you've ingested something that wasn't all that good for you." He gave her a knowing look.

"NO!" Paige exclaimed.

"Are you sure? The lab report will tell us, but it will also save us a lot of time if you tell us the truth so we know what you ingested."

"If Paige said she had nothing, then she had nothing. I know her. She doesn't use drugs." Linc stepped between the doctor and Paige.

The doctor shrugged his shoulders. "I'm a doctor. I have to ask questions, even uncomfortable ones, if I am going to help a patient recuperate."

Paige clasped Linc's hand tightly. "I didn't. Linc, you know I never would use drugs." But did he really? Did he know her well enough to know that? God, here was another thing against her. Now they believed she was a drug user. If the police get wind of this, they'll think I burned my house to support my habit. She had to get away from here before there was nothing left of her life. "Do I have to stay in the hospital? I mean, is there any reason I have to stay?"

The doctor flipped through the chart and glanced at Paige. He frowned as he read the chart. "As far as the accident is concerned, no. I'm more concerned by what caused you to become ill."

Paige leaned her aching head on the pillow. "The only thing I put in my mouth today was a cup of broth that Emma made."

"When?" Linc leaned forward.

"Just before Ada got sick." Paige popped up off the pillow, "Oh, my God. I was on my way to get her heart medicine. She was deathly ill when I left her."

Linc placed his arm tightly around her shoulder. "Calm down. I'll check on her." He turned to the doctor. "After I check on Ada, could I talk with you?"

"Certainly. Just check in with the nurse and one of them will know where I am."

As they left the room Paige could hear the doctor giving Linc directions to the nearest phone.

What was that all about? Why would Linc want to talk to the doctor alone? Surely he didn't think she was doing drugs. Maybe he thought she had done something to Ada. No, he couldn't think that. What was all this about him being her fiancé? When she last saw him she was giving him hell. Or was she? God, her thinking was so muddled.

Linc returned without the doctor. "Doc says you can go home, but you have to rest."

Relief engulfed through her. If she could go home, she would do anything they asked of her. Anything to get out of this place. She just didn't like hospitals. "What about the test? When do I do those?"

"The Doc says they have the blood test, you can return tomorrow for the rest." He patted her shoulder lightly.

Paige release a long breath. "Thank you."

"Paige." Linc hesitated.

"What?"

"They brought Ada in by ambulance. She called 911 for help. I just saw her, she's going to be fine."

"Thank God. I sat the phone on the bed beside her and told her to call if she got worse. I was so afraid she would wait too long."

Linc studied her. "Mara tells me that you and Ada never got along."

Paige waved her hand. "I was just a child. I didn't want to like her because she took my mother's place." She sighed. "I guess she's not so bad. She's the only one who has stuck close to me and hasn't made any demands except that I take care of myself." She shot a meaningful look at Linc.

He reddened under his dark skin, making his face almost a mahogany. "Paige, I am truly sorry. You were right, it was none of my business what you do for a living. But you were wrong about one thing—there is a commitment at least from me. I love you and want to marry you." His deep voice was filled with tenderness.

She gazed at the handsome man who had just proposed to her. He was everything that she wanted and she did love him. Yet she knew he was after her property. "It's not that I don't appreciate all of the help you've given me, but I know that you want my land for your tribe. To you this may seem as simple as me not telling you about my career but to me it goes much deeper."

He sat on the edge of the bed. "I don't want your land, the tribe does. I told them to forget it. I know how you feel about your home and I understand it." He gently placed his hand on her forearm.

"You don't understand. I overheard you speaking with a man at the casino." She remembered the scene and the man good-naturedly punching Linc in the shoulder. She was tired and wanted to go home but she might as well get this over with. "I heard him tell you that you are a real apple." Tears rolled down her face. She turned away from his pleading face. "I'll call Mara to come get me."

Linc placed his hands on her shoulders and gently turned her to him. "My crazy little sweetheart, when one Indian calls another an apple, that isn't a compliment, it's an insult. He was telling me that I am red on the outside but white on the inside. Don't you see? I was defending you and I always will."

"Really? But I thought—"

"Yes, really. And I know what it must have sounded like. But I never encouraged the tribe to go after your land."

Paige smiled into the chocolate eyes she loved so dearly. He was everything she wanted, everything she needed. She decided to take the advice of a good friend and grab Mr. Right. Ignoring her pain she threw her arms around him. "I love you too—and yes, I'll marry you. Yes! Yes! Yes!"

Twelve

Linc followed his grandfather through the field and the woodland path to reach Paige's property. He was glad to have this time of peace so that he could think. In the past few days since Paige's release from the hospital, many things had happened. Too many things, he thought as he glanced ahead at his grandfather's easy but determined gait.

The doctor had called and said Paige had either taken or been given an hallucinogenic drug. And that it had been close to a lethal dose. That explained the accident, but not the who and why. Jack and Mara felt certain it was Ada. Jack had even gone off to New York to investigate the woman.

But suspecting her seemed unreasonable. After all, what did she have to gain? Just in case, they never left Ada alone with Paige. But they didn't make Paige aware of their suspicion because she had enough to worry about. And if they weren't right, why spoil the reconciliation between them? He shook his head. Somehow, they would get to the bottom of it all.

Without realizing it, he had picked up his pace and had come close to running into his grandfather who had stopped. The old man stood quietly scanning the land. Then without speaking, his grandfather began walking again, reading the land, and listening to the earth. Linc followed his grandfather's example. He knew he still had a lot to learn from this sagacious Traditional Man and knew his grandfather would teach him. His grandfather's fine, silver-white hair lifted as a soft warm breeze rolled across the field and rippled the grasses like a wave on the open sea. Linc's heart swelled with love for the gentle old man.

Without speaking, they gathered dry twigs and kindling to make a fire. He watched as his grandfather placed each piece of wood in a specific position. When he was satisfied, he lit the fire.

Amber flame grabbed and licked the twigs, gathering momentum as it consumed the dry wood. Linc watched in admiration as his grandfather scattered the sacred tobacco on the flames and then lowered himself to the ground to begin the meditation.

The Traditional Man began softly speaking, pulling the smoke over his head, purifying his thoughts, invoking spiritual guides. He closed his eyes and deepened his chant. Linc watched, observing not only the man across from him, but trying to be ever alert to all that was around them.

Paige awoke with a start, feeling as if her troubles had been pulled from her. She felt light and free for the first time in a long time. She glanced around the room as if to see what had caused the feeling. Beyond the windows, the early morning sky was orange with the rising sun. Her gaze fell to the chair by the window. Mara was sleeping, her head cocked uncomfortably to one side. Poor Mara. That was no way to get any rest.

Paige reached for her water on the nightstand. Her hand slipped on the moist glass, sending it crashing to the floor. Mara awoke with a start. "Signs of life, I see."

"Almost." Paige smiled at her friend and patted the bed beside her. "Why don't you come over here. It's silly me being in this big bed all by myself and you sitting uncomfortably in that chair."

Mara stretched. "I think I will." She fluffed the pillow and laid her head back. "How are you feeling?" she yawned.

"With my hands." Paige smiled at her best friend.

"It's good to see your sense of humor returning. But I guess you haven't had a lot to laugh about lately."

That was an understatement. Nothing had gone right since her return. And the last two days had been immensely confusing. Although Jack and Linc seemed to be friends, she suspected they were putting on an act for her benefit. They all seemed to dislike Ada. Well, she could understand that; she hadn't liked her either. It was different now. Her stepmother was really trying, constantly coming in and offering to help or stay with her. But for some reason the others wouldn't let her. Paige pulled the blanket over Mara. "You don't have to stay with me. I'm fine, really. Besides, you have a new husband to be with."

Her eyelids heavy, Mara mumbled. "He's gone for a few days."

Paige quirked an eyebrow at her sleepy friend. "What could be so important he had to leave you behind? I mean, you just got married."

Mara giggled and yawned again. "He's on business. He'll be back in a couple of days."

"You still don't need to stay with me. I'm fine," Paige insisted.

Mara patted her friend's hand. "Yes, I do. I have my orders."

Paige watched as Mara's eyelids slipped down. She didn't have to ask who gave the orders; she knew it was Linc. She loved his concern but enough was enough. She was tired of everyone sticking to her like glue. Obviously whoever was trying to hurt her was gone. Everything had settled down, and maybe whatever had gotten into her blood was an accident. She really couldn't remember some of the things that happened after she and Ada went on their trip.

She could hear Mara's even breathing. The house was quiet, save for the birds singing outside. She watched tiny dust particles dance in the early morning sun that streamed through the window.

Paige wanted to walk in the bright sunshine and breathe deeply of the fresh air. She felt as if she was under house arrest. The only thing missing was the unarmed armed guard. She glanced in the direction of her sleeping guard and smiled.

Without making any noise, she quickly dressed and slipped from the house, quiet as a ghost.

A soft breeze whistled through the pines as Paige bounded down the steps, smiling to herself, satisfied with her escape. She drew in the fresh, clean air of the north country and felt vibrantly alive. Her headaches had gone and so had that feeling of malaise.

Her steps drew her closer to her childhood home. She stopped dead in her tracks as an all-too-familiar scent wafted over her. Smoke! She smelled smoke. A fire. Something was burning. Oh, God, not another fire. Please, don't let there be another fire. She quickened her pace but stopped short as she came upon the campfire. Linc and an older man were sitting in front of it. They were speaking in low tones.

Paige crept closer.

"The woman with red hair is responsible for the anguish surrounding this dwelling." The older man spoke with staid calmness.

Linc's eyes grew wide. "Red?"

The older man nodded slowly. "The woman with fire red hair."

Paige held her hand over her mouth to keep from gasping. She didn't know what was going on but she felt somehow this man knew what he was saying. His voice seemed connected to that feeling of well-being she had when she woke this morning. What did he mean the woman with red hair? The only one she knew with red hair was her stepmother. Could he be referring to Ada? How could that be? Ada had only come here to help her. She would not return to this "Godforsaken country," as she called it, for any other reason. She came because she was worried about her. Why would she want to harm her? Even as these questions raced through her mind, she thought the old man must be mistaken. She stared at their backs.

The older man spoke again, "Welcome. I knew you would come. Sit by the fire." He motioned without looking at her.

She quickly surveyed the area around her to see who he was speaking to. The meadow was alive with brightly-colored wild flowers, the freshness of spring, and songs of the birds. But there was no one else, so he must mean her. She moved toward the fire as if compelled by some mystical force.

She lowered herself to the ground and looked into the weather-worn face of the old man who had invited her. Though open, his eyes didn't seem to be looking at anything. Maybe he is blind, she thought. His melodic voice poured over her like a sweet aromatic oil. At this moment she felt better than she had felt in weeks.

She glanced in the direction of Linc. He smiled, his gaze sending her a message of assurance. Why were they here? What were they doing? The feeling it was for a spiritual purpose was confirmed when the old man began reciting beautiful prayers. She didn't speak, afraid she would break the spell. Somehow she knew to interrupt this wise old man would be sacrilege.

"Welcome, Linc's woman with golden eyes," he said to her, placing a callused yet gentle hand on Paige's arm. "You must be careful. Someone is out to harm you. They want what belongs to you."

A cold shiver spiraled down her spine. There was no doubt someone had wanted to harm her. She'd been to the hospital more in the past few weeks than in her whole life. But she had awakened with a feeling of euphoria this morning, so he had to be wrong. But, it could be simply the euphoria of being freed from that prison, she cautioned herself.

"The woman is evil."

Paige was startled from her personal argument by the old man's quiet but insistent pronouncement. She shivered. Was it...could it be...?

Before the old man could say more, a police car came to a stop beyond the clearing. "Miss Turner?" An officer asked as he stepped from the patrol car.

"Yes?" Paige rose, brushing the dust and ashes from her jeans.

"We would like you to come in with us to the station."

Linc placed himself between Paige and the officers. "Are you arresting her?"

The two officers looked at each other. "Just questioning."

Linc placed a protective arm around Paige. "Then I'll bring her to the station."

"But..."

"Unless you are making charges against Miss Turner, I suggest you report to your superior that Miss Turner will be there at a time convenient to both of us."

One of the officers climbed back into the vehicle. Paige could see him talking on the radio. After several minutes he emerged. "Is three o'clock all right?"

Linc glanced at Paige. She nodded. "Fine. We'll be there," Linc said, taking her hand in his. "I'll walk you back to the inn."

"I will stay a while." The couple turned toward the voice that caressed them like a gentle breeze.

"Grandfather, this is the woman with the golden eyes. Paige."

Paige held out her hand. "I'm pleased to meet you."

Linc's grandfather took her hand in his. "I've been waiting to meet you. You and my grandson must make life's flight together. Never part." He patted her hand. "You will be happy. The eagle has spoken."

She nodded. "Will you walk with us to the inn?" she asked, basking in the glow of love beaming from his ebony eyes.

The old man shook his head. "No. I will stay a while. Do not worry about me."

Linc pulled a pouch from his pocket and placed it in the old man's hand. "For you. I'll see you back at the house. Thank you."

They watched as he settled himself by the fire and returned to prayer.

When they were out of earshot, Paige asked, "What was your grandfather doing? It looked like he was praying to the fire. Does he have ESP or something?"

Linc shook his head. "It's funny how years of socialization haven't brought the Native American and the rest of society any closer to understanding each other." He smiled at her. "Grandpa was praying to the Almighty, not the fire. Most Native Americans believe that in the

Universe there exists an Almighty—a spiritual force that is the source of all life." His voice was reverent.

Paige squeezed his hand and gazed into warm brown eyes. "I've got a lot to learn about my soon-to-be husband and his family."

Linc nodded as he led her onto the path to the inn. "And I have much to learn about my soon-to-be wife and her family." He smiled down at her. "What are you doing out here by yourself, anyway?" His eyebrows knit together and the smile faded. "Don't you realize someone is trying to hurt you?"

"Linc, please, I'm not a child. I know, at least now I do. But you guys have been smothering me. I had to get away by myself, to breathe free."

"I know, and believe me, I understand. But I'm afraid for you. You were damn near killed. Whoever is doing these things is still out there. I don't want you alone for one moment."

Paige was thoughtful for a few moments. "You think it's Ada, don't you?"

"Don't you?"

"Kind of, but I don't want to. She's been so kind." But why would Ada want to harm her? "I don't understand this at all. She has no reason to hurt me. She hates Michigan, always has. She couldn't wait to get away when her mother became ill, then refused to return. Why come here and try to hurt me? What's in it for her? I can't imagine that she hates me so much. Actually until she showed up here, I thought she had put me completely out of her mind."

Linc twined his fingers with hers as they walked. "She has red hair, even if it comes from a bottle. Grandfather is never wrong."

Paige smiled. "Ada has always dyed her hair to help her pass for white. But why would she try to harm me? If anything happens to me the property goes to Mara if I don't have children. It's all in my will."

"That's what we're trying to find out."

Paige jerked a glance at Linc. "We? Who is we?"

"Jack and I. We're going to get to the bottom of this."

A smile spread across Paige's face. Maybe they hadn't been acting when they seemed friendly. "Does this mean that the life-long war between the two of you is really over?"

"You might say we've come to an understanding." His gaze searched the area around them. "I suppose Mara told you about the argument Jack and I had the night I brought you home from the Upper Peninsula."

Paige shook her head. "No. Actually, Mara is being a mother hen. She doesn't want to upset me." She scoffed. "I'm not as fragile as everyone seems to think." Now that she had said it aloud, she liked the sound of it. She wasn't weak. She had always believed that of herself but now she knew it wasn't true. She was strong and getting stronger every day.

He laughed. "I know you're not. I just don't want to lose you now that I've found you. And Mara is so damned happy you two are friends again that she is feeling a little protective."

"You couldn't lose me if you wanted to and neither could Mara. I feel bad that I misjudged Jack like I did, but I'll make it up to him." A warm smile lifted her face.

"Speaking of Jack and the argument...it seems that Jack and I have the same father." He dropped the news as if it were a fair weather report.

Paige stopped dead still in her tracks. "No! Is it true? Really?"

Linc nodded. "It's a long story. Remind me to tell you about it sometime."

A look of pleasure spread across Paige's face. Pleasure and satisfaction. "I'm so glad...so glad for you. Now you know about your whole family."

"It will take a little getting used to, but I have a brother and for better or worse, Jack is stuck with me."

She linked her arm through his and walked on. It was good to see him take it so well. "How did you find out?"

"Jack told me. I didn't believe him at first, but my mother confirmed it. Well, actually I did believe him, but I didn't want to."

"I think we can thank Mara for all these changes in Jack. Now the changes in you, I don't know who to contribute that to." She squeezed his arm.

He lowered his head and took her lips with his. The kiss deepened and he pulled her ever closer until she felt as if she might melt into him and become one. The thought shook her. To be one with Linc. To have him caress her skin, to taste her...she flushed just thinking about it.

"I love you, Paige. Nothing can harm you now. I won't let it, I promise."

Still floating with the clouds, she stared into his eyes. Those were easy words to say. She'd heard them before, tossed out like bait. But not from Linc. Never from a man like Linc. "I'm glad you're here. I need you."

"I'll always be here. Forever."

"Forever," she whispered in return. Again, his mouth crushed hers. His hand gently cupped the generous breast beneath her shirt.

He lifted his head and stared deeply into her eyes. "Paige, you must promise me you will be careful. I don't know what I'd do if anything happened to you."

She laid her head against his stalwart shoulder.

He tightened his hold. "I want to make love to you."

She raised her head and stared at him. Before her was the man she wanted. He was wild and free. No one owned him and that made him intoxicating. He was part of the earth, yet separate. His dark eyes quickened with the passion of a hot summer storm, mirroring her own surging emotions.

"Me too," she whispered softly.

No one was at the inn when they entered. A note from Mara on the bulletin board instructed Paige to stay put when she returned. The grandfather clock gently ticked away the seconds as they lightly made their way up the steps to her room. They entered in mutual agreement and she locked the door. Paige turned to the man behind her, the man she loved, the man she was prepared to give herself to.

She could see the flashes of pleasure in his eyes that matched her own. She unbuttoned his shirt, one button at a time, kissing his dark chest after each, until it was bare. She ran her hands over his sinewy muscles. Her lips tasted his skin.

He groaned and pushed his hands under her shirt and slipped it over her head. Under the lace of her bra he could see soft brown nipples pressing to be free. He slipped his hand behind her, reaching for the clasp and expertly slipped the piece of thin lace from her body. He cupped her breast in his hands and moaned in pleasure as he buried his face between the generous mounds. His lips moved up her throat to her mouth. His pants and her jeans soon followed as they pressed together and then apart for a mutual exploration of each other's body.

This was magic. Pure magic. She felt weak and willing with a single kiss. But what a kiss. This was her destiny and always would be.

His hand touched her bare midriff. She jumped as if burned. Burned? She was on fire. Her pulse accelerated, sending fresh blood to the heated area.

"Linc?"

"Umm?" His muffled reply came from lips pressed against the swell of her breast.

It took every ounce of strength to speak as she savored his touch, his smell. "Why are we standing here when there is a bed over there?"

He reached around her, picked her up and walked to the bed. He lowered her onto the comforter, her dark hair fanning out like a halo.

His hand caressed her arm and shoulder. "I love you, Paige Turner."

"I love you too, Lincoln Cross." She pulled him to her, her lips finding his.

"When will we be married?" His gaze probed until it met the depths of her soul.

"Soon. Very soon." This was what she had wanted for a long time. A man who loved her for herself. He didn't want a convenient bed partner or a summer affair. He didn't want to keep it light. He wanted commitment. She could read it all in the open book of his eyes. "The sooner the better."

"Good." His lips moved against her mouth and he laughed a throaty laugh.

All her hopes and dreams were wrapped up in this one man. Fantasies that she never admitted to having, even to herself, were coming to life. She quivered with the desire to surrender to him.

He kissed her tenderly, gently fondling her breasts until their dark peaks were aroused and tight. His mouth followed, his tongue teasing and tasting.

She quivered and writhed beneath his heated touch, a soft moan of desire passing her lips. Her breathing became rapid as she strained to feel him inside her, to become one with the man she loved.

"Easy, sweetheart. We have all afternoon, he murmured."

"Paige, are you in there?" Mara knocked on her door.

Linc and Paige froze, staring at each other.

"Maybe if we're quiet she'll go away," Paige whispered.

They laughed so softly no one could have heard them.

"Paige." Mara tried the door. "Paige...are you all right?" She rattled the handle again.

"I knew I should have taken you away from here," he whispered. "I should have taken you into the quiet wilds and made love to you native style."

Paige stared up at him. "You mean Native Americans make love different from other people?" she giggled.

"They don't do it with an audience." He glared at the door.

It was over. Mara had unwittingly seen to that. Linc flopped beside her on the bed. "Better answer it. She knows you're in here. She'll knock the house down at the rate she's going."

Paige sighed, doused by the cold water of her friend's interruption. She pulled her robe over her naked body and opened the door enough to peer through the crack.

"Paige. I was worried half out of my mind about you. When I woke up you were gone. The police were here a while back and..." She shoved her way in and stopped dead. She glanced at Linc who had barely gotten his pants on and Paige, clutching the robe to her chest.

"Oh, God. I'm sorry." Her hand flew to her mouth. "I didn't know, I had no idea..."

Linc reached down and retrieved his shirt. "Think nothing of it."

Mara didn't embarrass easily, but her face was lobster red at the moment. Paige laughed. "It's all right, really."

Linc pulled his shirt over his naked chest, leaving the buttons open. "I'll be back around two to pick you up." He leaned in to place a kiss on Paige's cheek. "If you take a nap this afternoon, either have Mara with you or lock that door."

Paige nodded. He was right. She would not take any more chances.

Mara wrung her hands together. "Hey, Paige, I'm so sorry. I didn't know. I really didn't." Her voice spilled over in apology.

Paige took her hand in hers. "I know you didn't. And, it's all right, really." But was it? This would have been the first time for her and Linc...a very special first time and it had been ruined.

Thunder and lightning flashed through the churning sky. Paige watched the storm through bars. She was in jail. Horror filled her. She screamed for Linc but he wasn't there.

A faceless woman with red hair walked toward the cell, a pistol in her hand, aiming it right at Paige. She was going to die. Paige screamed and awoke feeling cold and exhausted.

Strange, it was warm yet her skin was cold and icy, making her shiver. She sat up on the bed, running her fingers through her hair. Never in her life had she experienced such disturbing dreams.

Glancing at the clock, she jumped from the bed. She'd shower and change before Linc got there. She dreaded going to the police station. What did they want now? The officer said they weren't going to arrest her so what could it be? Should she call the lawyer? No, she'd wait for Linc. He'd know what to do.

Paige's ears perked as she heard a key turn in the locked door of her room. Her heart pounded painfully against her ribs. She stared at the door as it opened.

"Hello, darling. May I come in?" Ada knocked as she opened the door. "You're all right?"

"Yes." Paige breathed deeply to calm her racing heart. She looked at the older woman and answered, "The doctor says I'm doing fine. But how are you feeling?"

"Much better." That was so silly of me to let my prescription get so low without refilling it. None of this would have happened if I had taken better care of myself."

None of this would have happened if someone hadn't drugged me, Paige wanted to say. But she forced herself to keep calm, to put her best face forward. No sense in alerting Ada of their suspicions.

"Would you like me to get you a nice cup of hot tea or coffee maybe? I can have Emma make one."

Paige shook her head. "No. I'm fine. I'm just waiting for Linc."

Ada sat on the edge of the bed. "I'm moving to that little motel down the road. I'll feel better not being in the way."

She said it in such a way Paige knew she wanted her to ask her to stay. But it would be much better if they were parted. The more distance between them, the better. "You don't have to stay at all. I know how much you hate Michigan and I'm fine now, really."

Hurt flashed in Ada's eyes. "I can't leave you in this mess. What kind of stepmother would I be to do that? What would your father think if he were alive?"

Paige bit back from telling her just what her father would say. He'd have divorced her a long time ago...or at least she liked to think he would have. And then they would have come back to Michigan as a family, without Ada.

"No, really. It's all right. I have Mara and Linc. You can go home. I'm sure you have better things to do than look after me."

Ada stood. "Are you sure? I mean, I'd hate to leave you if you need me."

Paige pasted a smile on her face. "I'm very sure. You go home. I'll be fine, really."

"If you're sure. You know how much I dislike Michigan. But if you need me..."

"No. I'm going to be fine. Linc is going to take care of me."

"Then do you suppose someone could take me to the airport if I can make a connection today?"

"Paige, I..." Mara stopped short and glanced at Paige and then Ada. "Is anything wrong?"

Paige threw her a smile that held a message. "Ada is going home today. We were talking about someone taking her to the airport."

"I can do that," Mara offered a bit too eagerly.

Ada nodded. "Then I'll see if I can make a connection." She closed the door slowly behind her.

"What was that all about?" Mara whispered, her eyes still on the door Ada had disappeared through.

"She's leaving." Paige said simply. She could hardly believe it had been that simple. Ada was leaving.

Mara sat on the edge of the bed, her hands folded in her lap. "I know you think Ada came because she wanted to make up for the years of mistrust between you. And I can't prove that isn't so, but that earring you found and thought was mine?"

"Yes."

"It's hers."

Worry lines crowded Paige's eyes. "How do you know that?"

"She has one just like it in her right ear...the left one is missing."

Paige turned to the dressing table and lifted the lid of her jewelry box. "Here it is." She handed it to Mara. "But she had both earrings in, didn't she?"

"She has two holes in each of her ears. The first holes have earrings. In her second holes, one was missing. I noticed when she had her hair up one day. I got a real good look. This is hers. She was in your room before she called from the airport. Now that tells me she was up to something and I'll bet my life it was no good."

Paige put the earring back in the box and lowered the lid. Why did things have to be this way? She knew in the back of her mind that Ada was trouble. Yet she wanted to believe her stepmother had changed. That night at the Stafford Inn, that must have been she. It was too much of a coincidence to be anything else. It was good she was going.

"Not to change the subject, but what did the police want?"

"They want me to come in for questioning."

"About the fire?"

"I guess so...I don't know." What else could it be but the fire? She closed her eyes. She was so sick of this whole mess. She almost wished she had never come back to her home but then she wouldn't have met Linc.

"I have some good news for you," Mara said. "I think you'll be pleased."

"What?"

"You remember Linc's friend Winona? She called this morning while you were out."

"Oh?" Paige turned to her friend. "What did she have to say? Did she want me to call her back?"

"I don't think so. She wanted to tell you that our agent got her sister, Pazi, an interview with the Ford Agency."

"I knew it!" Paige exclaimed. "When I first saw her I knew she had that certain something that all models have. I'm so glad for her. Did Winona say how she was doing with her designs?"

"She said she was working for some designer as an apprentice and that he liked her work. She said she'd call again soon and to give you her congratulations on your engagement to Linc."

Paige was excited for the young women. She remembered when she and Mara had met on their first shoot. They were so naive and filled with the thrill of it all. She sat down beside her friend. "Mara, I haven't said it before but I am truly sorry for the way I acted when you gave me the news you were married." Mara started to protest but Paige hushed her. "You have always been there for me no matter what, and I am sorry. I think Jack is a wonderful man. And I'll be proud to have him as my brother-in-law."

Mara threw her arms around her best friend. "I probably would have reacted the same way." She stopped for a moment and then held Paige back to look at her. "Do you realize that we will be sisters-in-law?"

The women rolled on the bed laughing like a couple of teenagers. Through her giggles Paige said, "This is what

I've always wanted. Now I'll truly be your sister." She grew sober.

Mara sat up. "What?"

"Nothing. It's just that I need a maid of honor for my wedding."

"And?" Mara questioned pointing at herself.

"And now I'll have to settle for an old, married matron-of-honor."

This couldn't have worked better if they had planned it, Mara thought. She stood and pulled Paige to her feet. "I guess we owe John Devlin a big thank you for his philandering."

"Mara," Paige gasped. "I'm sure it wasn't like that. And if it was, don't let his sons hear you say that."

They fell on the bed laughing again. All was right with their relationship, which was a big load off both their minds. Paige closed her eyes and gave a prayer of thanks. Out of all this adversity something good had come.

Thirteen

"You've been cleared of all charges." The lieutenant dropped some papers in front of her and took his seat behind the messy desk.

Paige released a long sigh. "Just...just like that? It's over?" she asked, afraid to let herself believe it was that easy. After all this time? "But the officer that came to my property said you wanted to question me..."

"Yep. The investigation of the arson is fairly complete. We have another suspect. That's why we needed to question you." You're not under suspicion anymore, but it was still arson."

"So Paige is cleared of all charges? Including the arson and insurance fraud?" Linc stood behind her with his hands tightly gripping her shoulders.

The Lieutenant glanced in Linc's direction and nodded. "Witnesses couldn't give a good description of the woman who put the antiques in storage."

"What color was her hair?" Linc asked.

"They couldn't be sure. She had a scarf on her head and she wore large, dark glasses. We did a picture line-up. Not one of them chose Miss Turner's picture. Anyway the analysis of Miss Turner's handwriting proves she didn't sign the receipt."

"Have you considered her stepmother?" Linc relaxed his grip on her shoulders and took the seat beside her.

"After Judge Devlin called, we did. He lit a fire under a few butts to clear Miss Turner of the arson. Then he informed us that his nephew was going to New York to investigate." He looked at the couple in front of him. "Something better left to the police, I might add." When they didn't respond, he continued. "The Judge also made it clear that all of you think Miss Turner's stepmother is guilty. I can promise you we will investigate every lead."

Paige glanced at Linc and then back at the officer. "She's leaving today. My friend is taking her to the airport." Her gaze shifted to the wall clock. "They've already gone."

"We'll question her one way or another." He wrote something in his notebook. "Another thing. We got your reports from the hospital." He raised his eyebrows. "It seems you either took or were given an hallucinogenic.

Paige nodded. "So I've been told." She stared directly into his eyes. "I didn't take anything deliberately and I have no idea why someone would give me drugs without my knowledge or why someone would try to harm me."

"We've opened an investigation of that too." His full face reddened as frown lines appeared. "It seems the Judge decided you wouldn't take drugs, so someone must be trying to harm you," Lieutenant Jackson groused. "I'll be handling the case personally."

"Thank you." She eyed the Lieutenant. The man obviously was not happy with all of the outside pressure and interference but it wasn't as if she had asked for it. And it wasn't as if the police had treated her very well either—until they had to. This actually felt good. She smiled pleasantly at the ruffled man. "The Judge is right." Paige slipped her hand into her pocket and pulled out the diamond earring. "I don't know if this will help or not, but I found this in my bedroom before Ada, my stepmother, was supposed to be here." She handed the earring to the man whose interest was obviously piqued. "I thought it was my friend Mara's, but it wasn't."

"What makes you think it's your stepmother's?"

"Mara saw one exactly like it in Ada's right ear. The left one was missing."

"May I have this for evidence?"

Paige nodded. "Sure. It doesn't belong to me. Oh and another thing."

The lieutenant continued to scribble in his notebook. "Yes?"

"When I first arrived, Linc took me to dinner at the Stafford Inn. While we were waiting for a table, I could have sworn Ada was on the other side of the hallway. When I took a second look, she had disappeared. I didn't think much about it at the time, I thought she was just a woman who made me think of Ada, but now . . ."

The lieutenant leaned back and tented his fingers in front of him. "Looks like we have some real solid leads here . . ." He stood as if to dismiss them. "I'll get right on it."

"Are you going to arrest her?" Paige pushed, ignoring their dismissal.

The lieutenant opened his office door. "You leave the matter in our hands. If we need you, we'll call."

Paige got out one more question before Linc's gentle but firm tug led her out. "I know you're busy, but there's something I need to know."

"Sure." The officer lifted his eyebrows, waiting impatiently for her to finish.

"What about the insurance on my house . . . the original insurance that I took out?"

He held up his hands. "I can't see any problem there. We'll send a report to your insurance company and in the meantime you call your agent to get the ball rolling."

Paige held out her hand. "Thank you."

He took her hand. "Think nothing of it. It's our job."

"Come on, sweetheart, it's over. It's all over." Linc led her from the station and out into the bright sunny afternoon. "Care to walk with me?"

"Where? The truck's right here."

Linc pulled her close, twining his fingers with hers. "There's something I want to show you."

She smiled up at him. The aroma of his cologne brought her back to this morning before the interruption. "Let me guess." Her voice grew husky. "Is it the same thing you tried to show me this morning?" She ran her finger over his chin and down his chest, stopping at his belt buckle."

Linc held her away from him. "I think you are teasing the fireman." He paused to suck in a deep breath. "We could get arrested if I try to douse that fire right here."

"Well then," she teased in her most sensuous voice, "what do you want to show me, Mr. Fireman."

Linc laughed and spun her away from him. With his hands firmly planted on her shoulders, he said, "March the other way before we end up in trouble, you little siren."

The laughing couple strolled through the streets of Petoskey which were packed with summer tourists milling through the small shops and craft stores. Linc led her onto a path that was a shortcut through Pennsylvania Park to the main street. The park was quiet except for two small children playing while their mother changed a baby in the stroller. "Someday that will be me," she whispered in Linc's ear.

His eyes glowed with the passion of the day. "Not soon enough." His throaty whisper wrapped around her, causing her to shiver.

Paige surveyed the scene as they emerged from the park. Her gaze roamed down Mitchell Street. The city was revamping the buildings and the streets, trying to replicate a turn-of-the century atmosphere. This was the small town she remembered. Smiling faces greeted them as they strolled for the first time as a couple in love with no troubles. New York and the runway seemed so long ago and so very far away. It was as if she had turned into a different person and Paige Turner, fashion model, was now someone else.

"Earth to Paige." Linc gave a hearty laugh and squeezed her hand. "Will you be landing soon?"

She smiled at him, love glistening in her eyes. "I don't know. I love it right where I'm at." She stopped and gazed lovingly into his deep, dark eyes. "I don't know if I'll ever return to New York."

"Don't you want to work anymore?"

She gazed at him, trying to read his thoughts. "Do you want me to?"

"Hey, this is the new century. If you want to work, then you work. I'm behind you whatever you do. I just want us to be together while you do it."

She leaned into him and clutched his arm. "Don't worry about that. I'm never leaving you. Ever."

"Hey, Mr. Cross." A voice came from behind them, followed by pounding footsteps along the brick sidewalk.

Linc turned to the young man coming toward them. "Orin, how are you?" Linc's brows knit together as he scrutinized the man.

"Great. Anxious to go to work. I was wondering if you wanted me to start that job you told me about."

Linc turned to Paige. "This is Orin..."

"Green. Orin Green." A young man about their age, with a dark ruddy complexion and a mop of tight dark curls, filled in.

Linc looked to Paige. "I have been considering Orin to begin removing the debris around your place. It's dangerous being left like that."

"I think that is a great idea. The sooner the better." Her golden eyes danced with the joy in her heart. A thrill ran through Paige. Her house. She was actually going to see some progress. "When can you begin?"

"Paige," Linc said in a commanding voice, "I haven't decided on who will do it yet."

"Orin looks like he could do the job and I do so want to begin."

Linc shot her a stormy glance and then heaved a resigned breath.

"Does that mean I've got the job?" Orin's dark eyes flickered eagerly.

Paige nodded. "Sure. You look like you can do the job." She looked at Linc's face and for the first time noticed the clouds.

"Good." Orin nodded nervously. "Hey, see ya guys later. I gotta go." He rushed down the street at the same pace he'd approached them.

Paige turned to Linc. "I did something wrong?"

He stared at her for a minute and then shook his head. "I haven't run a background check on him." He shoved his hands in his pocket. "There is something about his over-eagerness that hits me wrong. He doesn't look like a man who has worked much. His hands are too soft."

"Oh, Linc, I am so sorry. I just thought—"

"Don't worry about it. I'll get that background check and keep an eye on him until then."

"Next time I'll consult you before we hire someone." She looked at her feet.

"I like the sound of that." He grabbed her hand and began walking.

"The sound of what?" She was walking twice as fast as Linc to keep up with him.

"We. You said, before we hire someone."

She smiled. "I guess I did." It was the first time but it would not be the last. She loved the sound of it, too.

He pulled her to the jewelry store window. "What do you see?"

She looked at him, her heart pounding. "Diamonds."

"Is that what you want?"

"A diamond?" she asked.

He tweaked her nose. "You know what I mean. I want to buy your engagement ring. Do you want a diamond or something else?"

"I do love diamonds, but not too big. I think the large ones look gaudy and fake."

He urged her into the quaint shop. "Then let's see what they have."

They studied the tray of diamonds the clerk brought out.   Paige found the one she wanted and handed it to Linc. He slipped it onto her finger. A perfect fit. The one-karat ring was surrounded by small diamonds. The wedding band fit into the engagement ring and semi-circled the large diamond.

"I like this one." She held up her hand, admiring the rings.

"We'll take this set," Linc told the clerk and turned to Paige. "There, it's official." He slipped the small velvet box with the wedding band into his pocket. "It will be even better when I can slip this on your hand and take you home as Mrs. Cross."

Paige didn't know if it was possible to feel any happier than she did right then but she was anxious to find out. "Let's set the date."

"Is my little siren getting anxious?" he whispered.

She playfully punched him. "No more than my fire-man."

"Five minutes from now would be good." His hot breath scorched her cheek.

She shook her head. "I'd love to, but I've asked Mara to be my matron-of-honor and I can't hurt her again." She gazed into steamy eyes. "One month?"

"Way too long. But you are definitely worth the wait." He looked around and then pulled her into his arms. "Let's go somewhere more private."

"I don't know if you can handle it. It could be a four alarm fire." She laughed lightly as they left the store.

"A fireman is always prepared."

"Isn't that a boy scout?"

"I'll be whatever it takes." He pulled her close as they walked with matched steps back to the truck.

This time Linc took her where no one would find them.

"What is this place?"

"This is my private place, where I can be by myself when I feel the need."

Inside the rustic cabin that held its own charm, a bed stood ready for the lovers. The quiet of the forest hung over the small dwelling as the sun shone orange behind the tall trees silhouetted against the evening's misty sky. Birds sang and the leaves on the trees rustled in a gentle breeze. But it was all lost on the two lovers inside.

He pulled her naked body into the circle of his warm arms. His lips slowly and gently moved over her soft mouth, then down her chin to the pulsating hollow in her throat. Without lifting his lips from her, he lowered them to the soft bed covered with a handmade quilt.

"Mmmm," she moaned. "I've never felt like this before." The words were just barely a whisper.

"That's because you have never been in love with any-one like me," he chuckled. He shifted his weight and covered her like a warm blanket.

The kiss that had at first been gentle, deepened, become passion driven, consuming her, drowning her in his love. Not only her lips burned for him, but her whole body was on fire from wanting him.

His tongue traced her mouth, her jaw, teasing and tasting her. The dance they were about to partake in was one that stemmed from the dawn of time, so primitive it was buried deep within and erupted like a gushing volcano.

"I love you," she whispered, arching against him, needing him, wanting him more than life itself.

"No more than I love you." He kissed her mouth again, his hand tenderly caressing her breast and marble-hard nipple.

She gasped as his hand lowered between her legs, writhing at his touch, aching for him as an all-consuming fire threatened to devour her.

She in return traced the sinewy muscles of his chest, delighting in his gasp of desire. His hands moved against her, igniting a hot flame that spread throughout her being. She felt his urgent need as he plunged deep within her. Together they rode the waves of passion that lifted them from earth and took them to a place where only lovers dance. Slowly drifting back to earth, they lay enveloped in each other's embrace and drifted into a peaceful sleep.

"Will you stand still?" Mara turned Paige in front of the mirror. "How can I get this to fit right with you fidgeting. I think you've lost a little weight."

In the week since Ada had left, Paige had been cleared by the police, and Linc and she were going to be married in less than a month. Tonight was to be her engagement party. Could anything be more perfect? Nothing could spoil this...nothing.

She couldn't believe that everything was turning out so perfectly. Her heart still squeezed at the thought that Ada could be at the bottom of all her problems. She'd never gotten along with her stepmother, but she didn't want to think Ada hated her that much. After all, her visit had been one of concern and kindness. Maybe the police investigation would prove who the guilty person really was.

She was pulled from her thoughts by Mara's statement and said, "More than a little, I'd say." She could remember a time when the only important thing in her life was her weight and her race. Ada had made sure it overshadowed everything. Now it wasn't worth thinking of, except of course that she couldn't wear her clothes. "I can't wear this. It's too big." She shrugged from the black cocktail dress she had considered wearing when she met Linc's mother. She threw it on the bed.

"What else have you got in here?" Mara flipped through the dresses hanging in the closet. "God, girl, you brought nothing but simple country things. Wait right here. Don't go away." She rushed from the room.

Now just where did Mara think she'd go in her satin undies? She glanced at her reflection in the mirror. Mara had done wonders with her hair. She'd pulled it atop her head in a wild, casual style.

"Here we go." Mara came back with a cream, beaded sleeveless evening gown made of a woven knit and an ivory silk crepe, jacquard cape. She laid the cape on the bed. ..ry this on. You've always been a little smaller than me and this has always been too tight." She slipped it over Paige's head.

"Then why did you bring it with you?"

"You know me. I bring everything I own."

It had been a long time since Paige had been in a designer gown. She'd forgotten how good she looked.

The plunging neckline showed perfectly her generous cleavage. The gown smoothly fell over her hips and clung to her shapely, rounded bottom. She moved across the floor listening to her dress as it whispered against the hardwood floor. Mara held the cape as Paige slipped her arms in and let it fall off her shoulders. Twirling in front of the long mirror she gasped, "It's beautiful. Linc will love it."

"Girlfriend, there isn't anyone who won't think you are drop dead gorgeous. Of course, they always do." Mara turned her around. "You never looked better." She went to Paige's jewelry box. "Now a little jewelry, not much but...how about this?" She held up a simple gold chain. "Just the right touch, huh?" She clasped it around Paige's neck. "Simple but beautiful."

Paige glanced in the mirror. "Oh, quit. You're only saying it because it's true." They giggled, and it was like old times.

"Now, I've got to get ready and see that Jack dresses properly." Mara left Paige alone.

The engagement party had been Mara's idea, not that Paige minded. A girl hopefully becomes engaged only once and the occasion deserved a party. It was to be a small, intimate affair with family and close friends.

"Stop daydreaming and come on, your guests are waiting." Mara rushed in, still fastening the earring through her ear. "If we don't get down there, Linc will think you are having second thoughts about marrying him."

"Wow, who are you trying to impress?" Paige ran her gaze over the short, black silk dress that plunged to the navel in front and to the waist in the back.

Mara whirled around. "Like it?"

"Does it matter what I like? I'm sure Jack will love it. Has he seen it yet?"

Mara glanced in the mirror, pulling wisps of her hair free from its high knot to frame her face. "No, but he will." She threw a long black and silver fringed scarf around her neck and arranged the ends down either side of her back. The scarf reached to her diamond studded ankle bracelet but it was purely decorative, it concealed nothing.

Paige was a little nervous. Nervous? Hell, she felt like the first time on the runway in front of the most prestigious fashion designers. Only this time it was Linc's mother she'd be parading for. She hadn't seen her since that disastrous dinner party. What was she going to say to her? How should she act?

"Come on!" Mara grabbed her arm and urged her toward the stairs.

"Here comes the bride!" Mara sang out in her loud New York voice.

Linc stood at the bottom of the staircase, his hand on the newel post, his dark eyes flashing with love, admiration and approval. He mouthed the words, "I love you."

Strains of soft romantic music drifted through the house. The room buzzed with people, but she only had eyes for the man waiting for her. Linc with his ebony hair carelessly spilling onto his forehead, his cocoa eyes telling her many things and those marvelous lips moving, declaring his love for her.

His double-breasted black suit made him even more handsome than she could have imagined. The white shirt and black and white tie accentuated his mahogany skin. If anyone in the room made a fashion statement, he did. Her heart throbbed against her rib cage.

He held out his hand and she slipped hers into it. "You're beautiful," he whispered. "I don't know if I can stay here all evening and keep my hands where they belong."

"You're not so bad yourself," she said, her saucy voice dripping with innuendo. "I don't think I want you to keep your hands where they belong."

"Mmmm." He pulled her close.

Private laughter bonded them as they joined their friends and family in the large living room. Flowers filled every unoccupied space, infusing the room with mingled, delicate fragrances. Gold and white streamers hung from the ceiling, while color-coordinated balloons swayed in the breeze.

Paige blinked in surprise as someone popped from behind a balloon tree. "Winona. What a surprise!" She hugged the girl.

"I had to come back. Nuna told me about the party and I didn't want to miss it."

"I'm glad you didn't. It wouldn't have been a party without you and..." She looked around. "Didn't your sister come with you?"

"No, Pazi is on a shoot, but she sends her best. Since I had some spare time, I came for the both of us."

"This is wonderful." Paige glanced around the room. Jack and Mara were there of course. Nuna was there too, and looking strangely out of place and uneasy. "I'll talk to you later." She stepped across the room.

"I'm so glad you came." Paige held out her hand. "It means so much to me and of course even more to Linc."

Nuna took her hand. "I wouldn't miss it. And I hope you are very happy."

Paige felt something stirring between them. "I know you wanted something else for your son, but we love each other. I want you to know I love him with all my heart and will do all in my power to make him happy."

Nuna smiled. "I know you will. Welcome to our family." She squeezed Paige's hand.

Paige knew she had gained a new friend and ally. Nuna had accepted her and that made her life complete. She glanced around. "Didn't your father come?"

Nuna shook her head. "No, he returned to the reservation. He only came to help you and Linc. He doesn't like to leave often."

"We'll just have to go to him often then." Paige's smile warmed thinking of him.

"He's here in spirit," Nuna said gently. "I'm glad you've been cleared of the arson charges. Linc has lost a lot of sleep worrying over it."

"Thank you. It has been a bad time."

"It's over now. You and Linc can get on with your lives without anything hanging over your head."

Paige reached out and hugged Nuna. "I want us to be friends, really friends."

"We will," Nuna said in a voice that told Paige she had made a friend. "We will."

"I guess I should mingle." Paige excused herself as Winona came their way.

"Happy?" Linc joined her as she made her way around the room, placing his arm around her waist.

"Uh-huh," she sighed.

"Are we going to let all that music go to waste?" He gathered her in his arms and swept her across the room. "You feel good," he whispered into her hair.

Paige closed her eyes and let him guide her to the music. His very nearness intoxicated her. She tried to listen to the music to avoid leading him to her room right this minute. She recognized the song, "Unchained Melody"; the same song that played on their first date, when he had held her so closely on the veranda.

"Did you arrange the music?" she teased.

"Did you think I'd forget?" He peered into the depths of her dark, liquid eyes.

"I'll sing that song long after I've gone to bed," she whispered.

"I'm not going to let you go to bed alone tonight." His words drifted through the spell that had been weaving.

"I didn't expect you to." She molded her body to his. The tinkling of a crystal bell and Emma's voice broke in on their mood. "Dinner will be served when the honored couple take their seats at the dining table."

They looked around and saw they were the only ones still dancing. The others had gone to the dining room. Sheepishly they followed Emma to the room where everyone sat waiting. They slid into their seats at the head of the brightly-decorated table and glanced in Jack's direction.

Jack stood beside his chair, a bottle of champagne in his hand. "To the happy couple. May their wedding day be blessed with the happiness Mara and I share." He filled Paige's flute first, then Linc's.

"To Paige and Linc." Jack beamed.

"Hear, hear," the guests chimed in unison.

The glowing couple gazed into each other's eyes, twined their arms and sipped the bubbly. "To us, sweetheart. To us, forever." Linc spoke, barely able to bring his voice above a whisper.

Everyone clapped as Emma brought in a large turkey on a cart with all the fixings.

"It's like Thanksgiving," Mara exclaimed, her hands clasped together gleefully.

Emma's face reddened, unaccustomed to the attention. She spoke to everyone but directed her speech to the couple. "Paige said she hadn't had a home-cooked Thanksgiving meal since she could remember. So this is for you." She placed the first piece of turkey breast on Paige's plate.

"You see?" Linc kissed her cheek. "Everyone loves you. Who else gets Thanksgiving in June?"

"I hope you do," she whispered. The roses in her cheeks deepened as she flashed him a playful glance. She looked up at the woman who had served dinner. "Emma, thank you but you are an invited guest. Why—"

Emma stopped her. "I didn't want all those strangers in my kitchen." Everyone laughed and dug into the wonderful meal that had been prepared with loving hands.

With everyone busy, Linc found a second to respond to Paige's whispered hope. "I hope I do too." Their gaze met and held. Slowly his lips found hers, kissing her hard and deep, his tongue teasing her lips, forgetting the crowd of people at the party. "Every day with you will be a holiday," he whispered against her mouth.

"Okay, you two. You're at the dinner table, remember that," Jack admonished, producing laughter from everyone as he leaned toward Mara, giving her a kiss as well.

The meal was one that produced warm, family feelings. Paige felt at home, with family for the first time in a very long time. She never wanted to leave. She wasn't going to ever leave, not without Linc.

After dinner Linc took Paige into the living room. "Here is my engagement present to you." He handed her a thick envelope. "If you don't like it, we can change it."

"What?" Her fingers fumbled with the sealed flap. She drew out the papers and unfolded them. She gazed at Linc. "It's a contract...a building contract."

"For your house. The builders are prepared to start whenever you give the word."

She gazed at him. She had been told by most builders that it would take months to begin construction. Their good building season was short and they were booked. Somehow he had pulled strings and now she would have her dream come true. "Our house...if you're interested." Her voice strangled with emotion.

"Interested?" He pulled her into his arms. "Just try to keep me away."

Everyone applauded the happy couple. Their struggle to be together had been met and dealt with. Now the glowing years lay ahead of them. Linc pulled her into his arms and glided onto the floor. "Remember this. Whatever is right for you, is right for me. We'll fill our new house with love and happiness. And children, lots of children." They moved around the floor lost in mutual silent musings. Linc's beeper startled them both. He read it and whispered, "I'll be right back. Hold my place for me." He brushed her mouth with his and then walked quickly to the phone in the hall.

Others had heard the beeper and watched as he made his way to the phone. "Who could that be? Anyone of importance is already here." Jack laughed at his own joke.

Linc stepped back into the room. "Sorry, folks. There's a fire. I have to go."

"Oh, no," Paige cried. "Not tonight." She prayed their life wouldn't be wrought with one crisis after another.

"Sorry, love. The fire's right in the middle of town—and it's threatening other businesses."

Paige knew he was right. He had been there when she'd lost her home and he would be there for others. That was the kind of man he was. And she loved him for it.

He bent to kiss her good-bye. She wrapped her arms around his neck. "Be careful," she whispered. "I'll be waiting."

"I'm coming with you." Jack jumped to his feet and kissed Mara goodbye.

"You be careful, too," Mara called as he disappeared through the door, following Linc.

Paige wasn't going to let this mar her happiness. The party had been a good one, even if it had broken up early because of the fire. She would have to get used to her husband's civic duties. She recalled her childhood, when her father had done the same thing. He had told her that in a small town everyone had to pull together if they were all to survive.

Paige, Mara, and Emma busied themselves cleaning up. It gave them something to do while they waited for the guys to return.

"I don't know about you, but I'm beat." Mara yawned. "It's been a big day."

"You go up to bed. I'll wait down here for a little while."

"Are you sure?" She moved to the stairway. "I think I'll get a shower and wait for Jack."

Paige nodded. "I'm sure. And I'll wait down here for Linc."

The inn was quiet. All of the guests were in their rooms and Emma had retired when the cleaning was finished. A soft breeze moved through the pines outside and ruffled the gauzy curtains at the open window.

The night called Paige outside. She shoved open the patio door and stepped out onto the porch.

A car pulled into the drive. Orin Greene emerged. "Miss Turner?" His excited voice alarmed her.

"Yes," she answered urgently.

"Mr. Cross sent me for you. He's been hurt."

Paige gasped and her hand flew to her mouth. "Oh, sweet Jesus, no."

"He asked me to bring you to him right away."

She didn't think of her evening gown or the high heels on her feet. All she thought about was Linc. Don't let it be serious. Please, God, don't let him die.

Orin opened the door and Paige slipped into the passenger side of the car. He jumped under the steering wheel, backing the car out at breakneck speed.

"Care for a drink?" He pulled out a flask.

"No, thank you." She glanced at him, thinking that was an odd thing to offer—but then she knew some thought alcohol should be used in times like this.

"Thought you might like something to calm you down." He raced the car through Harbor Springs, hardly slowing for the residential section.

"How badly hurt is Linc? Is he burned?"

"I don't rightly know."

What did he know? "Are you a volunteer fireman too?" she asked. What had he been doing at the fire if he wasn't? "Where are we going?" She looked back at the disappearing highway as he turned onto a dirt road. Something wasn't right. Prickles of fear swished across the back of her neck.

"To the fire. It's just down the road a piece." He rounded several curves and came to a secondary paved road heading north along the shore.

"Is he hurt badly?" she prodded. "Why wasn't he taken to the hospital?" Every nerve in her body was on the alert. If Orin wasn't taking her to Linc, then where? She peered into the darkness, wildly searching her surroundings.

He didn't answer her as he offered her the flask a second time. "Better take a drink. It will calm your nerves."

Paige shook her head. She didn't need a drink, she needed to be with Linc. "I don't see any smoke or flames. How far away is this fire. I thought Linc said it was in the middle of town." Her voice cracked.

She watched as Orin turned the truck down a dark road. She peered through the dimness at Orin. Was it her imagination, or was there a sinister glint in his eye? There was no fire, no Linc. Ahead she saw a cabin with a faint light in the small window.

"Okay, we'll have to do this the hard way." He braked and pulled a syringe from his pocket, then plunged it into her arm before she could fight him off.

She grabbed her arm, her eyes grew wide with realization. "What are you doing?" she screamed, reaching for the door. She couldn't find the handle. "Where are you taking me?" Her eyes began to blur, her head whirled, then nothing.

Fourteen

Paige fought to gain consciousness. Her head throbbed and nausea muddled her thoughts. Where was she? She tried to force her eyes open, to focus, but she was so tired, her lids so heavy. The nausea intensified and she was afraid she was going to be sick.

Slowly she raised her head and compelled her eyes to open. Darkness enveloped her, she couldn't see a thing. When she moved she could hear wire springs straining against each other. She knew she was on some kind of bed or cot. Her hands were tied above her head and her feet were bound. Her mouth—she wasn't gagged. Maybe she could scream. No, she thought, then he would know she was conscious.

He? In her mind's eye she could see Orin's dark, craggy face as he turned toward her to plunge the needle into her arm. His eyes had been void of emotion. His mouth had twisted in an angry sneer. Why? He had told her that Linc was injured. She'd gone with him willingly. Gone where? He had taken her for a long ride on a bumpy road, to a cabin in the woods. She flinched as she remembered the pain of the needle as it went into her arm. Her arm still ached at the spot. What was happening?

"Linc?" she whispered into the night. No answer. She was alone in forced captivity. She tried to raise herself to a sitting position. Dizziness spun her head, forcing her to lie still on the musty-smelling cot.

Orin. Orin had done this. Who was he? What did he want? Where was Linc? Oh God, Linc. She prayed he wasn't injured. She prayed he would come for her. A tear escaped and rolled down the side of her cheek.

The hot air was rank with musty odors. As her eyes grew accustomed to the dark she slowly moved her head, surveying her surroundings. Her eyes weren't focusing well but she could make out the dim outline of a door. Faint traces of moonlight filtered around a window that had been crudely covered. She closed her eyes.

How long she lay drifting between two worlds, she had no idea. A noise brought her alert. Her eyes popped wide open and her heart pounded loudly. She held her breath to quiet the runaway pump in her chest. She'd heard something. What? She listened, alert for any movement. There it was again. She strained to listen. Was someone in this crude place with her? Was it Orin?

The door flew open, slamming against the wall. Footsteps pounded loudly on the rough floor. A light flashed in her face, blinding her. She flinched at the pain and turned her head away.

"You're awake, I see." It was Orin's threatening voice.

Paige squinted her eyes. "Why?"

Orin laughed. "You'll find out in time."

"Linc?" she questioned, fearing the answer.

Again Orin laughed. "Probably out looking for you. But he ain't never gonna find you. We got you hid real good. And don't try screamin' either. It ain't gonna do you no good. Ain't nobody around to hear ya anyway."

Her mind whirled. "We?"

"Yeah, we," he said without giving her an answer.

"Why, Orin? What did I ever do to you?"

Someone entered the room behind Orin. "Enough said."

"What? I wasn't saying anything. Besides, who's she gonna tell?"

Ada! She could never mistake that voice. Linc, Mara and Jack had been right. Until this moment she had held a slim hope that everyone had been wrong.

Ada walked into the dark room carrying a lit kerosene lantern. She leaned over the bed. "So, how does the little princess feel now?" she scorned. Paige had heard that same ridicule when she was a child. She had cowered from it then and the same youthful fear gripped her heart now.

The older woman scoffed. "Not so good, I'll bet."

Paige pulled on her reserve strength. She knew it wouldn't do any good to cry. Not with Ada. "Why?"

"Because you were too damned stubborn to die in that car crash or when I pushed you into that cellar. Damn, but you're a stubborn one. So, I have to make sure of it this time."

Orin grabbed Ada's arm. "Hey, you ain't gonna kill her are ya? You said..."

Orin quickly removed his hand under her burning glare.

"I know what I said. Still, she has to be dead before you can inherit. It's that simple."

Inherit? What in God's name was she talking about? Inherit what? Everything I own goes to Mara.

"You can't do this. You'll end up in jail for the rest of your life."

"Oh, my darling daughter, I am in New York at a play." Her eyes gleamed with pleasure. "That bag lady was more than happy to have my clothes and sit in my seat. And I've actually done something humane. She got a new outfit and a night out of the weather."

"Linc will be looking for me." Her heart was choking at her throat but she knew she had to say something.

"He'll never find you. But Orin will find Linc. When he does, he'll tell him that you had a terrible accident. He'll come running to you." She sighed. "Isn't love wonderful." She flicked an imaginary piece of lint from her slacks. "Then we'll have you both! When the police find you, you'll both have had a terrible accident." She reached out and smoothed back Paige's tangled hair. "Poor Paige, poor Linc. What a tragedy that car accident was that took their lives just before their wedding."

Paige jerked her head away.

"Tsk, tsk. I don't understand your attitude. So ungrateful. We're letting the two of you go together. We'd never think of separating you," she mocked.

"The police are investigating you," Paige said. "They'll know what you've done. If anything happens to me, they'll know it was you."

"Maybe, but they won't be able to prove it," Ada answered.

God, she prayed. Please let me free. Don't let them get to Linc. Don't let them hurt him. Please, if you've ever heard me, hear me now. She tugged at the ropes. She held her breath, not knowing what to say next.

Ada filled the void. "I can see you are concerned for my well-being, but don't worry your pretty little head. Or should I say big head. Whatever." She waved her hand carelessly in the air. "The police don't bother me. They don't know as much as they think they do," Ada boasted.

"Why do you hate me so? What did I ever do to you?" Paige decided if she was going to die anyway she should know why. And maybe she could keep her stepmother talking long enough to undo the ropes or maybe—just maybe—Linc would find her in time.

"Light the other lantern, Orin. Let me tell the little princess a thing or two." She pulled a tattered, over-stuffed chair close to the cot. "What did you ever do? First of all, you were born."

God, she really hates me, Paige thought. "I was born?"

"Yes, you were born. You thought your dad was such a wonderful, loving husband and father. I was your father's lover. Your mother wasn't much of a wife to him, sickly all the time. He had to have a woman, most men do, you know. I gave him the pleasure your mother couldn't."

"I don't believe you," Paige spat, sickened by the suggestion.

Ada shrugged. "I don't care if you believe me or not. People in town thought I was just the nurse he hired to take care of your mother, but I was your father's lover for many years. He paid for my apartment and my keep."

Paige shook her head, fighting back the sob that threatened to escape from her throat. She knew it wasn't true. It couldn't be. But it was painful to hear.

"Oh yes. That's exactly what happened! What your mother needed was a nursemaid, not a husband. She was so sick it's a wonder she gave him a child at all. It was a surprise when she had you. She almost died then." She drew in a deep breath before she continued. "You don't know how hard I prayed to God she would die and free your father and me. But God must have had been very busy then, because she lived. For twelve more years she lived, making all our lives miserable with her constant demanding, complaining, and whining."

Paige flinched at the harsh words more severe than a slap. Ada seemed to believe everything she was saying, but there had to be a logical explanation. Paige shivered, perspiration beading on her forehead and upper lip. There had to be a way out of here. There had to be. She eyed the irrational woman. As much as she didn't want to hear anymore—she needed to buy time.

"If what you say is true, what does this have to do with me? He married you, didn't he? You got what you wanted."

"Oh, yeah, he married me all right. But instead of your mother in my way, you were there. His little fat princess got all his attention. God is finally answering my prayers. I wanted to get rid of you a long time ago but I didn't have the guts. Years of watching your father fawn over you and then the fashion world, made me realize that I could do it. Yes, I can do it now. For my son, I can do it now."

Paige glanced up at Orin. "Your son?"

"Yes, my son. Fate has a way of playing dirty tricks on people. I was so happy when I found out I was pregnant and so was your father. I was finally going to give him the one thing your mother couldn't. But that was short-lived, your mother saw to that. In a few months she spoiled my happiness by announcing she was pregnant. I could have killed her then."

"What are you saying?"

"Just what you're thinking. Orin here is your half-brother."

"I don't believe you." Paige choked out the words.

Ada shrugged. "Who cares. It's true."

"It's not true. Dad would have told me."

"Oh?" Ada sneered, and cocked her head to one side, clicking her tongue. "So, daddy would have told the little princess he had a son by his mistress?" Her words were edged with hate. "He wouldn't let me bring Orin with us when he married me. That was one stipulation to our marriage. Orin had to go live with my sister in New York and I was never to mention him to you. Oh, yes, he protected his little princess. Well, let's see him protect you now."

Paige felt sick. In fact, she was going to be sick. She leaned her head over the side of the cot and wretched, her wrists straining against the ropes that held her to the bed.

Ada shoved the chair back and jumped up. "Get me the syringe from my purse," she ordered Orin.

She removed the cap from the needle and snapped the ampoule with her thumb. "This should keep her quiet for a few hours."

Paige was horror-stricken. She didn't want to be unconscious or worse yet, dead. She stared at her stepmother.

"Don't worry," Ada said as she drew the liquid into the syringe, "it's only amobarbital. It won't kill you, just keep you knocked out for awhile." As she was about to plunge the needle into Paige's arm, Paige thrashed, pulling out of Ada's one-handed grip. "Hold her still," Ada ordered.

Orin clamped his hands on her arm and held her fast as Ada drove the needle into her soft flesh.

Paige moaned in pain and prayed she could fight the effects of the drug.

"Hurt, did it?" Ada mocked.

Anger and hatred exploded along Paige's veins. Hatred toward her stepmother, hatred for Orin who Ada had proclaimed to be her flesh and blood.

"Why? Why now?"

"Because Orin is going to come into your inheritance."

Paige had a hard time focusing, concentrating on what Ada was saying. "Inheritance? What inheritance?"

"You really don't know, do you? I asked your father not to tell you, but to arrange it with his lawyer, not to let you know until your thirtieth birthday."

"What?"

"That invention of his, that pipe-thawing device he worked on in the shop? He patented it and sold it for a small fortune. He put it all in trust for you on your thirtieth birthday. Well, since you won't be around to collect, your brother will. He'll finally get what's his by right as first-born. He is not only first-born, but your father's son, his only son."

"Come on, Ada, we got things to get done," Orin hesitantly interrupted.

Ada and Orin left the room, taking the lamp with them. The door failed to latch properly and swung partially open. Paige could hear them laughing. They were only fuzzy figures. Her eyes closed.

She jerked them open and watched Orin sprawl in the chair. Ada moved toward Orin and then looked in at Paige as she pushed the door closed.

Paige twisted and fought the ropes for as long as she could, burning her flesh before the drug finally did its work. Slowly, slowly she was pulled toward a deep black chasm. "Linc," she murmured as she was swallowed by darkness.

"Paige?" Linc called when she wasn't in her room. The bed hadn't been slept in either. He looked in the bathroom. Nothing.

He bounded down the stairs and searched through the house. Where could she be this time of night? He looked outside, front and back. She was nowhere to be found. Surely she wouldn't go off walking this time of night. He raced back up the stairs.

"Something wrong? I heard you calling." Jack came into the hall, still wet from his shower, pulling a green robe around him.

"I can't find Paige. Does Mara know where she is?"

"Can't find Paige?" He turned to the bedroom door. "Hon, have you seen Paige?"

"No," Mara's voice filtered into the hall. "Why?"

"She's not here."

Mara stood beside Jack in a matching robe. "She said she was going to wait for you. She was downstairs the last I knew." Mara pushed her heavy mane of hair from her face.

"That's strange. Her car is here."

"She was so adamant about waiting for you to return. What could have happened?" Anxiety grew in her voice.

"You heard nothing?" Linc asked.

Mara shook her head. "No, nothing."

Mara rushed toward Paige's room and thrust open the door, flipping the switch for the overhead light. Her gaze flew over the neatly made bed. "Did you check downstairs and outdoors."

He nodded. Worry lines gathered over his brow.

Mara picked up the ivory jacket she'd lent to Paige, which had been too warm to wear. She thrust open the closet and began searching. "The dress isn't here."

"What dress?" Linc asked.

"The dress I lent her for the engagement party. It isn't here." She whirled around, searching. She grabbed the ivory cape and gasped as she held up Paige's purse. "She never goes anywhere without this and her phone." She held out the purse.

"Then she's still in the evening dress." He was trying to think. Understand what this meant.

"That's my guess."

"Shoes. What kind of shoes was she wearing?"

Mara looked in the closet again. "Ivory satin pumps. And they're gone. She must still be wearing them."

Linc turned to Jack. "She couldn't have walked very far in those."

Jack ran his fingers through his wet hair, pushing it back from his forehead. "Maybe Emma heard something."

Linc and Mara followed Jack down the back stairs to the kitchen. Jack lightly tapped on Emma's room. "Emma, are you awake?"

"Jack?" She opened the door, sleep written across her face.

"Have you seen Paige?"

"Paige? No, not since she said she was going to wait on the porch for Linc to return, why?"

"She's missing."

Emma frowned. "Missing?"

"She's not here and her bed's not been slept in."

Emma came into the kitchen, closing the bedroom door behind her, tying the belt of her robe. "I don't understand. She wanted to wait for Linc. Where could she have gone?"

"I'm going to call the police." Linc lifted the wall phone.

Jack reached out and stayed his hand. "Now don't be so hasty. You know you can't get the police to do anything when a private citizen calls in. To get real action, you have to be influential."

"Jesus, man, I can't fool around. I've got to find her. She might be hurt someplace." Linc grabbed the phone from Jack.

"I know, but we have to go where we can get help. If I call my Uncle Richard...our Uncle Richard, he may help us by cutting through a lot of red tape."

Linc's face brightened. "Good idea!" He handed Jack the phone.

Jack made the call, describing the situation to Richard Devlin. "He promised to make a few calls and see what he could come up with. Then he's coming here."

Mara's voice quivered. "Paige has been through enough already."

Jack slipped his arm around her as she rested her head against his shoulder. "Yes, sweetheart, she has. And we're going to find her just as soon as we can. Uncle Richard can move the police a little faster than we can."

She pushed her head into his chest. "Maybe she just went for a walk."

"I feel so helpless. Damn, I should be able to find her." Linc stood in the middle of the room, feeling empty and alone. Could she have gone to her property? "I'm going out to her property. She's been so damned anxious to get the building underway that she's been over there almost every day. You know how she feels about the place. And I did give her the bid and proposal on the new house tonight." With a hopeful glance at Jack, he rushed out the door.

It didn't take him long to reach the house site.

"Paige, are you here?"

Nothing but the tranquil sounds of night answered him. He used his flashlight and looked into the burnt-out cellar where he'd once found her. Thank the Almighty Spirits, she wasn't there this time. But where the hell was she?

Linc closed his eyes, gathering in his thoughts. If he could clear his mind, he might be able to feel something, anything.

He walked back to his truck. What had he expected? He wasn't his grandfather. He wasn't wise enough, or pure enough. Sometimes he felt like the apple his friend had accused him of being. He ran to his truck and sped back to the inn.

❊ ❊ ❊

"Heard anything?" Linc asked as he entered the kitchen by the back door.

Jack shook his head and poured some freshly brewed coffee from the carafe. "Have some. You look like you need it."

Linc took the cup and turned as the sound of a car slowed and pulled into the drive.

Jack opened the door and anxiously stood waiting. "Uncle Richard, come in." He almost pulled the older man into the house. "You know Linc."

Richard Devlin reached out his hand, switching the manila folder he carried to his left hand. "Yes, I know you, son."

"It's good to meet you, sir." Linc studied his father's brother as if seeing him for the first time. "I'd appreciate any help you can give us."

The judge nodded, smiling warmly at his nephews. "I've contacted the police. They are out looking. Meantime, let's all sit down and get to the bottom of this thing." Richard took the seat at the head of the kitchen table. "Jack asked me a few days ago to inquire into Ada Turner's, shall we say, business dealings. I had to call in a few markers but the investigation proved fruitful."

"What?" the trio urged in unison.

Richard shook his head. "She's a nasty one. She is one of those women who began living off men from the time she could use her womanly charms to attract them."

Mara moaned and laid her head in her hands.

"So I ran a complete background check," Richard continued. "This has been one busy lady. She had been married twice by the time she got to Joseph Turner, and twice since. She always used the scam of getting pregnant even if she wasn't. She got the man to marry her or pay her to disappear so as not to cause a scandal for the family involved. She was quite successful at it until she got a little older. Then it didn't work quite so well."

"Paige never liked or trusted Ada. She should have trusted her first instincts; she was right," Mara said softly. "I wondered why Ada came to Michigan when Paige got hurt. It didn't make any sense to me. It still doesn't."

"Hear me out. It will make sense." Richard replied. "Ada was the first Mrs. Turner's nurse. She hated waiting for Paige's mother to die, some say she helped her along. But that's never been proven. Shortly after the funeral she had moved in, lock, stock and barrel, under the pretense of taking care of Paige.

She knew Joseph was on to something with this invention of his, some kind of pipe thawer for professional plumbers. Anyway, when he sold it to a large corporation for a small fortune, she moved in for the kill. He had just lost his wife and he was vulnerable. She convinced him that Paige needed a mother. Her. Ada thought she was going to cash in on all that money. Joseph was a little smarter than she thought. He placed most of the money in trust for Paige. When Paige turns thirty, she will be a very wealthy woman."

Mara sat straight. "But...this doesn't make any sense. If anything happens to Paige, I inherit from her and if anything happens to me, Paige inherits from me. How does this do Ada any good?"

Richard pulled a paper from the back of the file. "According to my sources, and believe me, they're very reliable, Ada conned Joseph into signing a codicil that stated, should anything happen to Paige, the money from the invention goes to Ada. She was there when he invented it and even helped get it patented. She used that to get him to rewrite that portion of the will."

"Oh, my God." Mara gasped. "Then Paige could be in real trouble."

Linc slumped back in his chair. "This is all very informative, but it isn't helping us find Paige."

Richard tilted his head. "Not so fast, son. I smell Ada all over this disappearance."

Mara leaned forward. "But I put Ada on the plane myself. I watched her fly out of Pellston."

"Maybe...maybe not," Richard said. "Ada is an expert at fooling people. She may have flown out of here, but did she stay gone?"

Mara frowned. "I don't know. I never thought about that."

"I picked up another little tidbit of information. I don't know if it means anything or not, but she's gotten herself a young lover."

Linc felt a chill. "A young lover, you say?"

"Yes, unsavory young chap with a record as long as your arm. Been in and out of trouble with the law since he was about eight years old. Strange thing is, he came to Michigan with her."

Now Linc did feel weary. He felt hopeful when he thought it might be Ada alone. After all, Paige was no wimp, she'd be able to outwit and out-muscle the older woman. "What does this guy look like?"

Richard opened the folder he had carried in with him. "A friend of mine faxed me this photo of him." He handed the black and white picture to Linc.

"Damn it!" Linc jumped to his feet. "This is Orin Greene."

"Who is Orin Greene?" Jack reached for the picture.

"The guy I hired to clear the debris from Paige's place. He wanted a job and came to me for work. Paige said to go ahead and hire him."

Richard nodded. "If this guy is still around, you can bet your life Ada is, too."

Linc felt cold, as if someone had walked over his grave or was digging it. Ada and this Orin must have taken Paige.

Richard lifted more papers from the folder. "According to Paige's medical records she was being drugged. Someone was giving them to her, probably Ada."

Mara reached out and clasped Linc's arm. "We know all that. You suspected Ada had done it but couldn't prove it."

Richard took the picture of Orin and handed it to Linc. "If this guy has been around the area long, he will have been at the bars. He likes to drink and frequents trashy places. Show his picture around and see what you can find out." He slid the chair into the table and turned to Mara. "And you, you stay by the phone in case Paige is able to contact anyone. If she does, this will be the first place she'll call."

Mara frowned. "But I want to come along. There must be something I can do. Something is wrong. I can feel it. I always feel when things are wrong."

Richard put his arm around her. "Of course you'll be doing something. You'll be here if she calls. Think how awful it would be if no one was here to answer her call."

Mara was silent for a moment before she spoke, "But Emma is here."

"And so will you be." Jack kissed her. "I'm going to get dressed so Linc and I can get out of here."

Linc held out his hand to Richard. "Thanks. You've done a lot for us."

"Think nothing of it. What's family for if not to help one another?"

The word *family* shook Linc. Richard had referred to him as family.

"Do you have a beeper?"

"I do." Linc's hand automatically went to the little box at his belt.

"Give me your number and I'll give you mine. We'll stay in contact."

After the exchange of numbers Linc paced the floor waiting for Jack. "When I get her back, I'll never let her out of my sight again."

Mara nodded. "When we get her back." Her voice cracked as she sat the coffee cups in the sink.

Fifteen

Lights flashed by as cars approached from the opposite direction. The night was black and street lights gave off that strange orangish glow.

"Do you want to start here?" Linc pulled into a seedy-looking little bar on the north side of town.

"Might as well. We'll work our way into town, unless we get lucky before then." Jack checked his watch. "It's a little after midnight. We've got two hours until the bars close." He climbed out of the truck. Jack studied his brother's face as they stood in front of the bar. "Have you thought of what you'll do if we find Greene here?"

Linc grunted. "I'll thrash him within an inch of his life."

"That's what I thought you were thinking, brother. But you have to control yourself. You have to think about Paige. If we happen to run into Greene, you be diplomatic. Leave the thrashing until later."

Linc glared at him. "That's easy for you to say, it's not Mara he's got."

Jack stayed his entrance to the bar. "And you don't know for certain he has Paige either. That's what we're trying to find out. Now keep calm and let me do the talking." He raised his brows. "Okay?"

Linc slacked under Jack's hand. "Okay. But I could kill when I think..."

"I know. But if we're going to find him we have to play the game and play it cool."

Linc knew Jack was right. He didn't want to do anything that might jeopardize Paige. He nodded. "Let's go."

Linc pulled the door open and let Jack go in first. Stale beer, body odor and tobacco smoke stung his nostrils. Dim lighting cast dark shadows over the interior. The two men stopped while their eyes adjusted. Nothing could adjust their nostrils to the dank odor. Loud music pulsated from the juke box in the corner, cranking out a whiny country song from long ago. The clicking of the cue stick against wooden balls on the pool table echoed over the fraternizing customers.

Linc and Jack sauntered in and threw their legs around a stool at the bar. A big, burly, bald-headed man with a large mustache came toward them, wiping his hands on his once white, multi-stained towel.

"What can I do for you gents?"

Jack pulled the picture from his pocket. "Just a little information, friend. Have you seen this fellow in here?"

The bartender took the picture, pursed his lips, shook his head and slowly looked up. "You police?" His gaze roamed over their clothes. Linc knew they were severely overdressed for this bar.

"No." Jack shook his head. "We're just looking for him. He's disappeared and we need to find him. Family emergency, you know."

The bartender looked at the picture and then at the two men. "Must be a distant relative," he cracked as he handed the picture back without a second glance, a surly smirk creasing his mouth. "Don't recall ever seeing him around here," he added as he wiped the bar with the towel.

Jack turned to the man to his right who was nursing a straight-up whiskey. "You ever seen this guy in here before?"

The man looked and shook his head. "No. Never seen him." He returned to his drink, obviously bored by the intrusion.

No other customers recalled seeing Orin and no one acted as if they cared whether they had or not.

"Well, I say we move on." Jack folded the picture and put it in his pocket. "No one here remembers seeing him, or won't admit to it if they have."

They drove on to the next bar and the next and the answer was always the same. No one had seen Orin Green.

"There's one more place I can think of." Jack jumped in the truck as Linc turned the key bringing it to life. "Go back to that first place."

"Why?" Linc asked. "Nobody remembers seeing him."

"Just a hunch. The bartender acted like he knew more than what he was telling."

"You think?" It felt good to have Jack on his side for once, working side by side, putting the old animosities behind them. Now if they could only find Paige, things would be right again.

"It's a feeling I got when we were talking to him. Let's give it a shot."

They entered the first bar again. This time a waitress was working the tables. She came by with a tray held over her head, carrying iced glasses with frothy heads of beer.

The bartender spotted them as they once again approached the bar.

"Hey, I thought I told you guys I ain't never seen that guy you're lookin' for."

Jack ignored him and said, "Two Bud Lites, please."

The bartender nodded curtly and returned with two frosty bottles of beer. "That'll be four-fifty." He took the ten and gave Jack the change.

"You sure you haven't seen that guy in here having a beer? He likes to drink and he likes to talk a lot, so I'm told."

The bartender frowned, his heavy brows narrowing over his cadaverous looking eyes. "Like I said. I ain't seen 'em."

Linc leaned over to Jack and whispered, "Looks like your hunch went bust."

"Another beer with a whisky chaser." The man to their left began pounding the bar.

The bartender went toward him. "Hey, Ed. Don't you think you've had enough?"

The man called Ed frowned angrily. "I'll say when I had enough. I got to go home and face the old lady. And I want to be plenty plastered so I don't have to listen to her whining." He began banging his glass on the bar.

"Okay, okay, but this is the last." The bartender brought him his drinks and turned to serve customers at the other end of the bar.

Jack pulled out the picture. "Hey, Ed. Have you ever seen this guy around here?"

Ed shakily took the paper and squinted. "Hey, this fella comes in here regular. I don't know his name, but I know he's a mean one."

"Mean? Explain that. How mean?" He shot Linc a look.

"Aw, he likes to pick fights, to show how strong and big he is. Tried to fight with me once," he slurred, "but I don't wanna fight. The old lady'd knock the crap outta me if I come home with a black eye or two." He laughed and downed his shot of whiskey in one gulp.

"When did you see him last?"

Ed pressed his lips and squinted. "Last night, I think. Said he had a big date. He was gonna do this girl."

"Do a girl? What girl?" Linc jumped into the questioning. Prickles grew on the back of his neck at the implication.

Ed burped and wiped his mouth with the back of his hand.

"What girl, Ed?" Jack urged, this time giving Linc a 'calm down' glance.

Ed shook his head. "I dunno'. Some girl he was supposed to work for."

Linc sat rigid. He was talking about Orin—and Paige. He had to be. He began to rise but Jack stayed him.

"You sure about this?"

"Sure, I'm sure. He's always doing some gal or other."

Linc relaxed. Maybe it wasn't Paige.

"Did he say what her name was?" Jack asked.

"Naw, just he was gonna do her." He gulped the beer. "I gotta go home. The old lady is gonna kill me now. Hey Pete. Put this on my tab. I'll catch ya Friday." He struggled to his feet.

Out of the shadows a figure moved toward them. "Come on, Ed, you can tell the gentlemen more than that."

Linc recognized him. He hadn't seen Bill since he'd opened the museum for him and Paige.

"Hey, Linc. Long time, no see." He slapped him on the back. "What you looking for?"

Jack pulled the picture from his pocket and handed it to Bill.

Bill thrust it under Ed's nose. "Where is this guy? You know where he lives?"

Ed pulled his brows together, thinking in an inebriated haze "I don't..."

Bill squeezed the back of his neck. "Come on, friend. Don't kid a brother. Where is he staying? Our brother here needs to know."

"Brother? He's a brother?" Ed stared at Linc.

"He's a brother. Now why don't you be honest with us and tell us all you know."

Ed pulled away. "I told you. He was gonna do this girl. He bragged about it. That's all I know, honest."

"What girl?"

Ed shrugged. "Just a girl."

Jack eyed the bartender nervously watching them. He nudged Linc in the ribs. "Wait here. I have an idea." He moved along the bar and leaned toward the bartender. "You have something to tell us?"

The bartender shook his head.

Jack reached into his pocket and pulled out a twenty, twisting it between his fingers under the man's nose. "Will this help?

"It's a start."

"Damn greedy bastard," Jack uttered under his breath and dug deeper, pulling out a fifty. Before he could exchange one bill for the other the bartender grabbed them both and shoved them in his shirt pocket.

He leaned in toward Linc and Jack, his voice barely audible, "He has a place near Goodheart, see. An abandoned cabin. No electricity, no water."

"Do you know how to get there?" Jack urged.

"It's one of those places off...oh, hell, let me draw you a map. You'll never find it if I don't." He pulled the pen from his pocket and laid out a bar napkin.

"You been there?" Jack asked.

"Yeah. But I don't want to be involved with him and that loony redhead he's shacked up with. They're into drugs big time. I don't want no part of it. I went one time but never again."

"Redhead," Jack spat. "Ada."

Linc jerked a glance at Jack. Ada? His grandfather's words came rushing back. The woman with red hair.

"Yeah, the broad is old enough to be his mother. And he's doing her, too." He glanced up at Jack and Linc. "Sick little bastard if I ever seen one."

Linc took the map. "Thanks." He turned toward Jack. "Come on, let's get going."

The bartender called after them. "I don't want no trouble. Leave me outta this. Ya hear?"

Jack and Linc rushed outside. Bill followed them out.

"Hey, man. You need some help? I can go with you."

"I don't think so. You've been a big help already." Linc shook his hand. "I won't forget it."

"Maybe you can help me."

"How?" Linc climbed into the truck.

"I need a job. My family..."

"I gotta go right now. Come see me at the office in a few days. I got something you might be interested in."

Linc spun away, gravel flying behind the truck. Goodheart. Abandoned cabin in the woods. He could spend all night looking for cabins in that area. There were plenty of them, but he had the map. It should lead them right to it.

"We did good. Got a map." Jack laughed, echoing the pleasure he felt at all they had just accomplished. "I was getting worried for a minute there."

Linc turned the truck onto the Harbor-Pestoskey road and put his foot to the mat.

"I'm going to give Mara a call." Jack picked up the car phone and punched in the numbers. "See if she's heard anything."

"Hi, Hon, it's me. Have you heard from Paige?"

"No. Where are you?" Mara's voice grew high-pitched with anxiety.

"Call Uncle Richard and give him these directions. Tell him that we think we've found Paige and are on our way.

Tell him to alert the police. We'll phone when and if we find her." He hurriedly gave her the directions.

"Jack, I want to be there. She'll need me."

"Sweety, it's bad enough that we have one of the women in the family in danger, we don't need two. You stay there in case she calls, in case we're wrong. I'll let you know the minute I know anything. Okay?"

"Okay." Her voice grew quiet. "I'll tell Uncle Richard." Jack pushed the phone back into the box on the seat. "Mara is going crazy waiting at home."

Linc shot him a sideways glance. "She's safer right where she is."

"I know. I hope she stays there."

Both men thrust forward as Linc covered the two-track road at breakneck speeds.

Paige's head was swirling. She tried to open her eyes but fell back into her dreamlike state. She wanted to be there, the love of her life was there, in her dreams. She stepped into the shower. Rivulets of water rushed down Linc's naked chest. She gazed at his perfectly muscled, bronzed physique, and then let her gaze move back to his face. "Linc?"

He smiled warmly at her. "Yes, baby it's me."

Paige collapsed in his arms as he locked her in his warm embrace. A heavy sigh escaped her lips as he pulled her tighter against his wet body. She was safe in his arms. How had he gotten here? It didn't matter. "You are here. I knew you'd come," she whispered.

Tilting her chin, he gazed into her eyes, "I'll always be here when you need me." His lips tenderly captured her mouth.

"Linc, you need to take me home," she whispered urgently as a chill ran down her spine. Suddenly Linc was roughly pulled from her arms. Paige reached to grab her lifeline, the man who would save her; he was fading into the mist. He reached his arms toward her and then disappeared completely.

Her eyes flew open as she was jerked back into her nightmarish reality. The fog began to lift. Paige moved her head back and forth trying to shake free of the drug. I can't think. Yes I can, she thought. If I am going to get out of this, I have to think.

I can do this because Linc came to me, I know he is looking for me. I know the spirits are guiding him, she thought.

She twisted and pulled, trying to loosen her hands. She pulled her head under her wrist and squirmed until she locked her teeth tightly on the biggest knot. It had to come loose. She couldn't go this way. Not now. She had just found Linc. And she had just discovered that she was a real person. No one, especially Ada, could ever put her down again. A whirling dizziness swept over her, and she lowered herself to the bed. She would get those knots out if her life depended on it. And it might.

It was still dark, or was it the next night? She'd lost all track of time.

Water. Her mouth was dry, as dry as the bed of a pine forest in a drought. She shook her head. Forget water, she chided herself. No sense thinking about things you can't have. Concentrate on the ropes. Try to get free. She bit at the knots again, pulling until her skin broke. She collapsed against the musty mattress, trying to ignore the pain the chafing caused, ignoring the exhaustion from her futile efforts.

Her eyes slowly adjusted to the low light from the lantern in the other room. Ada and Orin had either gone or were in another part of the cabin.

Her mind tried to put the pieces of the puzzle together. Orin couldn't be her half brother. Her father wouldn't have been unfaithful, he loved her mother. If he had a son, he wouldn't have ignored him either. He would have taken care of him. Ada was lying, she had to be.

She forced herself to work on the knots again. The painful thoughts drove her harder. She had to get loose. She had to. Her eyes searched the dimly lit room for something sharp. Perhaps Ada had left something. Damn, nothing!

She drew in a deep breath. Water. What she wouldn't give for one glass of ice cold water. Her tongue stuck to the roof of her mouth and her lips burned. She tasted the saltiness of tears intermingled with the coppery taste of blood on her tongue. That damned drug, she thought. It can't control me. I have to be in control.

She had to get a grip on this situation. To get water, she had to escape her bonds. She tugged at the knots, trying to loosen them. She pulled on the ropes. The ropes were tied securely several times around the sturdy headboard of the bed. She wasn't going to get away by trying to break the bed. Years of weight resistance training had defined her muscles, but she wasn't strong enough for this.

Damn, she needed a tool to cut through the ropes. But what? Where was she going to get it? Her eyes searched the room again. Beside the bed was a box of old magazines. Could something be in that box?

She studied it. Squirming around she was able to touch it with her bound feet. Thank God for long legs, she thought. Using her toes she began to move it. Perspiration dripped into her eyes, stinging them. She blinked frantically and gave the box a shove with her toes. It spilled. She jerked as she heard voices from the other room. Quickly she pulled herself back on the bed and feigned sleep.

"Better check on the little princess." Ada's voice filtered through the darkness.

Paige drew in a deep breath and slowly let it out. This was the performance of her life. Literally. Thank God for her modeling career. It had taught her to keep her face expressionless in front of crowds of people. She went limp and closed her eyes, praying her lids wouldn't flinch or flutter. It seemed forever before someone finally spoke. Then she felt the flashlight in her face. She forced herself to remain still, to play the part of being unconscious.

"She's out," Ada said. "I told you she'd be out till tomorrow. I gave her enough to knock out a horse."

"It was the same dose I gave her in the car," Orin said.

"Some of it was still in her system. Now she has double the dose. And I have more if we need it," Ada said matter-of-factly.

Paige held herself steady. If Ada realized the dose wasn't strong enough, she would give her enough to kill a horse.

The light went off. "No sense staring at her. Let's get busy. We gotta get things ready for Linc. We gotta be ready to do him next."

Linc? Yes, they planned to harm Linc. She'd forgotten that! What were they going to do to him, drug him too? How could she warn him when she was tied up like an animal ready for slaughter? She heard Ada's clicking heels receding from the room.

❋ ❋ ❋

Orin lingered. Paige fought not to be sick or cringe as he moved his hand up the slit in her dress toward her hips. His fingers inched up her inner thigh. Paige held her breath, praying he wouldn't rape her.

"Orin!" Ada called. "What the hell you doing in there?"

He jerked his hand away.

"Later. When this is all over."

Paige held her breath until she heard him leave. She fought the bile that rolled into the back of her throat.

"Turn right here." Jack held the flashlight on the napkin the bartender had given them. The truck bounded over the rutty unkept two track road. "He's got one mile, then turn left and one mile to the end of the road."

With those directions, Linc veered the truck onto a dusty, narrow dirt road lined on both sides with dark dense trees.

"This Orin sure knew how to pick an out-of-the-way place. We'll be lucky to find it with a map," Linc said.

Except for the truck lights, it was dead dark. Driving down this road was like picking their way through a dark forest with a candle. He could imagine Paige's terror as she was dragged through here. Don't think of that, he told himself. Concentrate on finding her. He sucked in a deep breath, letting the earth's fragrance brace him. He held the breath. Paige was here somewhere, he was sure. He could feel her now. And for some strange reason, he knew she was alive. That thought alone kept him going.

"Better slow up," Jack warned. "In fact, we should shut the lights off and roll forward. I think we're getting close and we don't want the lights to tip them off."

"Right." Linc shoved in the light button with a vengeance.

Now it was dark, black as midnight. It took a few minutes for their eyes to adjust to the darkness. Linc could just barely make out the thin ribbon of dirt in contrast with the silhouetted trees. He rolled forward, slowly, inching toward their destination and hopefully Paige. Feeling around in the dark to find his way, he gave thanks to the Almighty for his keen eyesight.

"Up ahead." Jack leaned forward as if it would give him a better view. "Isn't that a light?"

Linc followed his gaze. In the distance a dim light penetrated the darkness. "I think you're right." He stopped the truck. "Should we walk from here?"

"Go ahead just a little. If we can have the truck near, that will be to our advantage."

"Right." Linc eased the vehicle forward, barely creeping along. When he got close, he pulled the truck to the side of the road and backed it around so it was headed out.

Jack got out and reached under his seat and pulled out a case.

"What's that?" Linc watched him unzip it.

"A gun. We're dealing with some damned seedy people." He slipped the snub-nose .38 revolver under his belt. "Come on. Let's see what we got here."

Together they moved toward the shack that was almost hidden behind tangled brush and pines. The seconds it took to reach the cabin seemed an eternity. Linc peered through the dirty window. Orin and Ada stood within. He wanted to leap through, but he couldn't take the chance that he might cause Paige more harm.

Then he saw Ada hold up a syringe, the needle squirting liquid as she expelled the air.

He nudged Jack and nodded toward the window. "That's them. But I don't see Paige. Ada's got a hypodermic needle."

Linc glanced down the side of the shack and saw another window. It was covered with a dark rag, but it didn't quite come together in the middle.

His heart pounded in his chest when he looked in. Paige, tied like an animal, lay on the cot. God, he wanted to rush in and pull her into his arms.

Jack stood beside him and picked up on his feelings. "Easy. Don't do anything that puts her in jeopardy," he whispered. "We have to have a plan that won't backfire in our faces."

Overhead in the tall white pines an owl hooted, mournfully. A breeze came up, rustling the leaves and whistling through the pine needles. Linc gathered his strength from the spirits around him. If ever he needed help, it was now.

Linc crept to the first window. Ada and Orin were laughing. Ada put a cover on a small box she had just placed the needle in and watched as she moved into the other room.

"Come on. They're separated. We have the element of surprise." They crept to the door. Just as Linc reached for the doorknob he heard the sound of a gun being cocked behind him.

"Easy boys. Real easy. Turn the handle and go into the cabin, nice and slow." Ada's hardened tone penetrated the darkness. "You shouldn't have stepped so close to the window. I saw your shadow. Not enough to tell me it was a person, but better safe than sorry, I always say." She poked the cold metal of the gun into Linc's back. "Inside, boys."

"Damn!" Jack exclaimed.

Linc's mind raced. What a hell of a mess! Now they were all in deep shit. He cursed himself letting for this happen.

"Look what I found outside." Ada again pushed the cold steel of the gun muzzle into Linc's back, urging him inside.

"Damn!" Orin exclaimed in wide-eyed shock. "How'd they find us way out here?"

Ada moved to face both men, her gun leveled at them. "Good question. How did you find us?"

"You were careless," Linc stated simply.

She frowned. "Careless? How?"

"Do I have to explain it to you? Isn't it enough that we followed you here?"

Orin moved beside Ada. "Maybe it's not so bad. I mean he's here, ain't he? Now we don't have to go looking for him. We can do 'em together without no trouble."

Ada was silent for a few moments, thinking. "It would be, if it were only him, but what about him?" She nodded toward Jack.

"Just kill 'em," Orin replied offhandedly.

"Right. Maybe we should kill everybody. Then we'd really have the police down our necks," she snapped sarcastically. "I gotta think this out." She looked them over. "Check for weapons."

Orin frisked them and found Jack's gun. "Hey, lookie here." He held up Jack's gun.

"It looks like you boys were looking for trouble," Ada sneered.

Linc was startled to hear a moan from the room that held Paige captive. Had they hurt her already? God, if they had harmed her in any way...

Ada glanced at the darkened doorway. "I'm going to check the princess. You keep that gun on these guys.

Don't let them move a muscle." She disappeared into the other room.

Linc caught Jack's eye, hoping he'd catch the message he was sending. He flicked his eye movements toward Orin.

Orin leaned against the chair, fingering the gun lovingly. "Pow, pow." He laughed, blowing imaginary smoke from the steel barrel of the gun and twirling it around his index finger as if trying to impress them.

Again Linc slightly nodded to Jack and lunged at Orin. Jack made for the other room. The gun in Orin's hand went off in a deafening explosion. Linc wrestled Orin to the floor, all the while fighting to keep the gun facing away from him.

Orin twisted away from him and made for the bedroom. Linc was right behind him and grabbed him as he aimed at Paige. The gun blasted once more.

Linc stumbled toward the bed where Paige lay, smeared with blood.

"Oh God, no!" He lunged to the cot. Jack lay in a pool of blood beside it. The bastard got both of them. Before he could release Paige from her bondage, someone hit him from behind. Orin, he thought, as he struggled to keep himself from falling to the floor.

Paige's gaze frantically searched the room and saw Ada slouched against the wall, covered with blood. She turned her head to avoid the sight and a scream escaped her throat as she saw Orin bludgeon Linc. She fought the ropes trying to free herself to help him. "Mara!" she screamed as her best friend appeared miraculously at the door.

Mara ran to the bed and pulled at the ropes to untie Paige. Paige could see the fighting men were unaware of Mara's arrival. "How...where...? Paige whispered to her best friend.

Mara spoke quickly. "They gave me directions to give to Uncle Richard." As she pulled on the last rope, she added, "Did they really think I wouldn't use them?"

Paige shook her head as the last of the ropes came free. Out of the corner of her eye she saw Orin thrashing wildly for the gun that lay just beyond his reach.

Ignoring the pain in her arms, she dove for the gun, sending it spinning across the room.

"Jack!"

Paige heard Mara's heart-rending scream. She glanced in her friend's direction and saw her crumpled over her husband. Grief and anger tore at her heart. She glanced at the gun and then back at Mara. Without thinking, she quickly crawled over the rough floor and grabbed the gun.

Orin had his arm around Linc's neck, squeezing the life out of him. She looked at the cold metal in her hands and then realized what she had to do. She pressed the gun in Orin's face. "You let go of him you son-of-a-bitch or I'll kill you." Paige trembled as she tightened her grip.

Orin's narrow eyes grew wide as he stared at the gun that was shoved between his eyes. He released Linc and lifted both arms in the air.

"You'd better pray Jack isn't dead." With trembling hands, Paige pushed the gun barrel further into the skin that separated his eyes.

Orin nodded slightly and then cowered to the floor.

"Are you all right?" she said as she glanced at Linc.

Linc nodded and then pulled himself to his feet. He carefully took the gun from her hands. "You're covered with blood. Where are you shot?" he asked.

Paige glanced down at her dress stained in red. "Blood? Shot? I'm not shot."

Over her shoulder he could see Mara bent over Jack. The sight thrust him into action. "Grab those ropes," he said in a calm but commanding voice.

He handed her the gun as she gave him the ropes. "Hold this while I tie him." He pulled on the ropes to make sure they were secure and then reached to take the gun from Paige's shaking hands.

He quickly covered the space between him and his brother. "Jack." Jack's shirt was wet and sticky with blood. Linc reached down and carefully felt for his pulse. Thankfully he had one.

"Not Jack!" Paige cried.

"He's alive." Lifting Jack's shirt he added, "It looks like a shoulder wound." Relief and joy filled his voice.

Mara held Jack close to her chest. "We've got to get help."

"Mara!" Linc gained her attention as he threw his shirt at her. "Roll this and then apply pressure to the wound."

Paige took a blanket from the cot and laid it over Jack. Mara gently lifted Jack's head and placed a pillow under it. She held Linc's shirt tightly against the wound.

Jack moaned.

"Yes, darling." Mara caressed his face with her free hand. "I'm here. I'll take care of you."

"There's a phone in the truck. I'm going to call for help."

Linc hesitated. "Wait, where is Ada?"

Paige laid a shaky hand on his arm and spoke quietly. "She's over there." She pulled another blanket from the cot and laid it over her stepmother.

Linc leaned over the woman and felt for a pulse. "She's dead."

They both looked up when they heard the sound of sirens.

Paige felt a tear slide down her face. "Now I can cry," she said as she sat down beside Mara.

Epilogue

Paige returned Uncle Richard's smile as she walked down the aisle toward the love of her life, Linc. Her heart swelled as the brothers turned to her. Linc first, wearing a growing grin and then Jack, who was adjusting the sling around his injured shoulder. Mara stood to the right of the aisle, giving Jack looks to quit fidgeting. Everything was right in her world. The pieces were back together and she had added some new ones.

Nuna was on the groom's side with Linc's grandfather, Winona and Pazi beside her. Paige briefly scanned the crowd. It could have been lopsided, but many of the tribal members had filled the seats on her side. She knew this was a real show of support. In the front row, behind Mara, Emma stood smiling and crying. She was proudly filling in for Paige's mother.

Linc held out his hand as she approached and pulled her to his side. "I love you," he mouthed.

Her body ached to have this over and be pulled into his arms as his wife. His soulmate. His lover.

"Dear friends and family," Uncle Richard's commanding voice drew everyone's attention, "I have the honor of joining these two young people in a life-long pursuit of happiness. And all of you here have the joy of witnessing it."

"Linc has something he would like to say to his bride." Uncle Richard looked to Linc.

Linc stepped down and went to Nuna. She handed him a tissue-wrapped object. He brought the gift to Paige and gave it to her. She removed the soft wrapping to find a beautifully handcrafted dream catcher. "This dream catcher was made especially for us by my mother."

Paige glanced at Nuna and offered her a smile of thank you. "It is traditional, made of red willow, sinew, leather and feathers." He turned to Jack who handed him two feathers. "It will not be complete until we have inserted the pivotal feathers from the brave spirit eagle who sacrificed his life for us. He handed her a feather and then inserted his in the center tassel, made ready for the two feathers.

Paige did the same.

"I have waited a long time to find the woman with golden eyes. And now that I have, she will fly with me forever." He held up the now completed dream catcher. "We will hang this over our bed. The web will capture bad dreams so they can't harm us. The bad dreams will be held in the web until they evaporate in the first rays of morning sun. Our good dreams will slip through the center of the web and stay with us forever." He paused, holding her hand tightly. With his eyes gazing deeply into hers, he slid the wedding band onto her finger.

"I am offering you my soul. Will you take it and cherish it for the rest of your life?"

Tears of joy brimmed on Paige's lower lids as she answered. "I accept your gift with love in my heart, for you and my new mother." She smiled at Nuna, whose own eyes had grown misty. She hoped Nuna was receiving the message that she was overjoyed that Nuna had offered to be her representative when she was adopted into the tribe.

She turned her gaze to Linc. "Linc, all I have to offer you is me and a simple band of gold. I come to you with a heart full of love and a desire to fly with you throughout eternity." She handed the dream catcher to Mara and took the wedding band. She took Linc's hand in hers. "I offer this circle of gold as a symbol of my undying love. Will you accept it and my love forever?"

Paige slipped the ring on his finger. He smiled as she pushed the ring into position.

Linc's gaze misted as he spoke, "I will cherish your gifts and hold them close to my heart. I will accept your love forever."

Uncle Richard turned the couple toward the crowd. "There is nothing left for me to say except, 'By the power vested in me by the State of Michigan, I now pronounce you husband and wife.'" The crowd applauded as the couple promenaded down the aisle.

"It was the most beautiful wedding I've ever seen." Mara adjusted the simple circle of wild flowers on Paige's head. "Not as beautiful as mine, mind you, but almost."

Paige smiled at her best friend. "We're truly sisters now."

"I know." Mara returned her smile. "And I couldn't have asked for a better one."

"I don't know about that." Paige tilted her head. " I made life miserable for you for a while."

Mara took Paige's hand in hers. "I understand. You were confused. And Ada compounded your bewilderment, by acting as if she had become your friend."

"She really had me convinced, you know. I had no idea there was any money from my father other than what he had given me. So when she did return, I honestly thought she had come for me." She sighed heavily. "I guess I wanted to believe it and she could see that."

"A natural reaction. She was a slick one, I'll give her that."

Paige shook her head. "I don't like to speak ill of the living or the dead, but those things she said about my father broke my heart." She rose. "But Uncle Richard cleared all that up for me. He is a real Godsend, don't you think? Those terrible lies could have gone uncontested to the grave with Ada."

Mara was opening the women's lounge door, to answer a light tap. "If you are ready, daughter, it is time for the tribal wedding." Nuna smiled shyly at the two young women.

Mara held the door while Paige followed Nuna to another room in the Big Bear Arena. Linc's grandfather had told Paige that the bear was her spirit guide. She thought it ironic that the two ceremonies were being held in this particular arena on the reservation. They entered a small room and were greeted by family. The only people present were Nuna, Uncle Richard, Jack and Mara. The Traditional Man, Linc's grandfather, stood in the front of the room ready to perform the ceremony.

Paige and Linc joined arms and walked to the Traditional Man. Their family gathered around to witness the binding.

"You have come, as the spirits had predicted, to be bound to each other in Ottawa/Chippewa tradition." His voice was soft and gentle as a warm spring breeze. He lit a pipe and let the smoke roll from his mouth. "You will be bound to each other and fly one course as the eagle spirit has spoken." He handed the sweet- smelling pipe to Linc. He accepted it and drew deeply from it and gave it to Paige. She followed their example and was surprised at the sweet flavor. Linc took it and handed it back to his grandfather.

After setting the pipe aside, the old man accepted a wedding blanket that Paige knew had been made by Nuna. He carefully unfolded it and then placed it around the couple's shoulders. When they were wrapped securely together, he continued, "You are now together forever. You will walk as one. He held up both hands and recited the traditional Native American wedding blessing.

> Now you will feel no rain,
> For each of you will shelter
> the other.

> Now you will feel no cold,
> For each of you will be
> warmth to the other.

> Now there is no loneliness for you,
> Now you are two persons
> but there is one life before you.

> Go now to your dwelling place
> To enter into the days
> of your togetherness.

> And may your days be
> good and long upon the earth.

> As unto the bow the cord is,
> So unto the man is the woman.
> Though she bends him, she obeys him.
> Though she draws him, yet she follows.
> Useless each without the other.

The family quietly left the sacred room and joined their other guests in the reception hall. Uncle Richard offered a toast to the two newlywed couples. "Here's to many years of happiness. From the four of you, I expect to see many surrogate grandchildren. Basketball players, everyone." The crowd cheered. I know my nephews will have no need of bodyguards." He raised his glass to the two now blushing brides. The crowd cheered louder.

Nuna smiled at Richard. "There is no one I would rather share my grandchildren with than my lifelong friend. I hope Jack and Mara will consider me a surrogate grandmother to their children and that I live long enough to see the basketball games." Applause rang through the hall.

Linc and Paige turned to Mara and Jack. They held their glasses high. "Here's to our brother and our sister," Paige said.

Linc pulled an envelope from his pocket. And for my brother and his wife, Paige and I have deeded one-hundred acres of the land adjoining yours for a golf course."

Mara squealed as she ran to hug her friend and now sister.

Jack rose slowly, his eyes growing misty. "If it's okay to say this, "I love my big brother and I cannot express the gratitude I feel. No one has ever been family to me." He choked up. "Thank you." He raised his glass to the newlyweds and led the crowd in another cheer. The festivities grew louder and rolled forward with great precision under Nuna's watchful eye.

Linc pulled Paige aside and into his arms. "It's time for us to go to our dwelling place, at least the one I have selected for tonight."

Her heart pounded happily in her chest. "I've been waiting for you to ask."

Linc drove deep into the forest on the reservation. He jumped from the truck and pulled her with him to a teepee. "Here is where we will begin out flight together."

"So this is the wilds you were telling me about? Where no one would disturb us?"

Linc cocked his head and smiled seductively at her. "This is where I show you how a Native American makes love to his beautiful bride." He linked his arm in hers and led her to the teepee, allowing her to enter first. "When we get home, I'll carry you over the threshold. And in time we will teach our children about their heritages, yours and mine."

Paige gazed at the beautiful flower-covered bed. "Not for a long time yet. We have other things to do first."

He pulled her into his arms. "Come here, you little siren."

She giggled again. "Dose this mean you are going to douse my fire?"

"And this time we won't have an audience." Linc reached up and pulled the flap down, tying it securely.

Acknowledgments

A special thanks to Elisabeth Dietz, author of *Now is the Hour*, for her time and knowledge in our quest for accuracy. We'd also like to thank Lynelle and Doreen for taking their time and being our readers.

And our grateful appreciation goes to the Ottawa/Chippewa Tribe for permission to use the traditional wedding blessing.